JADED

BOOK 1 IN THE NIRVANA SERIES

Kristy F. Gillespie

By Kristy Feltenberger Gillespie
2014

KEEP CALM PUBLISHING

Acknowledgments

Patrick, for always encouraging me to write "my stories."

My mom, dad, brother, Grandma and Pa Feltenberger, and Grandma and Pap Petrunak for being my support system.

My friends, especially The Sarcastic Broads Club, members of Write By the Rails, Gary, Claudia, Terry, Tammy, Sharon, Carrie, Kelly, Peggy, Karen, Danielle, and Megan.

Illustrator Beth Breen (Front Cover)

Illustrator Karri Klawiter (Back Cover & Spine)

Editor Linda Bradshaw

Eye Colors and Names

Commune Members (*Main Characters)

Red:
*Ruby- Jade's paternal grandmother
*Rust- commune leader
*Scarlet-Jade's aunt
*Carmine- Ruby's best friend
 Flame- nurse
 Terracotta- nurse
 Rufous- Jade's maternal grandfather

Orange:
 Amber- Jonquil's childhood name
 Tangelo- Jade's student
 Persian - Jade's classmate
*Peach (Peaches) - commune leader's daughter

Yellow:
*Jonquil- Jade's mother
*Saffron- commune leader's wife
 Naples-Jade's uncle
 Goldenrod- Jade's maternal grandmother
 Mikado- teacher
 Lemon- teacher
 Gold- commune member

Blue:
*Royal- Jade's father
 Navy- Jade's paternal grandfather
 Cobalt- funeral director
 Periwinkle- guard
 Maya- Ty's mother
 True- Ruby's friend
 Glacier- (John Blackburn) Founder of Nirvana

Green:
*Jade
 Olive- Jade's student
 Hunter- Ty's uncle
 Hazel- (Margaret Miller) Founder of Nirvana (one green eye, one brown eye)

Purple:
*Tyrian (Ty) – Jade's best friend
 Indigo- Royal's childhood name
 Fandango- Jade's classmate

The Blind

White:
Ivory
Magnolia
Antique

Outsiders

Brown:
*Bronze- commune leader's adoptive son

Gray:
*Slate- Jade's aunt and uncle's adoptive son

Chapter One

My heart is frost bitten. The ache in my chest is so pronounced it hurts to breathe. I feel as if I've just sprinted 400 meters, in temperatures below freezing, with my mouth wide open like a fish.

The surrounding withered tree limbs resemble my Grandmother Ruby's fifty-six-year-old arms and legs. In November, the month which unofficially welcomes winter in Nirvana, she was diagnosed with terminal cancer. It only took two months for this disease to ravish her body to the point where boney branches remind me of her.

I exhale slowly, and my breath fogs the window. I have no desire to erase it because the only view is a black canvas with endless oak trees and a gravel road which leads to the commune hospice. My grandmother is expected to pass away any day or perhaps any minute, so my parents and I are saying our final goodbyes tonight.

The air in my father's work truck is stifling so I wind the window down. I close my eyes as a rush of crisp air caresses my face.

"Jade, you could have turned down the heat instead," my mother says, turning the thermostat dial left, toward the peeling blue sticker. "Please close it."

I roll up the window and press closer to the passenger door, leaning my forehead against the window.

"Are you feeling okay?" she asks. Without even facing her, I'm certain the skin between her eyebrows is wrinkled, her lips pursed.

"I'm fine." Fine is the response I almost always give— it's easier that way.

"Here, sniff this." She shoves a jar of cream under my nose. I can't tell if its peppermint or eucalyptus since it has such a potent scent of menthol.

"Rub some on your temples if you feel a headache coming on."

I dip my pinkie fingers in the small jar and massage the cream around my temples. It feels cool and tingly.

"Feel better?" She asks before my skin has a chance to absorb it.

"Is there an herbal remedy for heartache? If there is, I'll smear the entire jar on my chest." I press a hand against my heart for emphasis.

"Oh, sweetheart." She sighs. "I know how dreadful this is for you." She laces her fingers through mine. "The bond the two of you have is like... flowers and bees." She pauses, as if debating what to say next. "You still have your father and me. We're here for you. And we love you so much."

I nod. I know how much my mother loves me. She often says I'm the best part of her. As for my father, I honestly don't think that he does. At times, he seems jealous of the close relationship I have with my mother. And envious of the bond I have with his mother, Grandmother Ruby. When she dies, perhaps the best part of me will too.

"It's not fair!" I exclaim. My once vibrant Grandmother Ruby is like a red rose that was plucked from their garden and quickly discarded; well before the end of the season.

"Let's be thankful for the time we had with her," my father says softly, which contradicts his usually gruff tone.

I haven't even had seventeen years with her. I'm closer to my grandmother than with anyone else in my small world, and yet she won't be there for me during my eye color procedure, when I get married, or have children. She won't be there for anything.

My heart may never thaw.

Perhaps if we lived on the Outside, we'd have more time. My father is convinced there are cures for certain diseases beyond our commune. In fact, he brought up the subject this morning while I was eavesdropping in the hallway. Usually I remain in bed until my mother sprays a cloying scent in my bedroom as a means to wake me. This morning however, I was craving coffee more than five extra minutes of sleep.

"What if they have the cure for cancer out there, Jonquil?" my father asked.

"Royal, keep your voice down. You'll wake Jade," my mother said.

"If our leaders weren't obsessed with intraocular operations and more concerned with finding the cure for cancer, our life expectancy would surely increase." With each word, his voice rose like the notes on a musical scale.

"Not now, Royal, please."

"If we don't talk about these things now, when will we?"

"Honestly, I'd prefer if we never do. It's just so unpleasant."

"Of course you would. Then we won't." He sighed.

"Good. What would you like for breakfast?"

"I don't know. Pancakes I guess." His voice dripped with resignation.

And just like that, the subject was dropped. I've often wondered why eye color matters so much in our commune. Like most babies born in Nirvana, my natural eye color is brown. Not hot chocolate brown or buttered biscuit brown, but brown like the Crayola crayon stuck in the original crayon box.

Fortunately in Nirvana, Virginia, artificial trumps natural eye color because artificial eye color determines who you marry and your lifelong occupation. It even determines where you're buried, but I try not to think about that. In our commune, children have green, orange or purple eyes and adults have red, blue or yellow eyes. Only Outsiders, people who live in Nirvana but travel back and forth from the Outside, retain their natural eye color. However, there's an exception to these rules; commune members and/or Outsiders who commit significant crimes are blinded.

Even though my current name and eye color is Jade, both will change in six months, when I turn seventeen years old. I'll choose my blue-eyed father's life path of winemaking, or my yellow-eyed mother's life path of teaching. There's a third option, but only the crazy, desperate people consider it.

My father makes a left turn on Samsara Street. The mile long gravel path is aligned with boxwood trees standing guard like green ghosts. But of course, ghosts aren't real. At least that's what we're taught at the Academy. Supposedly when someone dies their body and spirit are buried together. And yet when my Grandfather Navy passed away five years ago, I sensed his spirit. I thought I was crazy until Grandmother Ruby mentioned she had actually seen his spirit. She said he looked the same as the day he died except for a blue glow which radiated from him. I only felt my grandfather's spirit once, but the experience left me with a sense of hope. I wish I could sense his presence now because all I feel is numb.

At the end of the lane, my father parks the truck in the lot behind Samsara. Before the start of Nirvana, Samsara was the heart of a 5,500 acre tobacco plantation. The plantation home was built in 1759, long before the start of our commune which came to fruition in 1865.

With our shelter from the rest of the world and limited technology, it may as well still be the 18th century. Supposedly on the Outside, people take phones with them everywhere. It's hard to imagine phones without cords. And there are computers that spit out information within seconds; and cures for diseases. But it isn't one-sided. The Outside is envious of our advancements in ophthalmology. In fact they trade oil for tidbits of information.

I feel hollow like the chocolate bunnies my mother orders from the Outside. As if one bite could cause me to crumble. As a result, I thread my arm through hers as we approach the back porch. We reach the first step as a cold January rain descends.

"You just dodged the rain," a guard perched on a chair says. His eyes are a pale blue.

My father nods. "Good evening sir."

"Where are you headed?" The guard, who is well over six feet tall, with bulging muscles asks. In fact, all of the guards, male and female, are all bulky like sacks of potatoes. Perhaps they take an herb like bupleurum to feed their muscles.

"Wing C," my mother says.

"I'm sorry," the guard says.

"Thank you, sir." My father stretches his arms like wings. The guard runs his hands along my father's arms, chest, back, and legs. When he's finished, he stands in front of my mother and me.

"Celeste, the female guard, is on break. Do you ladies have any prohibited items?" He asks.

"No sir," my mother replies as I shake my head. He nods.

Before we enter Samsara, we take turns gazing into an iris scanner. I stand approximately five inches from the camera which takes a quick digital photo.

We walk single file up the narrow wooden steps to the forth floor, Wing C, which is the area that no one willingly treads. Wing A is for intraocular operations, Wing B is the hospital, Wing C is the hospice. The ground floor includes the Center, where we have weekly meetings, dining hall, library, parlor, and living area for our commune leaders. There's an elevator but it's restricted to guards and patients.

On Wing C, nurses shuffle quietly through the hallway, each with various shades of red eyes. Like a rainbow of reds.

"May I visit alone first?" I ask, a lump in my throat rising.

"Of course, sweetheart," my mother squeezes my arm.

"Don't upset her," my father says. As if I ever would.

I push the door gently and slip inside Room 41. I hang my jacket on the coat rack, tip- toe to the side of the twin bed, and gaze at my grandmother.

Grandmother Ruby's red-colored eyes are like faded embers, in contrast to mine, which are the shade of bright green gemstones.

"You brought your camera," she says. "Take a picture of us."

I didn't realize a camera was hanging from my neck because I'm so used to its weight. I feel almost naked without it. I'm sure my mother feels the same way whenever there are no flowers in her hair. My bulky jacket must have hidden the camera from the guard. I'd be punished severely if officials found out I had a camera inside of Samsara. My father would scold me, too. But since I have it, I might as well take a final picture of my grandmother and me.

Half-heartedly, I hold the camera away from our faces and snap a picture. When the Polaroid pops out, I shake the picture until it slowly comes to life. It's out of habit that I shake it; it's not good for the photo.

"How do I look, Jade?" Her voice is so low I lean in close to hear her.

"You look beautiful."

"Don't lie. Give it here." A small smile plays on her lips.

Reluctantly, I hand her the Polaroid picture. She's aged years in a few weeks. Before she became sick, she would sit in front of her vanity and brush her raven black hair at least one hundred times. Then she would meticulously paint her face.

"Where's the red lipstick when I need it?" She gazes at the picture for a moment, looking so sad. "What will you label this one?"

I carry my camera to the coat hanger and hide it beneath my coat. "Umm, how about Sarcastic Broads?"

She laughs, which quickly turns into a cough. She takes a sip of water. "That's perfect." She places the photo on her meal tray between an untouched tapioca pudding cup and a bowl of chicken broth. "You're so talented. Promise me you'll never give up on photography."

"I promise to give up breathing first," I reply which I immediately regret. It's an insensitive comment considering my grandmother is struggling to breathe. I redeem myself by bringing up a topic that always brings a smile to her face. "I still have the first camera you and Grandfather gave me. It's gray and black with a rainbow stripe down the middle." In fact, I have a significant camera collection with cameras of all shapes and sizes.

"That old thing? Your grandfather gave it to you on your fourth birthday! Do you remember that party?"

"Yes, but tell me the story again, please." No matter how many times she repeats this particular story, I always enjoy hearing it. It takes me back to a time when life was simple. Back when my parents were happy, when Grandfather Navy was alive, and when Grandmother Ruby was healthy.

"Oh what a party it was. At least half the commune was in your backyard. We grilled hamburgers and hotdogs, but you'd only eat the bun. We sang 'Happy Birthday' and passed out chocolate cake. You scraped off all the icing and threw away the cake. You get those traits from your mother. Your father always ate everything on his plate. Still does, too." She takes a wheezy breath. "Then you tore into all of your gifts which were mostly homemade clothing and wooden trinkets. You pushed those aside, grabbed a stack of cups, and handed them out to all the kids. You collected feathers, rocks, worms, twigs…whatever you could find in the backyard. When your party was over, all of the other kids dutifully dumped out their cups and went home. You, on the other hand, threw a tantrum when your mother tried to take the cup away from…" she stops to cough.

"Here, take a drink." I offer her a cup of water. Watching Grandmother sip from a straw reminds me of how she used to hold my juice cup to my lips whenever I was little and sick. I blink back tears. I'm sure Grandmother is fed up with people crying. All week, she's had visitors saying their final goodbyes, leaving get well flowers and teddy bears in their wake. These gifts are an absurd splash of color against the eggshell white walls.

"Thank you, dear. Anyway, while you were hollering, your Grandfather smacks his forehead. 'There's one more gift in the truck,' he says. As soon as he handed the gift to you, you ripped into the wrapping paper. Once you realized it was a camera, your eyes just lit up. Grandfather lined up all of your treasures and you proceeded to take pictures of every one. He had to hold the frog though because that sucker was jumpy."

"I was such a brat, wasn't I?" I laugh.

"No, you were just precious and precocious. You were always asking questions, always interested in everything down to the smallest ant. Don't lose that zest. Keep discovering the little things, even in winter. Even if you're nearly seventeen," she says.

"But January is such a blah month; so stark. I'm so sick of taking photos of naked trees and gray skies."

"You just haven't looked hard enough. Wait until it snows. What's the weather like right now?"

"It's probably still raining."

"I'd like to hear the rain one last time. Open the window, please." The words *one last time* jab at my heart like an ice pick.

"But Grandmother, it's freezing outside."

"I'm warm, see?" She touches her silk head scarf with one hand and blanket with the other.

What can it hurt? I walk the few steps to the window and lift the screen which sticks. When it finally opens, a gust of wind swirls through the room. A fog has settled and the sky is hopelessly devoid of stars as the rain falls. As bleak as it is, it's much more pleasant than the hospice.

"I'll never like winter as much as you do." I turn from the window.

"Every season is lovely in its own way."

"If you say so," I shrug.

Grandmother points to the door.

"You want me to leave?" I ask.

She shakes her head and motions for me to shut the door.

"Got it." I head toward the door.

My parents are sitting in plastic chairs in the hall. My mother is knitting a yellow scarf which will match her eyes perfectly, and my father is scribbling in a tattered notebook.

"Does she need anything? Water? More medicine? Another blanket?" My father asks, bolting from the chair.

"No, she's okay. She just asked me to close the door."

"You two are so secretive with one another." My mother smiles, but I can tell it's forced because her smile doesn't reach her eyes. She loves Grandmother nearly as much as I do. "Are you hungry? You barely touched your dinner. I have some granola in my purse." She starts to root through an oversized bag.

"I'm fine, thanks." Why do they ask so many questions all of the time? I realize they're just trying to help but it's really annoying.

"A few more minutes, and then let her rest," he says.

Doesn't he realize that cancer has whittled her life down to minutes?

"Okay," I reply as I close the wooden door.

I return to my chair and scoot it as close to the bed as possible.

"They're still sitting out there like guards, aren't they?" Grandmother asks.

"Of course they are… Grandmother, what am I going to do without you?"

"You'll be just fine, Jade. You're a lot stronger than you think."

"But I'm going to miss you so much." I hug her lightly, and the smell of laundry detergent envelops me. It's the only perfume she ever wears and much more soothing than the bleach bathed sheets and blankets.

She grabs hold of my hands with her gnarled fingers. Her firm grip surprises me and her fingers are as cold as the metal bed rail.

"I need you to do a few things for me, okay?"

"I'll do anything for you," I reply quickly.

"I have a diary at home in my bedroom. It's in the cubbyhole, in one of your Grandfather's old cigar boxes, wrapped in a floral scarf. You must read it and then destroy it."

"W—w—what? Why?" Why hasn't she mentioned this before?

"I've found out things about Nirvana...*some really bad things*. If anyone finds out that I've kept a record and shared it with you, your life could be ruined."

"What are you talking about? And why are you telling me?" My tongue feels thick and heavy, and the bitter taste of bile rises in my throat.

"I must share this with you. Don't think I haven't struggled with this decision, I have. When I was sixteen, if I would have known these secrets, my life would have been much, much different. But I don't regret how my life turned out because regardless, I've been blessed." She pauses to catch her breath.

"Then why tell me? Won't I feel blessed like you if I don't hear these things?"

"I want you to know these secrets so the decisions you make are based on fact instead of the fiction the rest of us have been fed. Promise me you won't share this information with anyone. Not your mother, not your father, no one. Not even Ty." Ty, whose full name is Tyrian, has been my best friend since grade school.

"If this diary could hurt us, why would I want to read it? What if I refuse to?" My voice sounds shrill, foreign.

"That's your decision to make."

"Maybe I should just destroy it— burn it!"

"What you do with it is your choice. Burn it, shred it, bury it, whatever. But if you do decide to read it, heed my advice: don't read it all at once, pace yourself."

"You know how slow I read. It will probably take me forever to finish it." I hang my head.

"That's okay, sweetie. You take your time reading." She pats my hand. "Don't be so hard on yourself."

I look up and meet her eyes. "I'll try."

"And Jade, when you find the diary, hide it immediately. All I really ask is that you keep this book to yourself. You promise me that."

"But…"

"Just promise," she pleads.

I nod my head and in turn she lets go of my hands.

"Another thing," she pauses as she strokes my long auburn hair. "You listen to your mind and your heart when choosing your life path. Don't let your mother or your father or what's best for the family decide for you." She cups my chin with her dry fingers. "Most importantly, don't close yourself off with two choices. There's always a third."

An icy chill runs down my spine. Grandmother Ruby isn't as lucid as I thought. Is there even a diary? Or is she rambling on like a blind mad woman?

"Don't look at me like that, Jade. I'm not crazy." She narrows her eyes.

"But Grandmother, if I try to escape, they'll blind me!"

She stares at me a moment before she says, "That's if they catch you. There are ways to escape. You'll see." She nods her head up and down several times. "Just make sure if you decide to remain in Nirvana, it's your decision and yours alone, okay?"

Unsure of what else to say, I reply, "Okay."

"You're a good girl, Jade; so loyal. In fact, you're loyal to a fault." She struggles to keep her eyes open.

I yearn to ask what she means by that but she's exhausted. "I love you, Grandmother."

"Love you." She closes her eyes.

"I'll let you rest." I kiss her on the forehead.

"Leave the window open. I like the sound of the rain," she whispers. "And sit with me a minute."

I wait until I know she's asleep before I hug my legs to my chest, bury my face against my knees, and sob.

JADED

When there are no tears left, I drag myself into the tiny bathroom. I splash cold water on my face and then dry off with rough paper towels. When I glance at the mirror, my green eyes look despondent and dull. I make sure to close the window before I leave.

KRISTY FELTENBERGER GILLESPIE

Chapter Two

I rest my head against the hard wooden bench and stare at the vaulted ceiling that is painted sky blue with puffs of white clouds. A rainbow banner hangs in the middle. Our commune's philosophy is scrawled on the banner "Nirvana: Simplicity, Tranquility, and Equality." The painting and banner clash with the rest of the room design that include white pillars, a black walnut staircase, and brass pinecones which symbolize fertility and prosperity.

My parents, my best friend Tyrian—who will only respond to Ty—a group of commune members, and I are seated in Samsara's Central Passageway, informally known as the Center.

Each Friday, our so-called day of rest, commune members are required to attend meetings at the Center. Activities begin promptly at 11am and continue until 3pm or later, depending on how late lunch is served.

After a quick eye scan, we undergo health checkups. Checkups can be a mere annoyance or humiliating. It all depends on the nurse, and you never know which one you're going to get. Once everyone has been poked and prodded like cows, we're ushered into the Center. Summertime is the worst because we're crammed like crayons in a box with limited space, and limited fans. During the winter months we are ice cubes in a stainless steel bucket.

Occasionally there are wedding celebrations and life path announcements. Sometimes commune members are punished so severely that I can't watch. More often we're stuck listening to Rust and Saffron, our commune leaders, drone on and on. They must enjoy hearing themselves talk. In fact, Rust provides a complete weather forecast each Friday. The problem is that his predictions are usually wrong. Grandfather Navy used to scoff at Rust's weather reports. He said that if he wanted to know what the weather was like he'd stick his head out the window.

Finally we gather for lunch which is often the only bright spot because it gives commune members a chance to gossip. Members that weigh in at a recommended weight are offered dessert. Those that don't are given a tall glass of ice water. So much for equality. Lunch won't be served today because it's not Friday but Tuesday. We only meet throughout the week for emergency events.

And this morning's tragedy is Grandmother Ruby's viewing.

My grandmother is lying in an oak casket adorned with artificial flowers. Sunlight seeps through the window shutters, illuminating her pale skin. She's wearing a floor length white dress with a high neck, several sizes too large. Whoever dressed her should have raided a child's closet instead. And they should have chosen a different color, anything but white. She hated the color white and fake flowers. She isn't even wearing lip stick. Why didn't they ask me? I could have told them exactly what she would have wanted! It's probably Aunt Scarlet's fault.

As usual I'm avoiding Aunt Scarlet, my father's sister, so Ty and I are sitting in the second row, directly behind my parents. Aunt Scarlet is dabbing her eyes with an ivory handkerchief even though she isn't crying. Is she willing tears to fall? Her fake eyelashes resemble spider legs.

My father and his sister are as close as the Atlantic and Pacific Oceans, so we hardly ever see her or Uncle Naples. Grandmother Ruby often said that she tolerated Scarlet, but found her difficult, if not impossible, to love. I find it hard to even tolerate Aunt Scarlet because she's callous. She didn't even visit Grandmother Ruby in the hospice. It makes me sick. Whenever we see her, my father and I barely speak to her. My mother is cordial but she's polite to everyone.

My mother is sobbing and leaning against my father whose face is dry and expressionless. My father only expresses himself through his artwork. I'm like him in that way.

"Hold still." Ty brushes his fingertips softly across my cheek.

I gaze into his stark purple colored eyes which remind me of twilight, the most mysterious, most beautiful time of evening.

"Make a wish," he says. An eyelash is on the tip of his finger.

I wish my grandmother was still alive. I blow the eyelash off of his finger. If only my pain could disappear as quickly as an eyelash. Grandmother Ruby used to tell me to make a wish every time the clasp of my necklace slid around to meet the charm. I feel my necklace and the clasp is resting on the nape of my neck. When I finally look up, he's watching me intently.

"Why are you looking at me like that?" I ask as heat spreads over my face.

"I worry when you're so distant. It's okay to show emotion, you know. It's okay to cry."

"I know that, I just can't right now." I cross my arms tightly across my chest. I glance at the program that lies on my lap. I chose the picture of Grandmother Ruby which was taken in November, right before she got sick. She's holding a striped umbrella with one hand and waving with the other. A lump rises in my throat. I'll never see her smile again. I'll never talk to her again. And yet, I imagine her face and her voice so clearly. If she were seated next to me, she'd be reapplying her red lipstick. And she'd complain that the classical music was melancholy.

"Why the mourning?" she'd ask. "Why not celebrate the person's life? When I die, I hope they play jazz."

I agree with Grandmother Ruby. If only they would have asked me what music to play. My father probably chose this haunting music because he finds beauty in sadness. Every note cuts into my heart like a shard of glass.

After the music finally fades, Cobalt, our ancient funeral director, shuffles up the aisle. He ascends the steps to the small stage, stumbles, and then catches himself.

"If I'm not careful, it could be me next," he says with a chuckle.

"How can he joke at my grandmother's funeral?" I whisper loud enough for my father to turn around and give me *the look*. His piercing blue eyes so easily harden like ice. He has a mean streak like Aunt Scarlet.

"Don't let him get to you," Ty whispers in my ear.

"Who?" I ask softly. "Cobalt or my father?"

"Both of them." He laces his warm fingers through mine, causing my heart to hammer so loud I'm certain he can hear it.

Ty's my best friend— not my boyfriend. But recently whenever he touches me I feel shivers along my spine. Nervously I caress the calluses that line his palm.

Cobalt's hair piece is askew and his back is so hunched it's as if he's wearing a turtle shell. Cobalt and his late wife were unable to have children, so he's unable to retire because there's no one to support him.

"Good afternoon, brothers and sisters," Cobalt begins. "We are here to say our final goodbye to Sister Ruby Red. She was a fine nurse, mother, and friend." His voice cackles into the microphone. I try to listen to the rest of his spiel but my nerves have gotten the best of me. Why did I offer to speak on behalf of my family? I feel like throwing up.

"You've got this." Ty whispers. He squeezes my hand before letting it go. I refrain from grabbing his hand back.

"What?" I ask as my heart picks up the tempo.

"He asked if anyone wanted to speak on your grandmother's behalf," he explains.

I manage to raise my hand even though my arm feels weighed down. In fact my entire body feels this way, as if I'm wearing wet clothes. Cobalt squints his watery eyes at me. "Young lady," he motions for me to come up to the stage.

I glance at my parents as I stand. My mother beams and for once my father's smile appears genuine. Miraculously, I climb the few stairs in my way too high heels without tripping. Unfortunately I make the mistake of looking at the faces in the crowd instead of at the back wall like I had planned. A multitude of red-colored eyes stare at me. Their presence at my grandmother's viewing is a sign of respect. Likewise, at Grandfather Navy's viewing, all of the blue-colored commune members attended.

Rust, our commune leader, and his wife Saffron, are also seated in the front row but some distance from my parents. He gives me an encouraging nod but Saffron stares straight ahead. She never acknowledges me but I'm not sure why. I'm curious to know what I've done to her. I smooth the crinkled notebook paper before I speak into the microphone.

"G—g—grandmother Ruby is, I mean was," I stutter.

"Introduce yourself," Cobalt hisses.

Even though everyone surely knows who I am, I say, "M—m—my name is Jade, and Ruby was my grandmother. This is really hard for me." When I lock eyes with Ty, I feel the strength to continue.

"I can't believe she's gone." A tear slides down my face, but I wipe it away and hold my head up high. I forgot my reading glasses, so I have to squint my eyes in order to read from the paper. "I wrote a poem for her that I'd like to read. It's called *In Your Dreams*:

'In your dreams
Rain will fall from the grey-blue sky forever
Your outfit will always match your umbrella
Our bond will never sever
In your dreams
There will be no pain whatsoever
Only beauty will endeavor
And we'll be together'

"I'm not that great with words, much better with pictures, so I also created a slideshow tribute. Thank you." I flick the switch on the projector before stepping off the stage.

All of the pictures in the slideshow were taken by me, beginning with the camera Grandfather gave me. The last twelve years of Grandmother's life flash across the screen. In every picture she's laughing. She's even smiling in the last picture I took of the two of us in the hospice room. When the tribute ends, I feel as empty as a snowman without a carrot.

When commune members start to clap, Cobalt mutters, "Maybe she should take over as funeral director." No thanks.

When the clapping ceases Cobalt asks, "Does anyone else care to say a few words?"

Carmine, my grandmother's best friend, shakes her head when our eyes meet. I hastily turn my head because her eyes are the exact color of dried blood which makes my stomach sick. I'm relieved that nursing isn't my life path, even if the medical field is highly respected in Nirvana.

"May I say something?" Saffron asks, shooting like a star from her seat.

"Why certainly," Cobalt replies.

As Saffron passes, the cloying smell of hairspray fills my nose. Surely she used an entire can because her blonde hair is perfectly curled. A long black gown hangs from her lithe frame, clinging to her breasts. Diamonds adorn her ears, neck and wrists. Her stilettos are inches higher than mine and yet she climbs the stairs effortlessly. She's like a poisonous golden delicious apple that is slowly rotting from the inside out.

Cobalt hands her the microphone and then hobbles off the stage. She waits until he's seated before she speaks. "I want to first share my deepest condolences to Ruby's family and friends. Ruby was a marvelous woman...and so beautiful. May she forever rest in peace. Let's have a moment of silence." She briefly bows her head. My grandmother would be mocking Saffron right now. In fact, she couldn't stand her.

She continues, "Ruby's death hits especially hard because she was my dear friend Scarlet's mother." Saffron is as artificial as Aunt Scarlet so they're an ideal pair. "I was planning on waiting until the Center meeting on Friday to announce the wonderful news but I just can't wait," she gushes. "Rust, darling, will you bring Scarlet's gift out? And hit the spotlight, please."

Rust nods and slips back stage.

"Scarlet, will you join me on stage, please?"

Scarlet is so eager that she practically trips up the steps. They clasp hands and beam, clearly enjoying their time in the spotlight. Scarlet is also very pretty but not nearly as thin or as glamorous as Saffron.

"What the heck kind of gift is she going to give to her?" Ty asks.

I roll my eyes. "I have no idea. This is supposed to be my grandmother's viewing, not a festival for Scarlet."

After a few minutes of silence, commune members start to grumble. A few even stand up, as if they would dare to leave. With armed guards at every exit, they wouldn't get very far.

"You mustn't leave yet," Saffron orders. Her golden yellow eyes glow like a candle flame. "I'll check on Rust to make sure everything is okay." She takes a few steps before Rust returns to the stage empty handed.

"Where is Scarlet's gift?" Saffron asks through clenched teeth.

Rust whispers something in her ear which makes her march backstage.

I've often wondered why Rust, who resembles a clothed version of Michelangelo's *David* and who brings grown men to tears, allows his wife to treat him like a third child. It's ludicrous.

"I didn't receive a gift when Sapphire died," a woman seated behind me says.

"When I lost Goldenrod, all I got was heartache," another woman says.

"Not very equal, now is it?" The first woman replies.

"Sure isn't." Woman number two says with a snort.

Their conversation ceases when Saffron resurfaces, dragging a small child by their arm. It isn't until they're under the spot light that I realize it's a boy. He's wearing a navy blue suit, one or two sizes too big. His hair is a pale blonde but I can't tell what color his eyes are because he's squinting. His features are delicate like fairies in picture books.

Surely this child isn't Scarlet's gift. She can't even take care of a dog- her last two ran away. However, something tells me that she'll keep a sharper eye on a child because at age seventeen, if he chooses nursing as his life path, Scarlet is able to retire.

"Meet Slate, your new son!" Saffron pushes the child toward Scarlet whose eyes are as round as buttons. "Naples, perhaps you should join us." Saffron laughs.

I'm too shocked to speak and evidently the rest of the crowd is too. I can hear Uncle Naples's heavy breathing as clearly as if he were seated next to me. When he joins Scarlet, he stands with his arms straight by his sides and his mouth propped open like a dead fish. I can't tell if he's overjoyed or petrified. They've never been able to have a child which my father says is a blessing. I can't help but agree.

"Slate came to us in the same way Bronze did," Rust explains. Bronze is Rust and Saffron's adopted son, who is from the Outside. Bronze and his parents were traveling through Nirvana, as some Outsiders tend to do from time to time, when they were in a horrific car accident. "It wasn't difficult to choose Scarlet and Naples as Slate's adoptive parents," he says.

"Poor baby," one of the women behind me says.

"What a shame!" a voice in the crowd exclaims.

As the noise from the crowd increases, Rust raises his powerful arm, demanding silence from the growing discontent. He glances at Saffron and she nods. "This viewing is now over. Thank you everyone for joining us. For those of you that would like to attend Ruby Red's funeral, it will take place in half an hour."

"Do you feel okay? Are you going to be sick?" Ty asks.

"What?" I ask.

"Your skin is really pale." He lays his hand on my forehead. "And you feel warm."

"I'm fine," I reply, even though my mind feels disconnected from my body like a button hanging from a thread.

Once again Ty grabs my hand. I scoot closer to him and lay my head on his broad shoulder. I close my eyes and match my breathing pattern to his. I used to do this with my father when I was little. Whenever I was scared, either from waking up from a nightmare or during a thunder storm, I'd crawl in bed between my parents and rest my head on my father's shoulder. Once our breathing pattern matched, I was able to fall asleep to the sound of "shhhh…"

"Wake up Jade." I hear Ty's voice but it sounds far away, as if he's under water. "It's time to go." His voice is louder now. Reluctantly, I open my eyes.

"Sorry," I mumble as I lift my head from his shoulder.

"I'm sorry you're in so much pain." His eyes, searching deep into mine, are so familiar and yet so unusual. Ty has been so tender these past few months. I would be lost without him. He hesitates before he adds, "We should join your family."

My parents, aunt and uncle, Rust and Saffron, and Slate are the only ones left in the room. And of course the guards are still here. Some will remain at Samsara and others will accompany Rust and Saffron at the cemetery. Slate is hiding behind Uncle Naples which is a difficult feat, considering how thin my uncle's legs are.

My mother crouches down to the little boy's level. "Hi Slate, my name is Jonquil."

"Aunt Jonquil," Scarlet corrects.

My mother whispers something in Slate's ear and he manages a crooked smile. When it's my father's turn, he bends slightly and offers his hand. "I'm Royal." Slate eyes my father's hand a moment before he accepts the handshake.

"Uncle Royal," Scarlet says. "And this is your cousin." She points at me.

I sink down to his level. "Hi Slate, I'm Jade." His gray eyes resemble the color of the sky before a massive storm.

Ty crouches beside me. "And my name is Tyrian but friends call me Ty. Feel free to call me that."

Slate's crooked smile returns. He's so small and fragile, just like a newborn robin.

"Well, we best get going. There will be ample time to chit chat later." Saffron ushers everyone toward the exit.

I quickly grab my coat and follow Ty through the wooden doors. He borrowed his father's beat up work truck, so I ride with him. His father heads construction in Nirvana, therefore his truck reeks of damp metal. A satchel of potpourri hangs from the interior rear-view mirror but it's clearly lost its potency.

"Sorry," Ty says as he brushes sawdust off the seat cushion.

"No worries." I eagerly climb into the truck in order to escape the wind.

"C'mon, Blue." He smacks the dusty dashboard with one hand and turns the key with the other. "Finally," he mutters as the engine sputters to a start.

"Is she gonna make it?" I ask.

"Yeah, she's a trooper." He winks.

"I'm glad one of us is. I just feel so broken." I lean my head back and close my eyes.

"You're strong, Jade. A lot stronger than you think."

My eyes snap open. "That's exactly what my grandmother said the last time we spoke."

"That's because it's true," he replies quietly.

For the next few minutes we don't speak. I try to concentrate on the sound of displaced gravel and the low hum from the cassette tape. If only my mind could rest for a few minutes.

As usual, Ty is the one who breaks the silence. "The picture tribute was amazing."

"Thank you." His comment makes my heart smile. Creating the slide show was emotionally exhausting but I'm proud of the way it turned out.

"And I liked your poem," he says.

"You don't have to say that, I know it was stupid." Why did I bother to read that embarrassing poem? A five year old could have written it. I should have just stuck to the picture tribute.

"No, it wasn't."

"I bet my father thought it was silly and immature," I reply. My father is the writer, not me. In fact, writing the poem was a struggle, especially rhyming.

"How can he not be proud of you? Your poem and pictures honored your grandmother." He glances at me. "It was beautiful."

"That means a lot, thank you." Without Ty, today would have been unbearable.

I gaze out the window, withered winter trees serving as the only scenery. A gray bird flies dangerously close to the window and I think of Slate. "I'm so irritated at Rust and Saffron. Aunt Scarlet, too. Couldn't they have waited until Friday?" I ask.

"Yeah, they definitely should have. That was a crappy thing to do."

"I feel so bad for Slate, too. He must feel so lost. What do you think his real name is?"

"I have no idea. I don't know many Outsider names."

"For some reason, he doesn't look like a Slate. Does that make any sense?"

"Yeah, that does make sense. Slate sounds a bit too edgy for him. Davy Gray would have fit him better."

"You're right. Davy's a cute name whereas Slate sounds cold and harsh."

We pass underneath an oversized rainbow colored sign that reads, "Nirvana Cemetery."

"Ugh, what an ugly welcome." Ty says.

"It's an ugly place." My parents and I visit Grandfather Navy's grave in the Blue Lot nearly every month. However, we never visit my mother's parents' grave sites. In fact, my mother never mentions them and becomes visibly shaken whenever I ask. One day soon I'll search for Grandmother Goldenrod's grave in the Yellow Lot and Grandfather Rufous's grave in the Red Lot in order to pay respect.

We drive past a sign which reads, "Red, Yellow & Blue Adult Lots to the Left. Purple, Green & Orange Child Lots to the

Right. White Blind Lots to the Far Right." I hope to never have to visit the Child or Blind Lots.

When we reach the Red Lot, Ty parks next to my father's truck as my parents are getting out of their vehicle. I shiver as the four of us walk toward my grandmother's final resting place.

"Want my coat?" Ty asks. Without waiting for a response, he pulls off his black leather jacket.

"Are you sure? Won't you be cold?"

"Nah, I'll be fine." He drapes his coat over my shoulders before reaching for my hand. The warmth and weight of his jacket coupled with the size of his hand in comparison to mine makes me feel so content.

Most of the trees are naked but the breeze is blowing through the ones that still have leaves, shaking them so only the hardy leaves survive. Every so often, a crow caws, piercing through the crisp winter sky. The sun hangs to my right and its rays are bright enough that I squint.

Finally we reach the Red Lot. The wrought iron gate, joined on either side by large rocks, is propped open. Nearly all of the wooden chairs are filled with commune members which are a testament of how much my grandmother was loved. Ty and I sit with my parents in the front row and my grandmother's best friend, Carmine sits in the chair to my right.

"I'm so sorry, sweetheart," Carmine says. Her round cheeks are flushed. She's breathing heavily from the lengthy hike.

I nod because I can't think of a single thing to say.

"This too shall pass." She reaches for my hand and I fight the urge to yank it back because her hand is sweaty and hot.

A line has formed in front of Grandmother Ruby's casket. Some people are laying roses in the casket. Other people whisper their goodbyes. I follow my parents to the front of the line, behind Aunt Scarlet.

When it's her turn, Aunt Scarlet clings to the handle of the casket and wails, "I'll miss you, dear mother." I fight the urge to roll my eyes. Scarlet doesn't have a genuine bone in her scrawny body. She works at the hospital and yet she couldn't be bothered to visit her mother in the hospice, one flight up.

Uncle Naples stops in front of the casket and simply bows his head for a moment. Slate clings to his legs and refuses to look. If

Slate would have known Grandmother Ruby, surely he would have loved her.

I kiss my grandmother's cheek which feels thin like rice paper. I place the last picture of us and my tattered poem on her chest before backing away slowly. Every part of my mind and body feels numb, except for my heart. When I was little, I dropped a steak knife on my foot and immediately felt a searing pain. That's exactly how my heart feels right now.

My mother places her hands on my back and guides me to the side of the coffin.

Cobalt says a few more words before Grandmother Ruby's casket is closed and lowered into the earth. My father throws the first fist full of dirt onto the grave. I notice a single tear gathering in the corner of his eye. My mother sobs as she throws her handful of dirt. As I reach for dirt, I spot a lone red pansy which I pick and drop into the grave. And as the flower hits the casket, I pray that my grandmother rests in peace.

Suddenly, my head feels dazed like a punctured balloon, and I start to hyperventilate. I'm overcome by waves of sadness slamming against my chest. I sway as I approach the wooden seats. Ty catches me as I start to fall. My mother and Carmine rush over.

"Drop your head and purse your lips. Breathe slowly," Carmine orders.

"You're okay, sweetheart, you're okay." My mother strokes my hair as I concentrate on taking slow breaths.

"Does she need water?" Ty asks.

"Yes, please," Carmine replies.

After my breathing returns to normal, and the pain in my chest subsides, Carmine tells me to take small sips of water.

"Are you feeling better?" My mother asks.

I nod. But when I notice that my grandmother's casket is completely buried under the earth, I sob cold January tears.

***

It's only six o'clock but the sky is black and shiny like tar as we drive along a path full of potholes that leads out of the cemetery.

The temperature outside has dropped into single digits and it doesn't feel much warmer in Ty's truck.

"Your teeth are chattering." I start to pull off his jacket. "Here's your jacket back."

"No, you keep it but c'mere." I slide against him and he places his arm around my shoulders. He smells fresh and clean, like the outdoors. As awful as today has been, I feel so safe in his embrace. I'm so glad he offered to drive me home, even though my father didn't understand.

"But it's out of your way, Ty. Jade should just ride home with us," my father said.

"Its okay sir, I don't mind," Ty replied.

"Suit yourself," my father said.

"We'll see you back at the house." My mother beamed. She loves Ty as if he were her son. She'd be thrilled if we chose each other for life mates.

Until recently, the thought of Ty as my life mate was absurd because we were best friends and nothing more. But recently, it's as if my feelings were placed in a pot and stirred. I wonder if Ty's heart flutters and if his body tingles when he looks at me? Or does he still think of me as just a friend?

As if reading my mind, he glances at me. A truck passes on our left, flooding Ty's truck with a bright beam, highlighting his chiseled face and full lips. When did he become so handsome? Why did my feelings for him change?

Ty pulls into my driveway but leaves the engine running.

"Your parents aren't here yet. Want to wait?" he asks.

"Sure." I could easily let myself in the house with my key but I'd rather linger in his truck. Lately no matter how much time we spend together, it's never enough.

"How are you feeling?" He asks.

"If I talk about my feelings, I'll start to cry again."

"Jade, there's nothing wrong with that." I'm still leaning against his shoulder. He takes strands of my hair and twirls them around his fingers.

"I know. I just…I'm not a crier. I swear I've cried more these past few days then I've cried in sixteen and a half years." Once again, tears start to spill down my face.

"I have tissues in here somewhere." Ty opens the center console and grabs a small pack of tissues. He pulls one out and gently wipes my face. His lips are inches from mine and the way that he's biting his lower lip causes my heart to thud against my chest. There's a glow from the dashboard, so I'm able to sink deeper into his intense purple eyes. This moment is beautiful. Now if only he would lean over and kiss me. And just as I'm sure he's about to, the moment is ruined by blinding headlights and squeaking breaks.

"Your dad needs a new truck, too." His voice sounds raspy.

"Maybe my father can trade a case of wine for a truck," I ramble.

We're still sitting there, looking at each other, when my father knocks on the window. I lean over and roll the window down.

"You made it here quick. Best not be driving too fast, son," my father says.

"No sir," Ty replies.

"Thank you for taking care of Jade today. Drive safely," my mother says.

"No problem. Good night," Ty replies.

I watch as my mother gently coaxes my father towards the house. I wind up the window and turn to Ty.

"Thanks for everything, Ty."

"Come here." He opens his arms and I am drawn to him like gravity. "You still have me," he says. I press my fingers into his muscular, rope like back. When his teeth chatter, I break away. I pull off his jacket and hand it to him.

"Good night, Ty." I kiss him quickly on the cheek.

"Night, Jade."

Reluctantly, I climb out of Ty's truck. I stand in the driveway, waving, until his tail lights fade like the stars when daylight breaks. I hurry into the house, leaving the pitch black sky behind me.

Chapter Three

The bright navy door is the only splash of color on this dreary morning as my parents and I traipse up the porch steps of my grandparents' home. We're encouraged to take anything of sentimental value but to leave the rest for a newly married couple who will move in within the next few days.

"Here sweetheart," my mother thrusts an oversized basket into my arms. "Scarlet phoned right before we left. She's already placed her name on the things that she would like to have—"

My father interrupts. "So her name's on everything." He crosses his arms tightly across his chest and grimaces.

"And she's already claimed Pearl." I scowl.

"Jade, we couldn't have taken Pearl and you know that." My mother's jonquil colored eyes flash. "This is hard on all of us, Scarlet included. If we find something special, she said we should take it, even if her name is on it."

"This is sick. I don't want to take anything. These are Grandmother's things," I reply, mirroring my father's demeanor.

"I agree," he says.

"Shall we box everything up for Scarlet, then?" My mother asks.

"No," my father and I reply simultaneously.

"Alright then, let's get to work," she says, clapping her hands for emphasis.

We pull off our winter jackets, scarves and gloves and hang them on the coat rack. We also kick off our boots which are dripping with slush.

"What do you say we tackle the kitchen first?" my mother asks with false cheerfulness.

"I'd rather start in Grandmother's bedroom if that's okay," I reply.

My father nods and my mother says, "That's fine." They head to the kitchen while I remain in the short hallway, transfixed by a picture of my father and grandfather ice fishing. In the picture, they're sitting on orange buckets, holding short fishing rods in one hand, and a beer from the Outside in the other. A few oily trout lay between the buckets on the thick clear ice. It's one of those rare occasions where my father looks content. It's also one of the best photos that I've ever taken. I peel the tag labeled "Scarlet" off of the photo and place it in my basket.

When I can't put it off any longer, I bypass my father's and then my Aunt Scarlet's childhood rooms and enter my grandparent's bedroom. It's silent except for the rhythmic tick-tock from the oversized wall clock. Tick-tock, tick-tock, tick-tock...

From the doorway I notice that Scarlet's name is plastered everywhere: on Grandmother's frilly, beaded dresses, which are too small for Scarlet: on untouched perfume bottles courtesy of Scarlet from birthdays past: on Grandmother's favorite pearl necklace. Sorry, Scarlet, the pearls are mine. I'll leave you the petite dresses and stinky perfume. I know that Grandmother would want me to have her necklace because I'll cherish it so much more.

Tears fill my eyes as I sink onto her bed and stroke the floral printed comforter. I bury my face into one of the throw pillows which smells fresh like mint toothpaste. I'm surprised that there are no labels on the bedding. "Oh, no!" I exclaim, jumping from the bed. What if Scarlet discovered the diary first?

I crouch in front of the cubbyhole and tentatively open the door. The hinges make a groaning sound. There are a dozen hat and shoe boxes which I slide out of the way. The cigar box is pushed in the very back corner. I have to lie on my stomach and crawl. As I reach for the box, dust fills my nose and I sneeze. I grasp the box, dragging it from the darkness. I smooth hair out of my eyes and lift the lid. I unwrap the floral scarf to find her diary.

"How's it going, Jade?" my mother calls from the hallway. I hastily wrap the diary in the scarf and shove it into the basket. I toss the pearls on top.

"Just fine," I reply as she opens the door.

"How'd you get so dirty?" she asks, joining me on the floor. "Oh, from the cubby hole, I forgot that your grandfather built this little closet. What's inside?"

"Nothing special, just hats and shoes."

She strokes the pearls and scarf. "Very pretty. You have a great eye."

Fortunately she doesn't continue digging through the basket. Instead, she licks her thumb and tries to wipe my face with it.

"Eww, yuck, I'm not six years old anymore."

"But you'll always be my baby." She smiles. "I know this is really hard for you."

I nod while opening one of the shoe boxes which is full of old pictures. "Gosh, you and dad look so young." My mother's eye color and name were Amber and my father's were Indigo. Her hair looks the same now as it does in the picture—long, light brown, and parted down the middle. In the photo, a crown of daisies compliments her simple yellow dress. My father's sandy blonde hair is disheveled and contrasts with his crisp gray shirt. They're holding hands and laughing.

She holds the picture against her chest and sighs. "Is the past really as sweet as I remember or do I just imagine it to be?"

"Mom, you sound all emotional like dad."

"If anything, you've been the one acting like your father." She cups my chin with her hand.

"Thanks, I guess."

"Not that there's anything wrong with that." She returns the photo to the shoebox. "I'm really glad you found these pictures."

"Me too. Did you find anything special?"

"Your father found a pipe that belonged to your grandfather. I've been transfixed by the snow globes but I didn't choose any yet. I was waiting for you. Ready?" She stands up, picks up my basket, and balances it on her hip.

"I'll be right there." I trace the intricate etching on the canopy bed post. When he wasn't working at the vineyard, my grandfather was an amazing wood smith. Besides the bed, Grandfather Navy crafted shelves, a bookcase, a hope chest, and other furnishings which will remain in the house. I hope the new occupants appreciate these pieces.

With a final glance, I vacate my grandparent's bedroom and join my mother in the living room. I kneel in front of the open curio cabinet like I've done countless times before and gaze at the thirty nine snow globes. I helped my grandmother make them by filling the mason jars with oil and crushed egg shell. I lift my favorite globe and shake it gently. The snow falls on the miniature oak trees, houses, a woman, and a child. Both figurines are wearing dresses: the woman in red and the child in green. They're walking on a path and at the end of this path a sign reads "Home" with an arrow pointing out of the snow globe.

"This is the one that I want," I say.

"Here's a towel to wrap it in." She hands me a dish towel. "Let's choose half and leave Scarlet the rest. That's only fair."

"You choose the rest. I need some air." I have got to get out of this stifling house. If I don't, I'm bound to start bawling.

"Are you sure?"

"I'm sure."

"Okay," she shrugs her thin shoulders.

I pull on my boots and grab my coat. It's sleeting but I don't bother to cover my head with my hood. I don't wear my gloves. Despite hating winter, there's something about cold weather that makes me feel alive. I walk along the slippery gravel path and try not to think of anything. But it's nearly impossible to shut my mind off, especially with everything that's happened these past few weeks.

Tomorrow, my parents and I return to work since we've used all of our bereavement leave. We're allotted two weeks for grief—as if that's long enough. My mother says that only time can heal but so far time has done nothing except make me miss my grandmother more.

On the right hand side of the road, there's a playground that's usually over run with children. I make snowballs and whale them at the "Nirvana Playground" sign. When my fingers are pink and cold, I plop on a swing. I pump my legs and soar as high as possible. I lay my head back and close my eyes. My long hair is surely tangled but I don't care. It feels so refreshing to act like a child again. I swing until my teeth chatter and my nose runs. On the walk back, I imagine my grandmother telling me to "search for a winter rainbow" but all I see are shades of gray. My gray mood quickly shifts to black when a guard driving a pick up truck pulls up alongside me.

"Well, what do we have here?" He says. His nose is crooked and his lower lip is puffed out like a chipmunk.

I wrap my arms tightly across my chest and keep my head down. I pray that another vehicle drives past soon so that I can yell for help; unless of course, it's another guard.

"What's wrong, you mute or somethin'?"

"No," I say, lifting my head.

"Yer pretty, even though your nose is runnin' and yer hair is wild. Where you headed? I can give you a ride somewhere." He smiles, exposing a chunk of chewing tobacco.

There's no way I'm getting into his truck without a fight. My father taught me a few defensive moves but I'll have to be quick and accurate. When he opens the door and climbs out, I place my hands in my pockets. I don't have my keys but I do have a pen. I notice a taser hanging from his belt but I don't see a gun.

"I'm not gonna hurt ya, I'd just like to get to know you better," he says.

My heart beats manically but my hands feel surprisingly calm. I wrap my fingers around the pen, pull it out of my pocket, and stab him in the cheek. Then I knee him as hard as I can in the groin. His blue eyes open wide in surprise before he doubles over in pain. As I turn and race into the woods, I can hear him moaning. Branches scratch my face and body as I run but I don't slow until I'm much deeper into the woods. When I near my grandparent's house, I take a few deep breaths and pull my tangled hair into a ponytail. I've just done something really ballsy; I've just made myself a target. If I mention what happened to my parents, my father will react and he'll become a target, too. I've learned that often it's better to say nothing at all.

When I return, my parents are loading boxes and baskets into the truck bed. My mother says, "Why were you out so long? It's freezing out here. And you don't even have your coat zipped. You'll get sick. What were you thinking?"

"People don't get sick by being in the cold," I reply.

"Then why is your nose running?" My mother pulls out crumpled tissues from her coat pocket and hands them to me.

Without waiting for a response she says, "You better take a hot bath as soon as we get home."

My father tosses a ring of keys to me. I wish I could tell him that pens work just as well as a means of self-defense. I know I don't usually make him proud, but I think if he knew what just happened, he would be.

"Jade, why don't you start the truck, we're almost done." I climb into the truck and start the engine. My mother places my basket into the truck bed. I should have taken Grandmother Ruby's diary with me to the park. I hope my mother didn't find it because she'll insist on reading it, too. But then again, it's probably best that I didn't bring the diary with me. What if the guard had gotten hold of it? Or what if I had lost it in the woods?

As usual, my mother sits in the middle and my father takes the wheel. He peels out of the driveway as if he can't get away fast enough. I don't turn around because without my grandparents, the house is just an empty mass of nails and wood.

"Well that didn't take too long, did it? That's team work for you." My mother says. "I'll phone Scarlet to let her know it's her turn and then it will be ready for the next couple—"

"Jonquil, please stop talking about this." My father interrupts as he narrows his crystal blue eyes and grips the steering wheel.

"I'm sorry. I didn't mean to upset you," she says softly.

"She's just trying to make us feel better. Why do you have to be so mean?" I snap.

"It's okay, Jade. Your father isn't being mean, he's just upset," she says.

"I apologize. That was one of the hardest things that I've ever had to do. I thought losing dad was tough." His voice breaks.

My mother loops her arm through his. "I don't know what I'd do without the two of you. When I lost my parents, I felt abandoned. Still do actually…" she trails off.

I'm relieved when we turn onto Paradise Place. A "Dead End" sign is posted next to our wooden mailbox. Sometimes I think that this sign should replace the "Welcome to Nirvana" sign on Samsara Street which is the only official entrance/exit to our commune. It's as if we're trapped in snow globes—like each of us is a snowflake created in the commune. And nearly every snowflake will melt within the globe. How depressing.

When we return, we go our separate ways. My father and Licorice, our black Labrador retriever, take a walk, my mother escapes to her yoga room, and I head for the bathtub.

In my bathroom I light lavender scented candles before turning off the light switch and turning the water dial to the right. I remove my clothes and drop them in pile. I twist my auburn hair into a bun before easing my body into the porcelain tub and laying my head against the tiles.

What a crappy week.

I tilt my head and gaze at the glow-in-the-dark planet, star, moon, and comet stickers I had placed on the ceiling several years ago. Along with his books, my father must have ordered them from the Outside because we don't have glow-in-the-dark anything in Nirvana. We're taught that there's no such thing as astrology or an afterlife or anything supernatural. Fortunately, my father's book collection is vast. It's been a slow process but from reading the Bible, which I hear is sacred on the Outside, I now believe that there is something after death, something special. I just know there's a guardian angel looking out for every one of us, even if we don't live on the Outside. Perhaps Grandfather Navy was watching over me earlier today; protecting me from the guard. What if the guard had somehow forced me into the truck? What if he had touched me? A cold shudder runs up my spine, so I turn the hot water on. I tuck my knees under my chin and will the guard out of my mind.

I visualize the actual sky and the Cancer constellation which is my astrological sign. This constellation is considered one of the darkest signs because its stars are faint.

Ty's astrological sign is the Leo constellation which consists of much brighter stars. In fact, Ty tends to light up a room when he enters whereas I barely make a spark. In that respect, he's like my mother and Grandmother Ruby. I'm much more like my father, quiet and reserved.

If I choose winemaking as my life path, will my father and I butt heads because we're so similar? Will my mother and I argue because we aren't similar enough? Every time I think about the upcoming intraocular operation, I feel shaky and sick. After the surgery, when I look in the mirror and I'm met with blue or yellow eyes, will I still recognize myself? Or will I become a stranger?

I wonder if Ty's anxious about the eye color procedure, too. His seventeenth birthday is a few weeks after mine. Not that anything will go wrong with the procedure; it's extremely safe. Regardless, I'll miss his captivating purple eyes. I'll miss his name. I'll miss spending so much time together when we choose life mates. Unless we choose each other. I wonder if he knows that I'm falling in love with him. Wait, did I really just think that about *my best friend?*

After my bath, I throw on a pair of jeans and a sweater, grab the diary, and walk out back to my work shed which consists of two rooms. One is for processing film and the other is to hang out and relax. I remove the tiny key from around my neck and unlock the wooden door. The sour-like odor immediately hits my nose. It's a smell that my father loathes, considering the smell of vinegar indicates tainted wine. There isn't any ruined wine in my dark room, only chemicals that are used for developing film.

I slip through the room divider, light a few patchouli scented candles, and lie against fluffy pillows. I slip my black rimmed glasses on and hold the diary as if it's a fragile egg. Its crisp pages are taunting me but even so, it takes a minute to gain the courage to open it. Maybe I should start a fire and use this as kindling… but as soon as this thought crosses my mind, I disregard it for I know I'll engulf these secret words as hungrily as a wild fire. Once I start to read, I realize there's no going back.

Chapter Four

Excerpt from Grandmother Ruby's diary- September 2, 2011

Yesterday I worked alongside my daughter for the last time. Perhaps now that we don't see each other every day our relationship will improve, but I doubt it. Regardless, I'm retired! Now I have time to do the things I'm passionate about, including writing in a diary, gardening and spending time with friends and family; Carmine and Jade in particular. Scarlet is most likely jealous of the bond I have with them. On the other hand, I've tried my best to improve our relationship but Scarlet doesn't seem interested.

I'm worried about her. I can understand her plight; not being able to have children must be devastating. But she's intolerable. She's grown as bitter and unsavory as unsweetened coffee. This morning she stopped by before work. Now that I'm retired, she's required to work full time; and she let me know just how unhappy she is about that. And nothing I said comforted her. In fact, she stormed off after she said that the only person who understands is her best friend Saffron. It's unfortunate that infertility is the tie that binds them.

In disbelief, I re-read the last sentence several times. "But Saffron has a daughter." I whisper even though I'm alone in my work shed. I know it surprised commune members when our commune leaders accepted an Outsider into their family instead of waiting for a second biological child. But maybe they had tried and for whatever reason couldn't have another. Regardless, Peaches looks just like Rust and must be his daughter. Grandmother Ruby must be mistaken. But what would make her think that? I painstakingly read a few more entries but she doesn't mention it again. I yearn to keep reading but my eyelids feel so heavy.

Once I'm in bed and under the covers, my body relaxes but my mind refuses to let go of incessant thoughts that scatter like a rack of pool balls. My father has a homemade pool table in his work shed but he never plays because it's covered with books and pages of his short stories and poetry. And empty wine bottles. If I choose winemaking as my life path, will he still feel such a strong urge to escape? Will he finally treat me like a daughter instead of some teenager that just happens to live with him? But if I don't choose teaching, will I break my mother's heart?

And then there's the diary. Should I rip out each page- tear them into little pieces? Feed them to the wind? That way my life will carry out as planned. I'll choose winemaking or teaching. I'll get married; have three children and a dog. I'll take photos in my spare time. Life will continue to be simple, tranquil, and equal. Isn't that what I want? Isn't that what everyone wants?

But if I destroy my grandmother's words, I'll always wonder, always yearn for the truth. And I'd feel as if I've betrayed her because she needed me to know. At some point my mind succumbs to sleep.

The next morning I wake before seven. I step into the shower before my mother has a chance to spray a crisp citrus scent. She says it's the smell of waking up, of energy and light. To me it's the scent that jars me from sleep. After I dress, grab my camera and a mug of coffee, I hurry outside. The luminous sun is shining but there are an abundance of clouds so it's frigid. My mother waits patiently at the end of the driveway, an enormous wicker basket at her feet. I'm surprised to see Slate standing next to her, clutching his brown paper lunch bag. I wonder if Slate will bring us closer to Scarlet and Naples. I sure hope not.

"Hi," he says softly, tucking his head. He reminds me of a bent daisy. He stares at the ground looking pale and afraid.

"Hi Slate. What did you bring for lunch?" I ask.

"A sandwich and chips," he says.

"Sounds good. I have a tofu salad."

He scrunches his face and says "yuck," which makes my mother and I laugh.

"What's with the basket?" I ask her.

"I made mini pies for the kids last night. You were sleeping and your father was held hostage by words, so I decided to bake."

"I like that description, Mom. 'Held hostage by words.' Dad would probably like that, too."

"I'm sure he would." Her response is short because she's irritated by the amount of hours he spends writing. She'd rather he spend time with her.

As we walk along Paradise Place, I think of how bland the month of February is. It's probably around thirty-five degrees, the trees appear emaciated without leaves, flecks of snow fall from the pale gray sky, there's stillness in the air…nothing special about it.

I focus on Slate. He's shuffling along, head down, and kicking rocks. His parents are dead. He's been plucked from his home, his school, from his life. I can't imagine the pain he's going through. And here I am feeling sorry for myself.

"What's hanging from your neck?" He wrinkles his brow. I notice his lips turn up slightly. I look at my mother and she winks.

"It's a Polaroid camera."

"It looks really old."

"It is old but it still works. Would you like me to take your picture?"

"Okay." He smoothes his hair and straightens his shirt.

There's nothing nearby but a dirt road and listless trees. I look around for a decent place to take his picture. "Why don't you stand in that patch of sunlight?" I ask. Slate runs to the spot and smiles so big that his eyes twinkle. I snap the picture. When the photo slides out, I hand it to him.

"It'll take a few minutes to develop," I say.

"That's so cool, even my camera phone doesn't do that!"

"You have a camera in your phone?" I ask, intrigued.

Slate nods. "I can't find it though. I think I left it in the car."

In the car; where his parents died.

We walk in an awkward silence, unsure of what to say. All we pass are homes identical to ours except for their door colors and trees stripped of their vibrant autumn costumes. I'm grateful when Slate finally speaks.

"Is that it? It looks small and old." He points to the nursery school on the left hand side of the road. The door is painted a sickly yellow and is in dire need of a fresh coat of paint.

"No, that's the nursery school. That's for kids four and under," my mother says.

"My brother was four," he says.

I glance at my mother. Her frown matches mine. His brother must have died in the car accident otherwise Scarlet and Naples would have adopted him, too. And no one came forth to claim Slate. The same thing happened to Bronze. The thought both surprises and saddens me.

Tears form in his eyes so I say the first thing that pops into my mind. "Yesterday I took a picture in my mother's garden of purple flowers. My favorite color is purple. What's yours?"

"It used to be red but not anymore."

"Why not?" I ask.

"Because of the scary red- eyed people," he says as he hunches his shoulders.

"I know how you feel. Scarlet has eyes like that too."

"She's just joking. Right Jade?" My mother says. She gives me the *watch what you're saying look* that she saves for her most mischievous students.

I crouch next to Slate and say, "I'm afraid of her too." He giggles.

The last thing that I need is to argue with my mother. "Of course I'm joking."

"Not really," I whisper in Slate's ear.

"Oh no," my mother says.

When I look up, a truck filled with guards is barreling towards us.

"Quick, move!" She shouts while pushing us roughly to the side of the road.

As luck would have it, it's the truck from yesterday, which means the guard with the crooked nose is most likely driving. My heart is beating a million beats per minute. Think fast, Jade. I pull my reading glasses from my pocket and slip them on my face. Then I pull my winter cap lower on my forehead. The guard that I attacked parks next to us. There's a slight indention on his right cheek from my pen.

"You didn't really think I was gonna hit ya, right?" Crooked says. When we don't respond he says, "Where ya headed?"

"To work with my daughter and my nephew. He's in our class." My mother says. Even though she must be scared, her voice is steady.

"What are yer names?"

"I'm Jonquil and this is Jade." She points at me. "And Slate." She holds him tightly against her.

One of the guards sitting in the truck bed leans over and stares at Slate. "So you're the newest Outsider. I bet you miss playin' those videogames."

"Shut up." Crooked says. He steps out of the truck with an iris scanner clasped in his left hand. "Just a routine stop, ma'am. Look in the scanner." He holds it up to Slate's eyes. Click.

I freeze when he holds the scanner in front of me. "Do I know you?" He asks.

I shake my head. Click. How did he not recognize me? He must harass so many girls that he can't tell them apart. The thought makes me sick.

Next it's my mother's turn. Crooked lingers in front of her, eyeing her up and down. "Didn't you used to date Rust, back in the day? I can see why he liked you." He strokes her chin which makes her grimace. Click.

My fingers wrap around the pen in my pocket and I yearn for a replay of yesterday. Instead I narrow my eyes and wish him ill will. As if sensing my anger, he turns away from my mother and leers at me.

"I bet you'll be as pretty as your mama one day." He grins, exposing large, horse-like teeth. The smell of chewing tobacco radiates from his mouth. I have to take a step back.

"Leave her alone," my mother snaps.

"Excuse me?" He moves closer to her.

She straightens her spine. "I said leave her alone."

"Let's go, Peri," the guard sitting in the passenger seat says. "We have a lot of rounds yet."

Peri spits a chunk of tobacco inches from my mother's shoes. "You take care now, you hear?" He returns to the truck. We watch as he drives erratically down the road.

"Now those are people to be cautious of," my mother tells Slate.

"Why are they so mean?" He shudders.

She takes his hand. "Because they're bullies. They've been given a little power and aren't able to handle it. Try your best to stay away from them, Slate."

"His name is Peri." A nervous laugh escapes my lips.

"Why's that funny?" Slate asks.

"Peri is short for Periwinkle."

"That's a baby name," Slate says. When he smiles, the skin around his eyes crinkles.

"Be careful what you say about the guards, okay, sweetie?" My mother says.

"Yes, ma'am," he replies.

My mother quickens her pace and we follow. I wonder if officials on the Outside treat people as badly. I assume they do.

After a quarter of a mile, we arrive at the elementary school house which is about the size of two homes glued together. The front door is cherry red and squeaks when my mother pushes it open.

"The restroom is here," she says, pointing to the last room on the left. "Next is our classroom." We follow her into the spacious room with scratched wooden floors and high windows. "Our classroom consists of nine and ten year old students. The other two rooms look the same. Mikado teaches seven and eight year olds, and Lemon and her son Persian teach five and six year olds."

"Where are the laptops?" Slate asks.

"We have three computers back there." She points to the back of the room. "But we don't have any laptops."

He sighs loudly. Clearly he misses the technology from the Outside. I'm sure that I would, too. My mother shrugs her shoulders as if she's at a loss. "Here's a stack of napkins, Slate. Please pass them out." She walks behind him, placing mini pies on each student's desk. In turn, I fill the students' bronze cups with water.

After we're done, I stand in the back of the room and watch my mother write neatly across the board using a yellow stick of chalk. *Lesson Plan: Spelling Quiz, Fractions, Reading Hour, Science Lab.* If I were a student in this class, I'd dread the spelling quiz. So many words aren't spelled the way they sound. It just doesn't make sense.

The mini pies look perfect on the child-sized desks, so I take a picture. I really do enjoy working with children, especially the silly, offbeat ones, like Olive.

"Yay, Ms. Jade's here!" Olive slides across the scuffed floor.

"Hi, Olive." I ruffle her short hair.

"Who's he?" She points at Slate.

"Olive, don't point, it's rude. His name is Slate. I'm sure you'll like him, he's very nice, just a little shy."

She stares at Slate as if trying to make up her mind. "Okay." Her attention is diverted to the mini pies. "Oooh, a treat!" She races to her desk.

Once all of the students have taken their seats, my mother raises her hand for silence. "Before you dig in, I'd like to introduce you to Slate."

All thirty students turn to look at Slate, who is sitting in one of the empty desks in the back of the room. His face turns a tomato color. I'm not sure how the class will react to him.

"Hi Slate," the class says.

Slate gives a tentative wave.

My mother says, "Slate is from the Outside, so make sure to make him feel welcome."

Soon all thirty- one students' mouths and hands are covered in berry juice. Slate fits right in. I grab my camera and start snapping pictures.

"Say cheese, Olive," I say.

"I don't like cheese, but I like pie. Pie." She says before smiling broadly. Click!

Afterwards I supervise small groups of students in the restroom, making sure that every student washes their sticky hands. I remind each of them to tell Ms. Jonquil "thank you."

"Thank you, Ms. Jonquil!" Each student hollers as they re-enter the class room.

I can't imagine being alone with all thirty- one of these children each day. My mother really needs my help. I know it's a relief for her to continue teaching while I take students out of the class for restroom breaks. I also speak to the students who are misbehaving. Today I remove Tangelo from the classroom several times for poking students with his pencil, laughing loudly and throwing papers.

"What's going on with you, Tangelo?" I ask. We're sitting on a step outside of the school house. I perch on the edge of the step because it's cold. Numerous clouds have parted and the sun is a brilliant shade of lemon yellow but once again, it's greedy with its warmth. I imagine gigantic icicles hanging precariously from the sun's rays.

"It's hard for me to sit still." He scowls and his orange colored eyes flicker.

"Well, why don't we have a secret signal? You can let me know when you need a break and we can hang outside or in the hallway for a few minutes."

"What kind of secret signal?"

"Why don't you flip your empty water cup over when you feel like you've just got to get away?"

"And then you'll take me outside?" He grins.

"I know what you're thinking; you can't just simply turn your cup over for the entire school day. How about you flip your cup over no more than three times each day?"

"How about five times a day?"

"How about three?" I say.

"Four?"

"Three," I reply. "And that's my final offer."

"Okay."

"You can only flip your cup over one more time today since we've been outside more than we've been inside this morning."

"What happens when you aren't here?" he asks.

"I'll tell Ms. Jonquil about our secret signal."

"But then it won't be a secret anymore."

"It will be a secret between the three of us," I reply.

"Okay," he says reluctantly as we walk back inside.

The rest of the morning passes quickly and after my mother teaches a math lesson, the students march outside with their packed lunches. On rainy and snowy days the students eat at their desks. On pleasant days, there's a picnic table for teachers, but the kids sit in the grass. It's chaotic but all three classrooms eat at the same time. It gives Mikado, Lemon, Persian, and my mother a chance to gossip. I slide onto the bench next to my mother.

"I made mini pies for all of you," my mother says to the other teachers. "There's raspberry and blackberry. Frozen berries aren't as good as fresh, so I apologize." She pulls a dozen pies from the picnic basket and sets them on the table.

"Everything you make is delicious, Jonquil. Thank you." Mikado grabs one of each.

"Yeah, thanks." Persian says with his mouth full.

"How can you do this to me, woman? Tomorrow is weigh in!" Lemon places her hands on her thick hips.

"Then don't eat them, Mom." Persian rolls his eyes.

"Turn down dessert made by Jonquil? You must be crazy." She reaches for one of each pie and puts them on her plate. "I hope I weigh in with a nice nurse tomorrow. Really, anyone but Scarlet." She covers her mouth with her hand. "Oh, I'm so sorry. I keep forgetting that she's your aunt, Jade."

I'd like to forget too. "No worries. I know how strict she is."

I move the lettuce around in the bowl. I stab a piece of tofu with my fork but I just have no appetite.

"So Jade," Mikado says. "Can you see yourself working here every day?"

A knot rises in my throat. Three pairs of yellow eyes and one pair of orange eyes stare at me. "Umm...." I know what they want to hear but I have no idea what I want to do.

"Help, help!" squeals Olive. "Tangelo has my animal crackers!"

I rise from the picnic table. "I better check on them."

And I'm saved by nine and ten year olds because the subject of my life path is dropped. I notice that Slate is talking to a sweet girl. They remind me of Ty and me when we were younger.

After I finish picking at my salad, I carry a garbage bag around for the students to dump their trash. Persian, who was in the same class with me but who I've never liked, follows. His orange-brown hair resembles pottery and is the same shade as his eyes as if it were natural. Freckles splatter across his face and his ears are too large. I wonder who his life partner will be.

"Jade, you're so lucky that you're a first born," he says.

"Why do you say that?"

"Because you actually have a choice. My sister chose dad's job, which is what I really wanted and now I'm stuck doing this." He throws his hands up and spins in a circle. "I think she only chose medicine to spite me."

"I'm sure that isn't true. You've got to think positive."

"Yeah, right. Are you going to choose this life path?" he asks.

"I haven't decided yet."

"Time's ticking. Tick, tick, tock."

I refrain from making a mean comment. I won't give him the satisfaction of knowing that he's upset me.

"Since you're an only child, you'll have to have three children one day. Maybe you aren't so lucky after all." He snickers.

He's got a point. Up until now, I've tried very hard not to think about this rule. But for the rest of the school day, I'm consumed by Persian's comment. It doesn't matter that my future self may not want three children or any; it's simply our duty to keep Nirvana as balanced as possible. And my parents weren't able to do that.

That evening Ty stops by my work shed unexpectedly. I'm in my dark room, listening to a Rolling Stones record, and hanging pictures on the drying rack, when I hear a knock on the door. I assume it's my mother, so I call out, "Be right there, Mother!"

"Actually it's me Jade," Ty responds. Oh no, I look a mess. My hair is thrown up in a haphazard bun, I'm wearing a faded black tank top and ripped jeans. I contemplate hiding in the closet but he knows I'm in here. I search in a junk drawer for candy to mask my coffee breath and find a lone stick of cinnamon gum. My heart thuds in my chest as I slip through the door. Ty is leafing through a book of poems.

"Hi," I tilt my head shyly.

"Hey." He glances from the book and grins. "Your poetry collection grows like weeds, I swear."

Since I'm an excruciatingly slow reader, I enjoy reading poetry much more than novels. "That's the benefits of being a wine maker's daughter. You know our wine sells well on the Outside. I'm thankful that my father lets me read all of these. He'd be punished if anyone found out but no one will. Unless you tell on us." I joke. "So what's up?"

"Just wanted to see how you're doing." He returns the Robert Frost Poetry Collection to the shelf. His purple colored eyes look expectantly at me.

I sink to the floor, among the throw pillows. "I've been better."

When he sits next to me, I breathe in his clean scent.

"I can't imagine how much it hurts to lose someone you love so much," he says as he runs his hand through his dark hair.

Ty hasn't lost anyone close to him and yet I've lost all four of my grandparents. It's not fair. Not that I want something bad to happen to someone that Ty loves. It just seems like some families are hit so much harder than others. And mine was hit exponentially hard.

He leans back against a pillow. "Ouch." He reaches into the pillow case and before I have a chance to stop him, he removes Grandmother Ruby's diary. "Jade, what's this?"

My heart sinks. As much as I'd like to confide in Ty, I promised Grandmother Ruby that I wouldn't. "It's private."

"I understand." He slips the diary back into the pillow case and moves it aside. I'm so relieved he didn't open it or press for more information.

"So how are you doing?" I ask.

"Work has been more stressful since my father's been missing quite a few days." He sighs.

"Is he okay?" I ask.

"Yeah, he should be fine. He wasn't feeling well the day of your Grandmother's funeral or else he would have been there. My mother was too worried to leave him by himself. By the way, both of my parents told me to tell you that they're thinking of you and to let them know if you or your parents need anything. You know how much they adore you," he says.

"Please tell them thank you. And I adore them too." If Ty and I are life mates, then I'll have wonderful in-laws. I feel my cheeks grow red at the thought. I pull the rubber band from my hair to hide my flushed face. Then I ask, "So what's making your father so sick?"

"We think it's just heartburn but he refuses to speak to a nurse. You know how they are. Remember when I was eight years old and broke my leg? I gained a bunch of weight and wasn't allowed dessert for weeks at the Center."

"But I always snuck you half of mine because I felt bad for you."

"What if they would have caught us? We'd probably still be on restriction." He rolls his eyes which makes me laugh.

It feels so good to laugh with Ty, and yet part of me feels guilty because my grandmother just died, as if I laughing should be prohibited. But just as I'm enjoying the sound of Ty's laugher, he grows serious.

"I was thinking about Slate for some reason today. How's he doing?"

"He seems fine, considering all he's been through. Why?"

"Does it seem odd to you that nearly every year there's a fatal car accident in Nirvana?" His purple eyes search deep into mine. When I say nothing, he continues. "And each time a child is the only survivor, a child from the Outside."

"Stop it, Ty. You're scaring me." I break eye contact.

"It could be just a coincidence," he says. But deep down both of us knows he's lying.

Chapter Five

Excerpt from Grandmother Ruby's diary- September 10, 2011

I readily accepted an invitation to join a Thursday night bridge club at Samsara. Saffron, who never worked a day in her life, fellow retired broads, and I had a lovely time playing cards in the formal parlor. That room is quite fancy with polished wood floors and red silk damask adorning the walls and brightening the black walnut shelves and doors. Saffron's maid served copious amounts of Merlot from my son's winery and chocolate truffles from the Outside. It was fabulous!

Toward the end of the evening, I excused myself to use the lady's room. As I strolled down the main hall, I overheard men arguing in the little parlor. Curious to a fault, I pressed myself against the wall and eavesdropped. I easily recognized Rust's voice. He was speaking slowly, as if he were talking to someone feeble minded. He ordered this person to stay away from their sister. He said that if they didn't, there would be severe consequences. At one point I couldn't help myself from peeking into the room. The room was dimly lit and the men were seated at a small card table. A hefty cigar hung from the corner of Rust's mouth. The man he was speaking to was his adoptive son, Bronze. Before I had the chance to step away from the doorway, Rust turned his head. His eyes, which were like dancing flames, met mine. My heart beat vociferously as I tiptoed back to the former parlor.

What is going on between Bronze and Peaches? Are they having an inappropriate relationship? Why else would Rust sound so irate? Did Rust recognize me?

I lean back against the wall and close my eyes. Why didn't she mention this particular evening to me? I used to beg her to tell me the minutest details about her evenings at Samsara. It reminds me of a castle in fairy tale books.

I'd drape a potato sack around my shoulders and ask things like: "Did you enjoy your time at the castle? How are King Rust and Queen Saffron faring? Did you catch a glimpse of Princess Peaches and Prince Bronze?"

In turn, Grandmother Ruby would say, "My dear peasant girl, I had the most exquisite time. Since I couldn't bring you, I brought a gift from the castle to you." Then she'd hand me a linen napkin filled with almond macaroons in every color of the rainbow. "Let me tell you all about my night…"

What else has she kept secret from me? I turn the page to the next excerpt—

Knock, knock, knock.

"Jade, breakfast." I hear my mother call from the porch.

"Be right there." I slip the diary into a pillowcase before meeting her at the door.

"You're becoming as bad as your father." She brushes a strand of hair off of my forehead. She's been comparing us a lot lately.

"Bad how?" I ask.

"Spending so much time out here." She points to my work shed.

"Dad offered to build you a shed, too."

"Perhaps he should build another. That way we can just live separate lives." She turns and strides toward the house.

I don't respond because I don't want to get her started. Arguing with her is futile because she just shuts down and pouts like a child.

When we enter the kitchen, my father is seated at the table, holding a novel in one hand and a fork in the other. I spoon some mixed fruit in a bowl and join him.

"It's Friday," my mother says brightly, as if she wasn't upset less than a minute ago.

"Mmm, hmm," he mumbles.

"It was difficult returning to work yesterday. Thank goodness Jade was with me. I'm not sure I could have made it without her." She smiles. "Royal, you would have been so proud of the way she calmed down Tangelo. He actually behaved for the rest of the afternoon."

"I think he just needs some extra attention," I reply.

"I think that's very true, Jade. Children require just as much attention as my grape vines do," he says.

"So do wives," she says with a sarcastic edge to her voice.

My father ignores the comment. He pops a strawberry in his mouth and chews slowly before saying, "I'm sure Jade will be a great help at the winery tomorrow as well."

I nod and concentrate on eating quickly. I feel like throwing up every time I think about making my life choice. I'm bound to disappoint one of my parents, which is the last thing I want to do. Having a sibling would make this choice so much easier. One of us would take over school teaching, the other winemaking.

While I take a hot shower, my mind drifts to Ty. I can't wait to see him after our meeting at the Center. Whenever I gaze into his purple colored eyes I feel like I'm drowning. There's a slight urge to struggle, to kick my legs and cry for help and yet there's a stronger desire to simply let go.

After I dry off, I spray honeysuckle perfume on each wrist and then rub them along my neck. I curl my thick hair and run my fingers through it, creating loose waves. I choose a pink cotton skirt, white tights, pink flats, and a form fitting ivory sweater. Since my sixteenth birthday I've become less of a tomboy. I never thought I'd be the girl to wear pink. But then again, I never thought I'd fall in love with my best friend. Or that I'd lose my grandmother before my seventeenth birthday.

"Aren't you forgetting something?" My mother asks as I walk out the front door. What is she talking about? Was she snooping in my darkroom? Has she found Grandmother Ruby's diary?

"What?" I ask casually.

"Your coat, silly." She hands me a jacket.

Sigh. So now I'm being ridiculous.

When my parents and I step outside, we're met by a brisk wind and bright sunlight. A dusting of snow covers our world. My mother and I climb into the truck as my father clears off the front and back windshields. I crank up the heat and am immediately greeted with a cool blast of air. This old truck takes forever to warm up.

"You look beautiful," she says. "I'm sure Ty will think so, too."

"What are you talking about? I told you we're just friends."

"Talking about Ty again, huh?' My father asks as he gets into the truck.

Heat spreads across my face. Are my feelings for Ty so transparent that even my father can tell? Most of the time, it seems as though my father lives in his own little literary world. Fortunately my parents drop the subject of my love life or lack there of, and move on to boring topics like what supplies we need from the market.

As soon as my father makes a left onto Samsara Street, the boxwood trees block the sun, leaving the street in a shroud of darkness. Once we're through the tunnel of trees, my father drives to the back of the plantation house. He parks between nearly identical work trucks.

"Are we late, Royal?" My mother asks, a hint of worry in her voice.

"No, its quarter to eleven, we're early." He hoists a case of wine onto his shoulder for today's offering.

A lump rises in my throat as I follow my parents along the gravel lane for I started to search for Grandmother Ruby in the crowd. Pull yourself together, Jade. Don't cry.

I concentrate on Samsara, the imposing red brick manor home with ivory pillars. I would never wish to live here. It's beautiful yet hauntingly unwelcoming at the same time. I stare at the brilliant red doors, willing them to open because my toes are already losing sensation from the cold. I should have worn boots and jeans not flats and a skirt. I grab onto my mother's arm and snuggle against her for warmth.

"It's not even that cold, honey." My mother says but she wraps her arm around me anyway.

Whenever any of our students spot us they exclaim, "Hi, Miss Jonquil! Hi, Miss Jade!" Most are bundled up in mittens and hats and trying desperately to form a ball from a teaspoon of snow. My mother and I can't help but laugh. I say hello to former classmates and other commune members I know. I scan the crowd for Ty but don't see him. I feel a pang of disappointment but I'm bound to see him at some point today, and hopefully this evening, too.

At eleven o'clock sharp, Rust and Saffron thrust open the double doors. Guards stand on either side like lions. We follow the throng of people until we're finally standing in the Central Passage Way. As a check in, one by one we gaze into a machine that snaps an image of our eyes. *Click.*

My father places six bottles of Viognier and six bottles of Cabernet Franc on the offering table, next to breads, fruits, and vegetables. Everyone that works in the food industry is expected to contribute to our communal lunch.

We wait in line for our weekly physical which takes place on the third floor, Wing B, which is the hospital. It's the crappiest part of my week.

"I shouldn't have eaten so much these past few days," my father says, patting his flat stomach.

My mother smirks. "No, you shouldn't have, but you could have joined me for yoga this morning."

"My heart would have been racing for sure after yoga," he jokes. "Would've burned tons of calories."

"Every little bit helps." She says, playfully poking his side.

We shuffle along, single file.

I lean against the wall and allow my scattered thoughts to drift above my head and pop one by one like needles to balloons. Why didn't Grandmother Ruby mention the argument between Rust and Bronze? Didn't she trust me to keep it a secret? POP!

We climb a few steps.

How can I decide which life path to take? I'm only sixteen and a half. What if I choose winemaking but regret it or vice versa? Maybe I should just flip a coin from the Outside and leave my life path to chance. Heads for teaching, tails for winemaking. But then that would eliminate leaving Nirvana which Grandmother Ruby mentioned. Is there a way to escape without ramifications? POP!

We climb several more.

I wonder if Ty has ever considered leaving. Where is he anyway? As we stand at the top of the stair case, I glance over the railing to the first and second floors but don't see him anywhere. POP!

On the third floor, we sign in, and then we wait until a nurse calls our name. I wonder which room Aunt Scarlet's in. I'd prefer not to deal with her.

"Jade Green, room three," a voice calls out. I walk into room three which is a simple bedroom with bare floorboards, mint green painted walls, and a single window overlooking a garden.

"Hello." A girl wearing a white nursing uniform with red trim enters the room. Her eyes are her only vibrant feature. She reminds me of a moth because her skin is so pale and she's too thin. She was two years ahead of me in the Academy, so she's eighteen or nineteen years old but she looks years younger.

"Hi, my name's Jade," I reply automatically.

"I know that, I was the one who called your name." She smirks as she closes the wooden door. I'm taken back by the sight of her teeth. It's as if the tips of her two front teeth were dipped in brown paint. What could have happened to them? "Why don't you step on the scale first?"

I slip off my flats, remove all of my clothing except for my pale pink bra and underwear, and place them on a chair. I dutifully step onto the scale which reads one hundred and eighteen pounds.

"You've gained three pounds since last Friday. You've got to watch it." She jots down my number on the chart.

"I just had my period, so it's only water weight." I step off the scale and cross my arms tightly against my chest.

"Doesn't matter," Moth girl says. "You're five foot five inches tall and sixteen years old which means you have to weigh one hundred and fifteen pounds in order to stay balanced. Two pounds in either direction is adequate but not three. You'll have to lay off the dessert."

What is this girl's problem? She weighs like ninety pounds and she's several inches taller than me. Her weight is anything but balanced.

As I get dressed, she asks a plethora of questions.

"When was your last period?"

"It ended like two days ago, so it would have started five days before that."

"Are you sexually active?"

I feel my face grow hot. "No."

"I have to ask. Sorry." She doesn't sound sorry at all.

I perch on the end of the examination table.

"Any recent physical or mental ailments?"

I shake my head although Moth girl is giving me a headache.

"Open up and say ahh." She places a stick on my tongue, shining a flash light at my face. "Looks normal. Now for your temperature." She places the thermometer under my tongue. "Ninety eight point five." She scribbles on my chart.

"Now to check blood sugar levels. Since you've been eating a lot of dessert lately, it's probably high." Moth girl has serious issues. I'll refuse to ever see her again: if that's even possible.

I reluctantly offer her my pointer finger which she pricks with a needle. She squeezes until a drop of blood appears which she wipes on a tiny stick before inserting it into a small gadget. "Seventy six, low actually. Give me your arm." She places a cuff around my upper arm. "Eight five over fifty five. Are you sure you're not dead?"

"I'm very much alive." I yank my arm away from her.

"I was just joking, relax," she says. Moth girl could also pass as one of those insects that look like a stick.

"Let me just check your eyes and then you may leave."

I dutifully place my chin and forehead against the cool metal bars of the slit lamp and stare into the thin beam of light. Moth girl views my eyes through a microscope. After a few moments, she says, "They look normal. Have a nice afternoon."

I gather my coat, scarf and purse and exit into the hallway without saying a word. I'm so flustered that I don't notice Peaches until I've plowed my shoulder into her back.

"I am so sorry! Are you okay?" I ask.

She turns around slowly, wincing and rubbing her back. "That really hurt."

"I'll go get an ice—"

"Just kidding, I'm fine. I have plenty of padding. Isn't weigh in the worst? Why can't I just stay chubby and happy?" She smiles which lights up her round, pretty face.

"I know, right? My nurse was so rude." I lower my voice so that the commune members milling in the hall don't overhear.

"Which nurse was it?" She whispers.

"She didn't say her name but she looked like an insect. Kind of like a cross between a moth and a stick."

She nods her head. "She's one of the worst."

"Peaches dear, it's time to go." Saffron says. She's standing a few feet away from us.

"Another stick creature," Peaches whispers. "It was nice seeing you, Jade."

"Nice seeing you, too." I wave. We don't know each other too well since Peaches was home schooled. Otherwise, we probably would have been good friends. I follow Peaches and Saffron down the black walnut stairwell. My parents are waiting for me in the Central Passageway.

"That seemed to take a while. Is everything okay?" my mother asks.

"Yes, everything's fine. My nurse was just insane, that's all," I explain.

"Well, it's over, sweetie." She strokes my hair before we take our seats.

My father finds a bench with room for the three of us. Even though I'm sitting between my parents and we're surrounded by hundreds of people, I feel alone and anxious. Crowds always make me feel awkward. I finger the tassels on my scarf.

"You seem out of sorts. Here breathe in some lavender." My mother hands me a small jar and I place it beneath my nose. It doesn't help, but I lie and tell my mother that it does.

I will myself to focus on the stage but my eyes reflexively shift to the left hand side of the Center where fifteen commune members align a wooden bench. The youngest is twenty-two and the oldest is seventy-six. At some point in their lives, each of them attempted to escape Nirvana. Now each of them is blind. Ivory, the youngest male, turns his head in my direction and I'm transfixed by his milky white, lifeless eyes. A million questions race through my mind. If he had it to do over again, would he try to escape? Has anyone ever escaped with their vision intact? What would drive a person to find out? I've never had the courage to ask him that. After a moment, I force myself to look away. I focus on the bright lights which adorn the stage, the surrounding chatter, and the delicious smell of baking bread wafting in from the dining hall.

Once Rust and Saffron take the stage, all side conversation comes to a halt. "It's so nice to see all of you. Thank you for coming," Saffron speaks slowly into the microphone. As if we have a choice. Sickness and death are the only excused absences. She looks like a caricature because her breasts are so massive and yet her waist is tiny. It doesn't look natural. Perhaps she's had a few plastic surgeries at a place on the Outside. That's what I've heard through the grape vine, anyway.

She rambles on for a bit while I scan the crowd. When Ty's eyes meet mine, I smile, revealing all of my teeth and probably my gums. I have to look away when he places his hands around his neck pretending to choke himself, because the last thing I want to do is burst out laughing during the Center meeting. We'd be called out and embarrassed in front of the entire crowd.

I force myself to focus on the stage. "Now for community news," Rust's voice booms into the microphone. His height and muscular frame are intimidating to most. Although his hair is brown like milk chocolate, the sunshine pouring in from the window is highlighting the red hues in his hair, nearly matching my hair color to a tee. I think of the weirdest things sometimes.

"We have a number of sixteen year olds approaching their seventeenth birthdays, some of which have chosen their life paths. Persian Orange, please join us." Persian climbs the steps to the stage.

"Son, what is your life path?" Rust asks, thrusting the microphone in Persian's face.

"I'm going to teach five and six year olds with my mother," Persian mumbles into the microphone. I nearly feel sorry for him.

"Have you decided on your adult name?" Rust asks.

"Yes, I chose Maize Yellow."

"Let's give Persian, who will soon be named Maize, a hand here. Good luck on your life path, son." Rust says.

Persian's mother Lemon is the first to jump up and clap. As the crowd joins in, Persian's face grows bright red.

"Next, will Fandango Purple come to the stage?" Rust asks. Several people snicker. I'm sure that Fandango will be thrilled to change his name. I don't know him very well because he's always been incredibly shy. He's tall and thin like Uncle Naples.

"Fandango, what is your life path, son?" Rust asks.

"A plumber, sir."

"Excellent. Have you decided on an adult name?"

"Denim Blue."

"Congratulations. Let's give Denim a round of applause." As we clap, I search the front benches for Bronze and Peaches who always sit together. I spot Peaches right away but I don't see Bronze. Perhaps he's on a mission on the Outside. I rarely see any other Outsiders because they aren't required to attend the Center. Bronze is the exception considering his adoptive parents are the commune leaders.

"I'm sorry to end our meeting on a somber note but one of our members was caught stealing six bottles of alcohol from Samsara. Gold Yellow, it's time to receive your punishment."

Commune members gasp in disbelief because Gold is an upstanding member of our community. Recently, she lost her son in a farming accident. That's probably why she tried to steal alcohol. With her head bent, Gold climbs the steps to the stage where Saffron is waiting for her with a wooden paddle.

"This is going to hurt me much more than it hurts you." Saffron says.

Commune members mutter insults such as "She enjoys this," and "Sadist." My mother holds my hand and squeezes it.

Gold bends over and grips onto a chair. Saffron lifts the paddle high above her head and then whacks it hard against Gold's behind. Gold let's out a yelp. I clench my eyes shut. Saffron hits her a total of six times, one for each bottle of alcohol stolen.

"Sweetie, it's over. You can open your eyes now." My mother whispers in my ear.

When I open them, Gold is hiding her face with a handkerchief and sobbing.

"I know, it's awful, isn't it? I'll never get used to it either," she says.

My father remains quiet but his jaw is clenched. He thinks paddling adults as punishment is inhumane and humiliating. I agree but there's nothing we can do about it.

After assembly, we gather in the dining hall. Grandmother Ruby used to sit on my right but now there's a little girl in her place. Familiar waves of sadness crash against my chest.

Noticing my discomfort, my father says, "Jade, why don't you sit between us."

I nod and take a seat. I push the chicken breast onto my bread plate and nibble on carrots, broccoli and potatoes. Even though my mother and I are vegetarians, they always bring us poultry and meat. At least they don't force us to eat it. My parents continue to talk about tomorrow's market day.

"I'd like a new yoga mat but I don't really need it," my mother says.

"There's not much that I need either," my father says.

"Jade, have you thought any more about trading some of your photos?" she asks.

"I'm not ready to do that yet," I immediately reply.

"I don't mean to rush you. It's just that you have so many incredible photos. Do you need any more film or supplies?"

"No, I still have quite a lot." I just haven't been taking as many pictures lately. I haven't been developing many either.

When dessert arrives, I only take a few bites of blueberry pie with vanilla ice cream because I'm not in a sweet mood. If it's so important to maintain such a strict weight, I wonder why we're given sweets each Friday. It's as though someone in charge is sabotaging us. And if I don't lose those three pounds soon, I'll receive ice water in place of dessert. That would be embarrassing. I feel awful for the people who never receive dessert.

While my parents sip coffee, I excuse myself from the table to find Ty.

"We're nearly finished. Why don't we meet at the truck in ten minutes?" My father says.

"Okay," I reply.

Ty is waiting for me in the hall. His arms are folded and he's chewing on his bottom lip. Even though there are other people in the hall, mostly children running around, I'm completely focused on his twilight eyes. I yearn to race down the hall, jump into his arms, and plant a passionate kiss on his lips.

Instead I lightly grab onto his muscular arm which causes butterflies to samba in my stomach. "Why so serious? Are you upset about what happened to Gold?" I ask.

"That was awful. She didn't deserve that, no one does. Plus it's just one of those days. Want to meet at the cabin at four o'clock?"

"Sure, is everything alright?"

His face relaxes slightly. "Everything's fine. I just need to talk to my best friend."

"I'll see you then. I have to go now, my parents are waiting for me." As I turn away, the term *friend* bangs around in my head like a tambourine. Will he ever call me his girlfriend or am I stuck with friend status, forever? Does he even feel the same way? If not, why did I bother to curl my hair and wear this outfit?

When my parents and I arrive home, I march to my bedroom and change into jeans, a long sleeve tee-shirt and boots. I also pull my hair into a ponytail.

My parents are drinking tea in the kitchen. "I'm taking a walk to Ty's house," I say.

"Why don't you take the truck?" My mother asks. "I don't like the thought of you walking back home in the dark. Especially with those nasty guards milling around."

"Did something happen?" My father's eyes narrow.

"No." My mother's eyes meet mine. We both know its best not to tell my father about bad things that happen because he tends to overreact.

"I'll be fine. Plus I need the exercise since I was told how fat I am during my physical."

My father peers over a novel. His reading glasses make his eyes look like marbles. "You look fine to me," he says.

"Jade, you're perfect just the way you are," my mother replies. "You're my daughter after all." She smiles wryly.

The corners of my mouth turn slightly. "I promise I'll be careful." I pull on a winter coat and scarf.

"Don't stay out too late," my father says.

I nod before I open the kitchen door and escape into the late afternoon.

Ty and I have been meeting at the cabin since we were eight years old. We used it as a club house but were the only members.

Even though we had numerous friends, the cabin was something that was only ours.

"Want to see something cool?" Ty asked when we were playing hide and seek in the woods one day.

"Sure," I replied.

"But you have to promise not to show it to anyone else, or else it won't be special anymore." Ty's front two teeth were missing and he had a habit of sticking his tongue through the space.

"Okay, let's go." I said.

"I'll race you there." Ty yanked one of my pigtails before taking off.

"Where?" I chased after him, the leaves crunching and crackling beneath my sneakers. "Are we going to your house?"

"No, but it's nearby."

I pumped my legs as fast as they'd go, as if I were on a swing in the school yard. My father told me that once he flipped the swing over the bar, while he was in it. He said that he was trying to reach for the moon but no matter how hard he tried, he couldn't reach it.

"Ta-da." Ty halted and threw his skinny arms up.

My mouth dropped open.

"Well aren't you going to say anything?" Ty asked, scrunching up his nose.

"Why is this slave cabin so far away from the others?" I asked.

"I don't know and I don't care because it's mine now. Mom made me a flag so that I could claim it." An eggplant colored flag flapped in the breeze.

Nearly nine years later the flag is still standing, but time has faded its color to a lilac.

We still don't know why this slave cabin is so far away from the others and why it's unoccupied. The rest of the slave cabins are about a half mile from the Samsara plantation and house the blind.

The wooden door squeals like a baby crying as I push it. The smell of must hits me and I breathe in greedily because I love the scent of the past.

Ty is seated on the single bench, gazing out the small, glassless window. I slide next to him, not as close to him as I would like, but close enough to smell his cologne, a combination of musk and leather, which smells even better than the musty cabin.

Through the window, gray clouds hover mightily in the sky. Birds are chirping but I have to strain my ears to hear them over the wind. Large oak trees extend their branches as if offering friendship to one another.

"I bet my father is praying to the sun gods right about now," I say.

"Why?" he asks, glancing at me.

"We've had way too much rain this season and too much rain causes the grapes to split. He says last year was a really bad year, at least for wine. It's too bad he's unable to visit other wineries outside of Nirvana. Sometimes he'll order wine from the Outside, but it can't be the same."

"Stuck in Nirvana, how ironic." Ty brushes a lock of dark hair from his forehead and sighs.

"It really is. What's wrong?"

"I have a lot on my mind. I'm afraid I'm not going to be the best company tonight."

"This will cheer you up." I pull an energy drink called ZOLT from my oversized purse. Even though I think it tastes like syrup, it's Ty's favorite drink. I always ask my father to order a few cans for Ty from the Outside. Ty's parents refuse to order it because they're health nuts and ZOLT is anything but good for you.

He smiles, exposing perfect white teeth.

"When we were little, I wondered if your adult teeth would ever grow in," I say.

"Hey, my mom said I was cute without front teeth."

"Let's just say you're a lot better looking with teeth." I feel heat spread over my face yet again.

"That reminds me; I meant to tell you how nice you looked at the Center." He tilts his head and grins.

"Thanks." I twirl my ponytail through my fingers. He could have used the word pretty but I'd settle for nice. I'm just happy he noticed.

For a few moments, we listen to the wind blowing the trees as if waking them from a long slumber. I shiver and Ty immediately takes his coat off and drapes it across my shoulders.

"Thanks again. So what are you thinking about?" I ask.

"I found something out." His purple colored eyes flash. "My uncle isn't dead."

"What are you talking about? I thought your Uncle Hunter died before his seventeenth birthday."

"I thought so too until I caught my parents in a lie. After your grandmother's funeral, I asked them why we never visit Uncle Hunter's grave. They stared at each other for like an eternity before my father said, 'Maya, it's about time we told him the truth.' But my mother shook her head. Her eyes were cold enough to freeze a flame. My father said nothing. I thought the conversation was over, but she turned to me and said, 'Son you don't need to know the details of your uncle's death. It isn't pleasant or necessary. But I will tell you there is no grave site for him, so don't bother looking.'"

"Wow, she told you that?"

He nods. "I knew she was lying. Every member of our commune, no matter what, has a grave site. That is if they're dead." He pauses to take a swig of *ZOLT.*

"You don't think he left the commune, do you?" I ask.

Ty stands and paces. "Why else wouldn't he have a grave site? And why else would my father suggest telling me the truth?"

"Well, how will you find out if he's still alive?"

"I figure I'll ask Bronze." He walks to the window and stares out. "Perhaps the next time he visits the Outside he can search for Uncle Hunter. There has to be a way to find him."

"Why would Bronze want to help you? You're not exactly friends."

"I'd have to bribe him of course." He rakes his fingers through his hair. "I'll think of something."

I join him at the window. "Be careful," I whisper.

"Always." He grins. "I'd also like to visit the cemetery."

"But your mother already said your uncle doesn't have a grave site."

"I'm sure he doesn't."

"Then what's the point of going to the cemetery?" I frown.

"To search for your grandparent's graves. You mentioned you've never seen them, right?"

"You're not implying that my grandparents may have left Nirvana?" My voice sounds shrill, unrecognizable.

Ty gently grabs hold of my arms. He opens his mouth to speak but says nothing for a moment. We stand there, searching each other's eyes. It should feel awkward but it doesn't.

I break the spell of silence. "How could they have left the commune in the first place?"

"Maybe they bribed the guards who helped them escape. I don't know but there just has to be a way out of here."

I stare at him in disbelief.

"You've never wanted to leave this place?" He asks.

"I've never wanted to risk my sight!" I exclaim.

"Part of me is seriously considering leaving Nirvana. With my sight," he adds.

"But Ty," I grab his hands, "Even if you found a way to escape; once you leave you can never come back. Wouldn't you miss your friends and family?"

"I wouldn't miss you if you came with me." His twilight colored eyes pierce my heart. I can't imagine losing Ty. Because if he left, no matter how much my heart broke, I couldn't leave with him. I just couldn't hurt my parents like that. I just couldn't risk going blind.

"Don't say things like that," I plead.

"I'm sorry I brought this up."

"I'm sorry you did, too. I think it's time for me to go home." I remove his coat from around my shoulders and toss it to him.

"Let me walk you home, it's getting dark and I don't trust the guards."

"They're never in the woods and I'll be fine by myself," I reply. Even so, Ty follows behind me, as loyal as Licorice. I take long strides along the dirt path. Fortunately I know these woods so well that even though it's getting dark, I know exactly where and when to turn.

I'm seething inside. How could Ty even suggest that my grandparents may have left Nirvana? How could they have deserted my mother? It's such a shameful act. It can't be true.

Grandfather Rufous and Grandmother Goldenrod died in a tragic fire. That's what happened to them. My mother wouldn't lie to me about something like that.

When we reach the 'Dead End' sign, Ty turns away from me. I watch him walk away until the darkness swallows his form. I feel a sharp pain in my heart as if a shard of glass has just punctured it.

Chapter Six

Excerpt from Grandmother Ruby's diary- September 21, 2011

At the Center today, I focused on the dynamics of Rust's family. For being such a powerful man, Rust succumbs to Saffron's every wile. It's as if she has a love, or more accurately a lust, spell on him. I wouldn't be surprised if she were a bona fide witch. Perhaps my daughter is one, too. My son-in-law Naples may as well be a rug, the way he allows Scarlet to wear him down.

Then there's Rust and Saffron's adoptive son, Bronze. He's an Outsider through and through. And he's trouble. He best stay away from my granddaughter. And there's something wrong with the way he touches Peaches. Granted they aren't biological siblings but even so, it's unsettling to see his hand placed protectively across the small of her back at all times. Rust must think the same since that's what they were arguing about the other night. Clearly Bronze isn't heeding his father's warning. And Rust isn't someone to cross. I wonder if he regrets accepting Bronze into his family.

I've often thought the relationship between Peaches and Bronze is a mirror image of mine and Ty's. And I've fallen in love with Ty and if I'm lucky, he feels the same. It sounds like my Grandmother was on to something.

It's been such an awful week. I miss Ty and yet I'm still so irritated by what he said. He hasn't called or stopped by since last Friday. This is the longest we've ever gone without at least speaking on the phone. Life is unbearable without Grandmother Ruby and Ty.

KRISTY FELTENBERGER GILLESPIE

I lie in bed and stare at the white ceiling. Eventually my eye lids grow heavy and I fall back asleep. Unfortunately my mother's voice wakes me, zapping me back to reality which is the last place I want to be. The citrus scent follows.

"You look exhausted. Are you feeling alright?" She perches on the side of my bed.

"I'm fine."

"Well, you don't look fine." She wrinkles her forehead. "And you haven't spoken to Ty in awhile. Did you two have a fight?"

"No, I just haven't been sleeping well. What's the weather like?" I ask in order to deflect the topic from Ty.

"It looks like the sun took a vacation, so dress warm. I'll make you some coffee."

"Thanks." I root through my closet, deciding on jeans, a T-shirt, sweatshirt and sneakers.

"Here honey." My mother thrusts a travel mug at me the minute I step foot into the kitchen. My father is leaning against the door with an identical travel mug.

"Don't forget the deal we made with Tangelo but don't let him flip his cup over more than three times." I say to my mother.

"I won't." She smiles and hands me a picnic basket. "Besides your lunch, there are mini pies for the blind. Have a great day." She gives each of us a kiss on the cheek.

"Are you sure you don't want a ride, Jonquil?" My father asks.

"No way. I enjoy my morning walks too much. Plus, Slate keeps me company," she says.

I pray the guards leave them alone.

When we step outside, we're greeted with a gust of wind. As I approach Licorice, his tail wags frantically. The best part of working at the winery is bringing Licorice. After he jumps onto the seat of the truck, he presses his face against the window. Every so often he barks at a squirrel, a person, and anything else that moves. His life is so simple.

During the three miles to the vineyard, my mind swarms like bees after an ignorant person throws a rock at their hive. Ty's words race through my head. 'I wouldn't miss you if you came with me.' Why would Ty want to leave the peace and safety of

66 | P a g e

Nirvana? What kind of life would he lead on the Outside? And why would he think I'd ever leave with him?

My father parks his work truck outside of the rust red barn. Even after he turns on the light, it's dim inside. I place my belongings behind the counter before filling Licorice's water and food dishes.

"So what's my job today?" I ask.

"Minding the counter as usual," he says. "But first, taste this." He pours a small amount of a ruby red liquid into a wine glass.

I swirl the wine, place my entire nose into the glass and breathe deeply before I take a sip.

"What can you tell me?" he asks.

"It's been aged in oak. There's a hint of spice on the nose, taste of black cherries, long finish. It's Merlot."

"Excellent. Now you'll know how to describe it when the customers arrive. Please label these bottles." He points to the cases behind the counter. "Shout if you need me." He puts on a pair of work gloves. "I've got vines to tend to." He takes the opened bottle of Merlot and a wine glass with him. I worry when he drinks so early in the morning. Does he drink because he's sad? Or does he drink because he's overwhelmed? I could help him so much more in the vineyard, if only he'd let me. Will he ever ask me to do anything other then minding the counter? If I choose winemaking as my life path, he'd have no choice but to teach me, considering I'd be taking over as winemaker when he retires. Perhaps he'd be proud then.

I place a case of unlabeled Merlot on the counter and pull out the first bottle. It pains me to affix the label considering the design is so ugly. It says "NIRVANA MERLOT" in white letters above a rainbow bordered by clouds resembling grape clusters. Who came up with such an ugly design? I'll be disappointed if my father did.

As if reading my mind, a voice says, "Do you like those labels? Saffron designed them." Rust stands in front of the counter with an impish grin on his face.

"They're very nice," I reply.

"Don't lie, they're hideous, aren't they? Not sure why your father agreed to those." He laughs. His eyes, which are the same color as the barn, light up.

Did he have a choice? I don't dare say this. "They're okay. Would you like a glass of Merlot?"

"That would be lovely." He removes his brown leather jacket and drapes it at the end of the counter before he climbs onto a wooden stool.

I grab a corkscrew, open a bottle, and pour a wine glass halfway with Merlot.

"Why don't you have some, too?" he asks.

"I actually don't like wine very much," I say.

"I'm sure you'll grow to enjoy it, especially if you choose winemaking as your life path. Have you decided yet?"

I shake my head.

"Jade, can you toss me a bottle of water?" My father asks as he walks into the barn. His blue eyes narrow when he notices Rust.

Rust climbs from the stool, towering over my father by several inches. He offers his hand and my father reluctantly shakes it.

"Hello, Royal."

"Hello, Rust." My father turns to me. "Jade, the water."

I grab a bottle from behind the counter and hand it to him.

"Wish I could stay and chat but I've got to get back to the vines," he says.

"Don't work too hard," Rust replies.

We watch as my father vanishes out the door.

I've often wondered why my father hates Rust. A lot of people find Rust intimidating but I don't. I know my mother doesn't either.

As if reading my mind yet again, Rust asks, "How's your mother doing?"

"She's doing well."

"I bet those students keep her busy."

"They do, but she loves them," I say.

"And I'm sure they love her. Jonquil has always been such a natural with children." Our eyes lock for a moment.

"Anyway, I best get going." He swallows the rest of the wine in one long gulp.

"Did you want a case to go?" I ask.

"Sure, a mix would be great."

I place four bottles of Viognier, Merlot and Cabernet Franc in a box.

"Please add that to my tab. Perhaps your parents would like to order something from the Outside. It was nice seeing you, Jade. Take care." He lingers for a moment, staring at me which makes me feel uncomfortable. For a moment, I think he's going to say something meaningful but all he says is "goodbye."

"Bye. Have a nice day," I say.

After he's gone, I resume the tedious job of bottle labeling.

Every once in awhile a customer stops in. One woman exchanges a bag of potatoes for a bottle of Viognier. Another trades four small bottles of chamomile essential oils and a bag of tea leaves for four bottles of Cabernet Franc.

"These are for your mother," she says, "wonderful in treating depression."

"What? But my mother isn't depressed. If anything my father could use these," I joke.

"Chamomile works very well." She nods. "Have a nice day, dear."

What is this woman talking about? My mother is one of the happiest people, if not the happiest person I know. She must have my mother confused with someone else. As she leaves, Carmine walks in. Licorice barks incessantly.

"Licorice, it's just Carmine. She's not a stranger." Regardless, he keeps barking until I have no choice but to shoo him outside.

"That was some welcoming." Carmine sits at the bar. "How are you doing, Jade?"

"I'm doing okay. How are you?"

"All things considering, I'm okay."

"What would you like a glass of? We have Chardonnay, Cabernet Franc and Merlot."

"Usually I'd say Chardonnay but Cabernet Franc sounds nice."

After I pour her a glass, she swirls the wine, closes her eyes, and takes a long whiff. "This smells heavenly." She takes a long sip. "Tastes heavenly, too." After a moment, she says, "I have something for you, too." She hands me a thermos.

"What's this?"

"It's an herbal tea that is as therapeutic as it is tasty."

I take a drink. It's spicy yet fruity, like an orange bathed in chili pepper. It's a bizarre yet delicious combination. "I love tea. Thanks so much."

"You're welcome dear. Now that I know you like it, I'll bring you more."

"What's in it?"

"That's my little secret." She laughs which causes her double chin to jiggle. Carmine is the perfect example of someone whose inner beauty doesn't match their outer beauty. She tilts her head. "You remind me of Ruby."

"I miss her so much."

"Me too. Before she passed, she gave me her favorite red scarf. Did she leave you anything special?" She stares intently at me.

I contemplate telling Carmine about the diary considering they were best friends since grade school. But then I remember Grandmother asking me to tell no one. "I have some of her snow globes and a strand of pearls."

"That's nice dear." She drains the rest of the wine. "I best get going. Take care of yourself, Jade."

"It was nice seeing you, Carmine."

After she leaves, I let Licorice back in and continue with the labels. Once they're finished, Licorice and I curl up on the old leather couch. During the summer, which is our busy season, my father often spends the night here. I turn on the space heater which envelops us in luxurious warmth. We cuddle under the blanket and within minutes Licorice is snoozing. I look out the window as tiny flakes of snow fall from the gray sky.

I hope it snows so much school is canceled tomorrow. That way I can spend the day developing pictures instead of worrying about my future and missing Ty and Grandmother Ruby. But the chance of that happening is slim to none because it just doesn't snow enough in Nirvana. Wishing for snow, I drift off to sleep. Sometime later, I wake up when I hear my father's voice.

"Jade, it's time for lunch," he says.

"I'll be right there." I switch off the space heater and untangle myself from the blanket which causes Licorice to groan. "I know your life is so rough."

I join my father at the small wooden table where we eat our lunch.

"Boring day, huh?"

I rub the sleep from my eyes. "Sorry, I shouldn't sit on the couch because I always seem to fall asleep. After Rust, we only had two customers. Oh and Carmine stopped by. I finished labeling all of the Merlot."

"It's okay," he says which surprises me. He pulls out sandwiches from the picnic basket. "This one must be yours." He hands me a much thinner sandwich than his. "What kind of sandwich is that?"

"Tomato, lettuce and mayonnaise on toasted wheat bread."

He shakes his head. "It's missing the bacon and turkey."

"Yuck." I stick out my tongue before I take a bite of sandwich.

He takes a long drink of water before he says, "Jade, be careful what you tell Rust, okay?"

"What do you mean?" I scrunch my face in confusion.

My father tightens his jaw. "He comes across as charming and pleasant but that's just a thin veneer."

I hunch my shoulders. "I don't know him very well but he's always been nice to me."

"He's not a good person, period. No matter how nice he seems. Please be careful around him, promise me that."

Although I'd like to ask my father what Rust has done to him personally, I refrain. I honestly don't think he'd tell me. "I promise."

My father rises from the table. "I'm heading to the cabins. Would you rather stay here or come with me?"

"I'll come with you," I reply quickly. The majority of commune members avoid the blind; as if they're afraid they'll lose their sight by association. Most of their family members shun them, too. My parents and I are among the few people who visit them and they're always grateful for our visit.

I grab my camera and the picnic basket and follow my father and Licorice outside. The truck is covered in a thin layer of snow and a chill hangs in the air. My father pops a tape into the cassette player and cranks the volume. "Peace of Mind" by Boston blares from the speakers.

"Why don't you ever listen to any Nirvana produced music?" I ask.

"If it was half decent I would. Unfortunately, it sucks."

"It does, doesn't it?" I laugh.

We pass Samsara Street, a few other trucks, and a multitude of oak trees before we reach the slave cabins. My father parks in the middle of the road because chances are likely we'll be the only visitors today. As soon as I open my door, Licorice bounds out and races toward the campfire where most of the blind are gathered. My father balances a case of wine on his shoulder and I carry the picnic basket.

"Licorice!" Ivory exclaims. "I just knew you'd visit today. Sit." Licorice obediently sits, tilts his head, and waits expectantly for a treat. Ivory pulls a piece of beef jerky from his coat pocket. "Slow," he says. Licorice daintily accepts the treat.

"Licorice still doesn't listen to me like that. I don't know how you do it," I say.

Ivory shrugs his broad shoulders. "Just one of my many talents, I guess." Before he was blinded, his name and eye color was Cerulean. The color cerulean resembles the sky on a crystal clear spring day.

Magnolia, a woman in her sixties, embraces me. "It's so nice of you to visit, Jade. How are you dear?"

"I'm doing well. How are you?"

"Besides the aches and pains from old age, I'm doing pretty well." She turns to my father. "Royal, I'm glad you came." They hug.

"I'm glad to be here," he says.

"Enough with the pleasantries. Did you bring wine?" She asks, rubbing her hands together. Everyone laughs.

"Of course."

"In that case, have a seat." Magnolia motions to two empty lawn chairs.

"My mother made mini pies. Should I pass them around? There are napkins here, too." I say. I don't take one because my stomach feels queasy.

"Yes, please," Magnolia says.

"I'm glad I still have most of my teeth," Antique, the eldest blind member, says. His front two teeth are missing.

"Maybe you'd still have your teeth if you'd stop eating so many sweets," Magnolia chides.

"Mmm." Antique takes a large bite of pie.

"He's hopeless." Magnolia shakes her head.

I remove my camera from around my neck. "Does anyone mind if I take some pictures? I haven't taken any here in a long time."

Everyone shakes their heads.

I snap a few pictures of the slave cabins and the people surrounding the fire. Then I wander further into the woods. A wave of sadness washes over me. Ivory, Magnolia, Antique and the others are such warm, welcoming people and yet they're treated like criminals. How can fighting for freedom be a crime? Why are we forced to live in captivity? Is the Outside world such a treacherous place? I suppose I'll never find out. I lean against an oak tree and sigh.

"You okay?" I jump when I hear Ivory's voice. "Sorry, I didn't mean to startle you."

"That's okay."

"I can't believe you didn't hear me. I'm like an elephant clutching a tree branch." He leans against his walking stick.

"No, you aren't."

"Mind if I ask what you were thinking about?"

I tilt my head to the gray sky. I can barely make out the faded sun. "I suppose I was feeling sorry for myself. I've taken pictures of just about everyone and everything in Nirvana. Soon there won't be a reason to take any more." I immediately feel awful for complaining about something so trivial. I have my sight, family and a home, whereas Ivory has nothing!

"There's a whole world out there, Jade,' he says softly.

I inhale sharply. "Do you regret it?"

He pauses for a moment. "No. If I hadn't tried, I would have spent my entire life thinking about it anyway."

"Will you try again?"

"Not now. I couldn't leave my family." He points towards the fire. "They need me." So he thinks of the other blinds as his family. I hadn't thought about that. "And besides, if I tried again, surely they'd kill me."

I wrap my arms around my chest. "I know some commune members have escaped unharmed. How do you think they did it?"

Ivory chews on the inside of his cheek before he responds. "As far as I know, there are at least two ways. One way is to disable a section of the electric fence; the other is to pay off a guard to blow out a generator."

"Which did you choose?"

He sighs. "I chose the latter, which was clearly the wrong choice."

"Did the guard turn you in?"

He shook his head. "He was caught."

"What happened to him?"

"Public hanging; you don't remember?"

"I try really hard not to." I place my hand on his shoulder. "Ivory, I'm so sorry."

"No reason to be sorry; everything happens for a reason right?"

"Right," I reply uncertainly.

"Let's relax for a minute." He sits down and rests his head against an oak tree. I sit Indian style next to him. I close my eyes and try to imagine my life without sight; concentrating on my other main senses. I feel the wind caress my skin, smell the faint smoke from the fire, and hear rustling in the brush from what I assume is a squirrel. Unfortunately, there's nothing to chew on besides dirt and grass and I'd rather not taste that. Eventually I open my eyes to the familiar sights of the forest. As lovely as it is, I yearn to see, feel, smell, hear, and taste other parts of the world.

"Do you know how to disable part of the fence?" I whisper.

"Yes."

"Will you teach me how?"

"Are you sure you want to do this?"

"No, I'm not sure but I'd like to know how to just in case."

He pauses for a long moment and I assume the answer is "no." But then he says, "Okay, I'll teach you."

Chapter Seven

Excerpt from Grandmother Ruby's diary- October 4, 2011

I made the mistake of confiding in Carmine. There are some things I just can't talk to her about, which now includes anything remotely negative about Nirvana. Actually, these days it's difficult to find any topic that doesn't offend her. I'm not sure what's gotten into her lately.

Regardless, earlier today, Carmine and I were drinking tea in my kitchen and I decided to tell her about the argument I overheard between Rust and Bronze. I thought it would be nice to share this information with someone I trust. Instead, she admonished me for gossiping about things I had no business with.

Obviously, Scarlet was eavesdropping in the hallway because she barged into the kitchen, her face the same shade as her name, and scolded me for speaking out against Nirvana. According to Scarlet, I'm bound to bring trouble to our family if I start overturning stones. I pretended to agree with her, so that she'd borrow a cup of sugar and be on her way. Carmine left soon after.

From now on, I'll keep my thoughts concerning Nirvana to myself. (I'd confide in Jade but she has enough to think about right now). My sixth sense is telling me that underneath the pleasant, rainbow colored façade; some very unpleasant things are going on in Nirvana. I'm determined to find out what they are.

I'm assuming Scarlet had prior knowledge of Peaches and Bronze's unusual relationship, considering how close she is to

Saffron. I'm sure she's sworn to secrecy and she's probably afraid if the scandal gets out, they'll blame her. Therefore, I can understand why Scarlet would be upset. But why would Carmine? Maybe she was just trying to protect my grandmother.

I've read enough for one evening. I return the diary to its hiding place, blow out the half dozen candles, and lock the door to my dark room.

I jog across the yard in an attempt to bypass winters chill. When I enter the kitchen, my mother is seated at the table, staring into her tea cup as if searching for something meaningful. I pull up a chair and inch close to her.

"Mother, are you okay?"

She slowly looks up from the cup. Her yellow colored eyes are dull and despondent. Exactly how my eyes looked in Grandmother Ruby's hospice bathroom.

"Did someone die?" I whisper.

"No, of course not. Why would you ask such a thing?" She purses her lips.

I shrug. "It's just that you look so… sad."

"I'm not sad, I'm relaxed. This chamomile tea is potent. Would you like a cup?"

Not if it's going to make me look like you. "What else do we have?"

"There's green, black, and that funky tea Carmine dropped off for you. I tried it but didn't like it."

"I'll take the funky tea, please."

When she rises from the table, sheets of notebook paper slip from her lap. I bend to pick them up, but she grabs onto my upper arm. "I'll get those." Taken aback, I watch as she plucks them from the floor and shoves them into the bread box.

"Mother, what are those papers?" I ask.

"Oh, just a list of things we need at the market." She pours hot water from the kettle into a cup before dropping a tea bag in it. "Voila," she says, placing the mug in front of me. Her movements are slow, controlled.

"Thanks." Why is she acting so strange? I didn't know Chamomile could cause someone to act like a zombie.

She runs her fingers through her long brown hair. "What kinds of pictures are you developing?"

"Nature shots in black and white." Why did I mention the black and white part?

"No color?" She pouts. "Don't get all melancholy like your father."

Or like my mother, I think. According to the woman from the winery, my mother is the depressed one.

"I won't just take pictures of rainbows and butterflies," I reply before I have a chance to bite my tongue. My mother clearly doesn't understand. Why try to explain it?

"Relax, sweetheart. Take pictures of anything you want." She takes a sip of tea. "On another note, I know you must be worried about the procedure."

I grimace. "I am."

"Well don't worry about it too much. Just follow your heart. It's your life path after all." Her response sounds rehearsed. "You were the first born baby girl," she strokes my cheek with her soft fingers. "If you would have been the second born baby girl, your life would have turned out much different." Her yellow jonquil eyes darken.

Assuming she's referring to her situation growing up, I reply, "I'm sorry you didn't have a choice, Mother. Would you have been happier as a doctor?" My mother's father, my Grandfather Rufous, worked as a doctor.

She slides her fingers from my face to my hair. "You have the most gorgeous hair, Jade. You didn't get that from me." She smiles sadly.

"Are you sure you're okay?"

"Sorry, I didn't answer your question. No, I would have hated being a doctor. You know how I faint at the sight of a drop of blood! And I love being a teacher. Besides it doesn't matter now because it all worked out in the end. Just like it will work for you too honey."

"I know," I reply, in order to appease her. Why did she seem so sad a minute ago? Is she thinking about her parents, who died in a tragic fire? Or her sister, who passed away before I was born? Surely that's why she's depressed. It's a wonder she's not upset more often.

She rambles on for twenty minutes about safe topics like yoga and students at school. I respond with requisite nods and smiles.

"Well, I can't seem to keep my eyes open, so I'm heading to bed," she finally says. She kisses me on the forehead. Her lips feel dry.

"Good night," I reply. I rinse our mugs and glance out the window at my father's work shed. The lights are blazing so I know he's out there. Licorice must be with him. I pluck the papers from the bread box and hurry to my bedroom. I flick on a lamp and sit crossed-legged on my bed.

Angel Feat by Royal Blue. A chill of excitement runs down my spine for it's rare that I'm able to read one of my father's stories:

Rosado's dark hair whips around her as she glides across the ice.

"Hello," she calls as she passes Azul. "Are you ever going to speak to me or just stare?"

"Hello." Azul replies after a slight pause but she doesn't hear him. She's already at the end of the frozen lake, spinning like a plastic ballerina trapped in a jewelry box.

"I'm here to comfort her in her time of need and that is all." Azul whispers as he walks away. He reaches to touch the steam from his breath but it disappears.

That night, Azul watches Rosado as she sobs into her pillow. A picture of her dead baby girl, Rosa, is illuminated by a candle burning on the night stand. He strokes her cheek and hair after she succumbs to sleep. Azul blows the candle out before leaving.

The next morning, Azul watches from a corner table in a cafe as Rosado flits from table to table like a brand new mother bird. He peers at her over the top of a newspaper.

"You again? I'm Rosado and you are?"

"Azul."

"Why are you following me, Azul?"

He yearns to tell her the truth— that he's her guardian angel sent from Heaven to save her from herself. Instead, he says nothing.

Up close, Azul notices the fine wrinkles which circle her grayish-pink colored eyes. They are like washed up pools of sadness. To Azul, she is still beautiful even though she is skinny and pale.

"What can I get for you?" she asks.

"Plain coffee, please."

She brings him the coffee, which he doesn't drink, as he's an angel. Every so often he dumps the coffee into the plant on the table. And every so often she refills his cup. Mornings go by this way and Rosado begins to enjoy Azul's presence. One morning, the shop is empty. Rosado sits at his table.

"You're a mystery, Azul. You come here every morning, dump coffee into a plant and then leave. Why?"

"I actually don't like coffee." He smiles.

"Then why come here?"

"I like being around people."

"Don't you see enough people everyday at work? Do you even work?" She asks.

"I'm considering retirement; weighing my options."

"Wouldn't that be the life?" She sighs.

"Would you like to go somewhere sometime? Maybe ice skating?"

"No thank you. I'm not looking for a relationship. Especially not with someone who feeds coffee to a plant." She grins.

"I'd like to be your friend," he says.

Rosado hesitates before she says, "Okay, I suppose I could use a friend."

Two days later, on her day off, they ice skate.

"Your hand is so warm," she says as they glide slowly across the ice.

He squeezes her cold fingers.

She stops skating and gazes into his eyes. "In fact," she says, "you have this way about you, Azul. Ever since I've met you, I feel lighter, hopeful even. It's like you're the constant sun in my sky."

"And I will continue to be, as long as you need and want me to be."

He lowers his head to kiss her— warm lips meeting cold.

***

"Gris, please make me mortal."

"Azul, you cannot be serious."

"I love her. I can't fully protect her unless I'm human."

"You'd give up all this?" Gris spreads out his massive silver wings.

"Yes."

"Would I be wasting my breath if I were to try and change your mind?" Gris asks.

"Yes."

"But think of what happened to Amarillo, Blanco, Verde, Marron...I could go on and on."

"I honestly don't care, Gris. I'd rather spend a few moments with her than an eternity without."

"There's no going back."

"I know."

***

At first, Azul's human love is enough. He works as a waiter at a nearby restaurant and moves into her apartment. They ice skate until spring takes hold of winter's chill. Even human, Azul doesn't care for the taste of coffee but he loves hot chocolate which he orders each morning before work. They bike ride in the spring and plant flowers in the communal garden. In the summer they swim in the lake and eat ice cream cones nearly every night. When the slick green leaves turn to a dusty brown— that is when Azul's human love is no longer enough.

"I no longer feel hopeful around you. I don't feel your warmth. It's like a black hole in the sky swallowed the sun, which was you, which was our love. I'm so sorry, Azul." Rosado breaks down and sobs for the heartache of lost love and for her dead daughter.

Rosado's baby girl, Rosa died last autumn. It is if Rosado is suddenly haunted by Rosa. She can't sleep, refuses to eat, refuses to take her medication, and loses her job. All she does now is sit in the rocking chair by the window. She speaks of Morado, her first love that left her for another woman, soon after Rosa died.

It breaks Azul's heart to commit Rosado to a hospital but he's learned that he cannot save her from herself.

He visits her faithfully each morning. He brings her a cup of hot chocolate no matter the season. He works double shifts to pay for the medical bills. Sometimes there is a glimmer of the old Rosado. She'll wash her long dark hair and brush it one hundred times. She'll clasp Azul's hands and grin. She'll ask him to walk with her to the hospital garden. She'll clap her hands like a child when a flower blooms. But more times than not she stares blankly into space with no recollection of their brief love.

Rosado never leaves the hospital but Azul never regrets becoming human. To Azul, true love, no matter how brief, is worth the price of mortality.

The End.

"What does this story mean, father?" I whisper. "Are you Azul and is mother Rosado? But then who is Rosa? And who is Morado?" This story must mean *something*. Why else would my mother act so bizarre? I fight back tears because there's no time to fall apart. I have to figure out what the heck is going on around here. I tip toe to the kitchen. It's dark so I have to feel my way around. I eventually find the bread box and slip the story back inside. Lights are still glowing from my father's work shed and it's nearly eleven o'clock. I'm such a slow reader that it took me an hour to finish his story. I fill a glass with water and return to my bedroom. I crawl under the covers and stare wide eyed at the ceiling.

What does his story mean? What should I do now? Should I visit the cemetery and search for Grandfather Rufous and Grandmother Goldenrod's graves? But if their graves aren't there, then what do I do? Bribe Bronze to find out information from the Outside? But what do I bribe him with? The only thing that I can think of is wine and I'd have to smuggle it out of the winery without my father seeing it. Somehow in the midst of agonizing about this, I fall asleep.

Fortunately, the next day I work at the winery and only a handful of customers stop in. I even get a chance to nap with Licorice again. For once I don't mind that my father is quiet and distant during our late lunch. I feel the same way.

"May I please use the truck after work?" I ask as I clean up.

"What do you need it for?"

"I'd like to take a drive to clear my head. I've had a lot on my mind lately."

"Sure, I like to do the same thing from time to time." His blue eyes sparkle like the Hope Diamond. "Why don't you go now? Clearly we're not busy and I'm sure if anyone needs me, they'll holler," he says.

"Really? Thanks." I'm surprised.

My father pulls a ring of keys from his pocket and hands them to me. Licorice hears the keys jingle and races over.

"Not today, Licorice." I scratch behind his ears.

"C'mon boy," my father says. "I'll get you a bone."

Leaving the winery in the middle of the day feels so… freeing. Is this what people on the Outside do? I feel guilty about lying to my father but this is something I have to do.

The door to the truck squeaks and the engine rattles. Will I even make it to the cemetery? The roads are empty as I drive along. Most commune members are at work and school doing exactly what they are required to do.

I contemplate parking in the Blue Lot in order to pay my respect to Grandfather Navy but I worry I won't have enough time to find Grandmother Goldenrod and Grandfather Rufous's grave sites before dark. Therefore I park in the Yellow Lot. After I climb out of the truck, I zip up my sweatshirt and shove my hands into the front pockets. At the end of the gravel path, my boots sink into the soft earth. Twilight is approaching which reminds me of Ty's eyes and I think of how much easier this would have been with his help. I shake the image of his face from my mind and concentrate on the multitude of graves in front of me. "Gold" seems to be a popular name and it tricks me into looking closer several times. Row one and two can now be ruled out. Midway through row three I spot the name "Goldenrod" but the date reads 1902, whereas my grandparents supposedly died around the time that I was born, in the year 1995.

"Can I help you find a grave, Miss?" A raspy male voice asks which causes me to jump.

"Sorry, I didn't mean to scare you. It's just I know this graveyard like the back of my hand. My name's True." He holds a cigarette in his left hand and offers his right hand to me which I shake gingerly. He's around my late grandfather's age. He must not have had a child to take over his life path. Like Cobalt, our funeral director, this poor man will never retire.

"Do you have a name?" he asks.

"Jade. It's nice to meet you but I really should be going." This obviously was a bad idea. I feel awkward standing in the middle of a cemetery, chit-chatting with a caretaker.

"Jade? You're Ruby's granddaughter?" His deep blue eyes shine.

I fold my arms protectively across my chest. "You knew my grandmother? From where?" She never mentioned knowing this man.

"From here." He spreads out his arms. "She visited her late husband's grave frequently. That's how we got to know each other. She was a wonderful woman. I'm sorry for your loss."

"Thanks…did you attend the funeral?" I'm curious to know.

"No, I didn't. I prefer to remember people the way they were. If that makes any sense." He sighs.

"It makes perfect sense." I can see why my grandmother liked this man. "That must be hard to do, working here."

"When anyone I care about dies, I ask one of my coworkers to take over. I do the same for them."

I'm not sure what else to say, so I nod.

"Well, for future reference, there's a listing of everyone who's buried in each lot," he says.

"Where is the list located?" I ask.

"It's in the mausoleum where our founders are laid to rest. Right in the center of the entire cemetery." He inhales deeply on his cigarette.

"Thank you, I appreciate your help. And it really was nice meeting you." I smile.

"No worries, that's my job. You take care."

Once I've exited row three, I jog back to the work truck. Once the engine reluctantly comes to life, I drive quickly to the mausoleum, anxious for this adventure to end.

Poison ivy covers most of the building from the outside, so I use the sleeve of my sweatshirt to twist the knob. Why isn't the mausoleum better taken care of? After all, our founders are buried here. But then again, so much of what happens in Nirvana doesn't make sense. I use the weight of my shoulder to push open the wooden door. The cloying smell of honey fills my nose as soon as I enter. The building is heptagon shaped with Nirvana's founders, Glacier and Hazel's caskets in the center.

I lift one of the candles from its holder and use it as a guide. The first side on the far left lists all of the commune members who are buried in the Red Lot. Grandmother Ruby's name is last on the list. I trace the etching of her name with my pointer finger.

I climb a ladder to the dates from the mid 1990s. I search for Grandfather Rufous' name to no avail. I'm not surprised that Grandmother Goldenrod's name is missing from the Yellow Wall as well.

Chapter Eight

Excerpt from Grandmother Ruby's diary-October 13, 2011

Scarlet and Carmine have repeatedly told me how worried they are for me and how I should stop searching for dark secrets. But what have I actually found so far? I've overheard Rust chastise Bronze concerning Peaches. I've realized that Rust has a valid point; Bronze does treat Peaches as more of a girlfriend than as a sister. That's basically it, mere speculations. I haven't even begun to scratch the surface.

It makes me wonder if Grandmother Ruby ever dug for secrets in her own back yard. Did she know that her in-laws, my Grandmother Goldenrod and Grandfather Rufous, fled Nirvana? If so, did she know why? Or did she know that both of my parents might suffer from depression? Did she know anything about the baby in my father's story? If she did know, why didn't she share any of this knowledge with me? I'm more confused than ever. It's like I opened a hope chest of truth and destroyed the lock of naivety.

At breakfast, I stare into my coffee cup, as if I'll find answers within the bitter black liquid.

"Earth to Jade." My mother's voice slices through my thoughts like a knife through a multilayered cake. "Do you mind going to the market alone today? Your father left for work already and I couldn't find a retired teacher to take my place this morning, so I'll have to go in."

"Okay." I stretch my arms above my head and arch my back. Perhaps the long walk will clear my head and ease some of my anxiety.

"Thank you so much, honey. Have a great day but be careful." She kisses me on the forehead. Then she thrusts the list and tickets at me. Each ticket is worth one bottle of wine which I'll trade for the items on our list.

I leisurely get up from the kitchen table, slip on a pair of slippers and a robe, and fix another cup of black coffee. Then I step onto the front porch and sit on the wooden swing. The chains squeak as I push the swing back and forth with my feet. It's chilly but the hot coffee helps as it travels through my mouth, down my throat and in my stomach. Coffee is truly the best part of waking up. I rest my eyes and enjoy the solitude of the gray morning.

I've spent the past week feeling sorry for myself. I've gotten through each day with a fake smile on my face and each evening holed up in my dark room. I've got to pull myself together.

After I finish my coffee, I take a hot shower and get dressed. I grab the list, tickets, and large basket and walk briskly out the door. I only have to walk about a mile to the center of town where the market is held. Hints of spring brighten my spirits along the way. Bluebell flowers are growing in patches so I bend down to smell their clean but faint aroma. If my mother was with me, she'd pause to make a crown. I pick a single bluebell and tuck it behind my ear.

When I arrive at the market, tents of every color of the rainbow align Lullaby Lane. Most of what is traded at the market has been made locally but there are some things that are imported from the Outside including oil. Half a dozen guards peruse the lane, staring with their beady eyes at the contents and activity in each tent. I never speak to a guard if I can help it. I search for Crooked but fortunately don't see him.

I glance at the list which consists of: vegetables, (asparagus, beets, carrots, green onions) fruit, (anything that's available) beef jerky, several bath towels and wash cloths, mint toothpaste, and cigars.

My heart races from the last item on the list because Bronze is in charge of the tobacco tent. Perhaps I'll be able to speak with him about the Outside. Usually I take my time browsing and haggling but this morning I exchange quickly. I don't even bother arguing with the elderly man who insists one towel is equal to one bottle of Chardonnay, when clearly I deserve two towels for one bottle of wine.

As I'm about to leave his tent, he yells, "Miss, come back. Ahh, you young people don't haggle hard enough. Take another towel. Your father's a good man and your wine is worth beaucoup bucks."

"Thanks." I drop the cotton towel into my basket. I'm not sure what beaucoup means so I'll have to look it up in the dictionary later. But the way he said it makes me think it's a compliment.

As I approach the brown tobacco tent, my mouth feels dry but my hands are clammy. Bronze is straddling a stool with a bored look on his face.

"Hi, how are you?" I ask casually.

He brushes a piece of long blonde hair from his forehead. "What can I get for you?" He asks, by-passing any niceties.

"Three of these cigars." I point randomly.

"Nah, your old man will like these better." He slips half a dozen cigars in a plastic bag and places them on the counter.

"How many tickets do I owe you?"

"Don't worry about it. My old man says he owes you." He blows a ring of smoke from his mouth.

"Thank you." I add the cigars to the top of the full basket. Then I stand there awkwardly.

"Anything else? We have these slim cigarettes for ladies." He slides a thin cigarette from a packet. "They're all the rage on the Outside."

"No, thank you, I don't smoke. Mind if I sit?"

"Sure." He motions to an identical stool.

I slink behind the counter, rest my basket on the ground, and perch on the stool.

"Getting close to your seventeenth birthday, huh?" he asks.

"Less than six months, why?"

"I seem to become popular with the ladies before their birthdays." He licks his lips. "I'm popular with the guys, too." He laughs.

"I've got to go." I stand up. This was a ridiculous idea. I'm not dealing with slime. I'll find out about the Outside some other way.

"I'm just kidding, sit back down. What do you want to know?" His brown eyes have a hard, metallic quality.

I bite my lip and glance around the market. People are preoccupied with the art of trading. Guards are milling around, sampling various food products. Most of them have round bellies. They must be excused from weigh-ins. Regardless they aren't paying any attention to us. It won't hurt to ask him a few questions, will it?

I scoot my stool closer to his. "Have you ever thought of leaving Nirvana? I mean forever?" I whisper.

"The thought has crossed my mind but I have a good life here, even though my folks kicked me out of their mansion." He shrugs. "It's better living alone anyway. But then again, maybe I will leave Nirvana. I never know where the wind is going to take me. Why, do you want to run away with me?" He grins before inhaling deeply on his cigarette.

Ignoring his comment, I whisper, "What's it really like on the Outside? I've heard rumors of course, but you get to travel back and forth."

He drops the cigarette butt and grinds it into the dirt. He immediately lights another one before he replies. "What exactly do you want to know?"

"Has anyone ever asked you to help find someone on the Outside?"

"Yes. Who would you like to find?"

I hesitate because I don't trust him but curiosity gets the better of me. A quick glance at the surroundings proves that no one is paying any mind to us. "My mother's parents, Rufous Red and Goldenrod Yellow. They left here in 1995."

"I'll see what I can find."

"I'm not sure how I can repay you. All I can think of is wine and I'd have to pay you in installments."

"I can think of some ways." He smirks.

"That's not going to happen." I feel my lips purse and my face flush.

"Relax. I'm joking. I'm not as much of a jerk as everyone thinks I am, you know. I'll let you know when I find something out."

"Thank you, I appreciate it."

"Don't say a word of this to anyone, you hear me? We could both get into serious trouble." He looks at me gravely.

"I promise." Suddenly I have a sinking feeling in the pit of my stomach.

"Looks like we have company," he says.

"Hello Bronze, Jade." Ty is standing in front of the tent, clenching his jaw.

"Hey man, she wanted to talk to me." Bronze throws his hands in the air.

"Thanks again, Bronze. I'll see you later." I scoop up the basket and join Ty on the other side. I try not to smile but its hard not to because he actually looks jealous.

"Can we talk?" I ask, looking expectantly at him.

"Yes." He looks at me and shakes his head. "What am I going to do with you?"

I grin. "I don't know."

He places his hand lightly on my upper back. "Let's get out of here."

We weave through the crowd and end up on a path which leads to the Secret Grove. Although the name is pretty, it's really just a group of congested trees. Once we're surrounded by a canopy of silence, Ty sits on a large rock.

"Want to sit here?" He pats the space next to him and I sink down. He wraps his arm around me and squeezes.

"I've missed you," he says.

I rest my head on his shoulder. "I've missed you, too." My heart is beating so incredibly fast. There's no doubt I'm in love.

"What were you doing talking to that scumbag?"

"I asked for his help." I lift my head and grab his hand. "Ty, you were right. My grandparents aren't buried in Nirvana. I asked Bronze if he could help find them on the Outside. I'm sorry."

"Jade, I would have talked to him for you. I want you to stay away from him, he's shady." He runs a hand through his dark hair. "Promise that you will." Our eyes lock.

"But I've already asked him for information."

"I'd rather talk to him. He knows how close we are, he'll understand."

I'm torn. On one hand, I'm flattered because I'm pretty sure he's jealous. On the other hand, I'm irritated because I'm a big

89 | P a g e

girl and can take care of myself. Instead of responding, I bite my lip.

"How are you doing? Still mad at me?" he asks.

"I'm fine. And you're the one who should be mad at me."

"I want to apologize for being so insensitive."

"No worries. We all have our moments. Except for me, I'm pretty much perfect." I beam.

"You're pretty close." He tugs on my hair and grins. "Why don't you wear pig tails anymore?"

"For two reasons, for one, I'm not seven years old and two, because if I did you'd yank on them constantly." I playfully swat his arm.

"You're right, I totally would. C'mon, I'll drive you home." He reaches for my hands and pulls me up. For a moment it looks like he might embrace me, but he doesn't. Holding his hand feels as natural as breathing and he doesn't let go until we reach his truck.

"It felt weird not talking to you." He opens the passenger door.

"I know. That must have been the longest we've ever gone without talking," I reply.

"Yeah, even when we were kids our fights only lasted maybe an hour." He says as we climb into his truck. When he starts the engine, it rattles. "One thing I'm really looking forward to is having my own truck. Maybe then I won't mind being errand boy."

"So you were sent to the market today, too?"

"Actually, I offered to go. I needed to get away from the site for awhile."

"What are you working on now? Surely not the roads." I grab onto the handle as the tires dip in and out of potholes.

Ty laughs. "As soon as winter ends, we'll fix this road. Right now we're working on interior jobs like painting, plumbing, electrical work… fun stuff, huh?"

"At least it's more interesting than minding a wine counter when only a handful of customers stop in each day."

"Does that mean you're choosing teaching for your life path?"

"I don't know. I'm so confused." I want to tell him about everything- Grandmother Ruby's diary, my father's story, my talk with Ivory, that I'm in love with him, everything. But I can't.

He glances at me. "Relax, you have months to decide. And either way, you'll be fine." I know he's right but it's not comforting.

Ty pulls into my driveway and cuts the engine. "I'll bring in your basket for you."

"You have to get back to work now?" I ask as we get out of the truck.

"Unfortunately I do. I promised to bring the guys some soda from the market."

We climb the few steps to the front porch.

"I'm glad we made up. I'll see you Friday." He cocks his head to the side.

"I'm glad too. Thanks for the ride home." I stand on my tip toes and give him a kiss on the cheek.

Ty's cheeks turn pink. Awkwardly, he ruffles my hair. "Bye Jade."

"Don't work too hard. Bye, Ty."

I immediately escape to my dark room. I have a lot to think about.

***

The next morning, I'm surprised to wake up without coaching from my mother. I glance at the clock and it's not even seven. Grandmother Ruby's snow globe catches my eye. I pick it up and shake it. Should I remain in the globe or should I break free? How do I make a decision like that? I replace the snow globe as my mother sweeps into my room with a spray bottle poised in the air.

"No need to spray the stinky citrus, I'm awake."

She perches on the edge of my bed. "Good morning, sweetie."

"Morning." I pull the covers to my chin.

"I have a favor to ask you. Scarlet phoned to ask if one of us could take Slate to Samsara this morning."

"For what?"

91 | P a g e

"She wants him to view the eye color videos."

"But why? Slate's an Outsider. He won't have an eye color surgery."

"She thinks it will help him understand our culture a bit more." She pauses before she adds, "Evidently he's asking a lot of questions."

Slate's bound to get in trouble if he continues. "Okay, I'll take him."

"Thanks." She rubs her eyes. "I don't know how I'm still tired; I've been sleeping a lot lately. Too much sleep probably."

"Grandmother Ruby always said there was no such thing as too much sleep."

"She did, didn't she?" My mother strokes my hair. "I'm so sorry she's gone."

"I miss her so much." Hot tears fill my eyes. A few escape and run down my cheeks.

My mother grabs a few tissues and wipes my face. "Only time will heal, Jade."

"I'll always miss her. No matter how much time passes."

She nods. "Believe me I understand."

I think about Grandfather Rufous and Grandmother Goldenrod. Are they alive somewhere on the Outside? And if so, why did they leave?

She kisses me on the forehead. "I'll bring you some coffee."

"Thanks." I take a quick shower, dress, and enjoy a cup of coffee before heading outside. I'm greeted with yet another gray morning. March is such a hit or miss month. Some days it resembles spring, others winter.

As I walk to Aunt Scarlet's house, my head starts to throb which I'm sure is stress related. I take several deep breaths and try to concentrate on the positive things in my life. I'm healthy and young, I love my parents and my best friend…I'll be devastated if he doesn't feel the same. I pick a daisy from the side of the road and pluck its petals. He loves me, he loves me not…the last petal proves that he loves me. If only it were that simple!

When I arrive at my aunt and uncle's house, I jog up the steps. Before I have a chance to ring the door bell, Slate flings open the door. Pearl barks and wags her tail fast like a windshield wiper.

"Good morning, Slate." I ruffle his pale blonde hair.

"Hi. I'm ready." He's already wearing a winter jacket and boots.

"Dressed already? You must be excited."

"It's boring here when I'm all by myself." He hangs his head.

"Well I'm here now, so cheer up. Let me just use the restroom and then we'll get going." I walk down the short hallway, and open the last door on the left. Scarlet and Naples' bedroom reeks of hairspray and nail polish remover which makes me gag. I flick on the light switch and grimace. Everything is red- curtains, bedspread, carpet, rug- everything. In the equally red themed bathroom I search the medicine cabinet which is stuffed with bags of various herbs. Nurse Scarlet must be raiding supplies from the hospital. I choose a tiny bag of powdered butterbur because it's perfect for headaches. When I return to the living room, Slate and Pearl are sitting side by side in front of the glass door.

"Slate, I'm making a quick cup of tea before we leave. Would you like hot chocolate or something?"

"Hot chocolate, please. The clouds look angry."

"Do they? I'm not surprised. Please grab umbrellas from the coat closet."

As I prepare our drinks, Slate wanders into the kitchen.

"Can Pearl come with us? She wants to go for a walk."

"Unfortunately dogs aren't allowed at Samsara. And anyway it looks like it might rain, right?"

"But I saw a dog there. He was laying in his dog house."

"That's Rust and Saffron's dog. His name's Chocolate. And even he isn't allowed inside."

"Oh. But won't Pearl be lonely if we leave her here?"

"No, Pearl will be fine. She'll probably take a long nap. Listening to rain always makes me sleepy. Let's get going."

We hold our umbrellas in one hand and mugs in the other. As we walk, we don't say much. We just listen to the pitter patter of rain against our umbrellas. Grandmother Ruby loved to dance in the rain when everyone else was holed up in their homes. During storms we'd sit on the front porch and count the seconds between a flash of lightning and its subsequent thunder. She taught me that a five second elapse meant the lighting was one mile away.

Today's storm begins as Slate and I reach Samsara Street. My tennis shoes and the bottom of my jeans are soon soaked. Slate's are too but that's because he's jumping into puddles. I can barely see the lightning bolt through the mass of trees but the thunder is unmistakable. We still have a mile to walk.

A black truck pulls next to us. Slate asks, "Who's that?"

"That's Bronze. He's Rust and Saffron's son." I'm both thankful and scared to see him. Thankful to escape the storm but scared to hear if he's discovered anything about my grandparents.

Bronze leans across the seat and pushes the passenger door open. "Get in."

Slate looks expectantly at me and I nod. He's smart for hesitating. He climbs in and I follow. The window is down a crack which does little to help dissipate the smoke from Bronze's cigarette. Slate immediately has a coughing and sneezing fit.

"Sorry bud." Bronze tosses the cigarette out the window and winds it down further. "It's a nasty habit, I know. Even though I work closely with the tobacco industry, my advice is that you never start smoking."

"I'm allergic to smoke and cats," Slate says.

I turn to face Bronze. "Thank you so much for stopping."

"No problem. I'm curious, why are you headed to Samsara?"

"Slate has to watch some videos to curb his curiosity."

Bronze glances at Slate. "It's not wise to ask too many questions, bud. Especially to the wrong people. But you can ask me anything. I'm an Outsider like you."

"Why did I stay in Nirvana instead of going home?" Slate asks.

"Now that's a question I've been asking myself for years. Unfortunately I don't know the answer to that one." He pauses to adjust the windshield wipers. "Have you been treated okay so far?"

"Yeah. Everyone's been nice, especially Jade."

"Yes, Jade is nice and very pretty. She reminds me of my friend Peaches." He winks at me. "You're lucky to have her. Let me know if anyone bothers you, okay?" Bronze offers Slate his hand. "Deal?"

Slate grins and shakes his hand. "Deal."

"Hey Jade, I need to speak to you at the Center tomorrow. Before lunch, okay? Because I have to make a few deliveries on the Outside afterwards."

My heart beat quickens. I can't ask any questions in front of Slate. "I'll be there."

Bronze pulls his truck as close to the back porch as possible. "Bud, remember I have your back." Slate nods his head solemnly.

"Thanks again, Bronze. You really helped us out," I say.

"No big deal. Be careful. Watch out for the little Outsider, okay?" A look of concern clouds his shiny brown eyes.

"Of course. See you tomorrow."

There are two guards on the porch this time, each with piercing blue eyes. I've noticed the guards that man Samsara seem to have a tad more empathy than the guards throughout Nirvana.

"Place your belongings in the storage bin," the male guard says. I drop the umbrellas, travel mugs and my key ring in the bin.

"Stretch out your arms," the female guard says. The male guard pats Slate down while the female guard checks me for any prohibited items.

"Where's your destination?" The female guard asks.

"Wing A," I reply.

Her eyes narrow. "For what reason?"

I protectively place my hands on Slate's thin shoulders. "Slate's adoptive parents, my aunt and uncle, would like him to view some videos."

"Very well." She motions with her hand like she's shooing away a fly.

"You look just like my Aunt Jen," Slate says.

"It's too bad I'll never meet her. Go ahead and scan in." She points to the iris scanner.

I guide Slate to the scanner. "All you have to do is look into the camera and it will take your picture. Just like when we attend meetings at the Center."

"Why do they have to take so many pictures?"

"No more questions for now, okay?" I whisper.

"Okay." He sighs but dutifully gazes at the iris scanner. *Click.*

"This way to Wing A, Slate," I point to the creaky, wooden stairs. When we reach the second floor, everything is white – the linoleum floors, the walls, the scientist's lab coats, and the equipment. The scientist's red eyes are the only exception.

"This place looks like a movie. Do we get to take a tour?" His eyes are wide open.

"That's a question, silly. I'm not sure, maybe after we watch the videos."

"I hope we get to take a tour. I want to see everything!"

"First things first and here we are." I halt in front of a door that reads "Media" in black letters. I push the button to notify a guard. Within seconds, a male guard appears.

He stares into an iris scanner and the door opens. *Click.* "Look into this." He holds a miniature iris scanner in his palm. Slate and then I do so. *Click. Click.*

"Why don't you hang up your coats." He points to the coat hanger in the corner. "And then have a seat." He points to the white leather couches situated in the center of the room.

"Yes sir," I reply.

When Slate sits on the couch, he grins. "This is as soft as marshmallows."

"What are marshmallows?" I ask.

"You've never had one?" Slate lifts his eyebrows.

I shake my head. "Am I missing out?"

He nods. "They're white, fluffy, and delicious."

"Then I can see why this couch reminds you of one. I could take a nap." My body sinks into the luxurious couch. I wouldn't be surprised if I did fall asleep halfway through the movie.

"Me too," the guard chimes in. "Anyway, I'm assuming you need to watch the intro videos?"

"Yes, please," I reply.

The guard flicks a switch before settling in on an identical couch. Evidently we aren't allowed to view the video on our own. I wonder how many hundreds of times this guard has had to view this. I remember watching these videos ten years ago with Ty and the rest of our class. For some reason I was scared so he reluctantly held my hand. I wonder if he remembers that.

Gradually, the lights dim and the video commences. A rainbow stretches across the screen as a soothing female voice begins:

"Welcome to Nirvana- a simple, tranquil, and equal commune. Margaret Miller and John Blackburn founded Nirvana in 1865." A black and white photo of Margaret and John standing in front of Samsara appears on the screen. *"Margaret's family's land and John's study of ophthalmology paired with their love of humanity was a winning combination. Margaret and John's fathers were slave owners and staunch supporters of the Confederacy. However, Margaret and John were quiet advocates of the Union. When Margaret's father passed away, he left her Samsara and all of its riches.*

John was instantly attracted to Margaret's unusual eyes. One was green and the other brown. This condition is called heterochromia iridium. John's eyes were unique as well: pale blue with a nevus, (freckle) under each pupil. Two sets of eyes flash across the screen. *John gave Margaret the nickname "Hazel" and Margaret called John "Glacier."*

Soon after Hazel's father died, she wed Glacier. A small ceremony was held at Samsara. Black and white wedding photos flash across the screen. *After a brief honeymoon spent in southern Virginia, Glacier immediately ordered equipment for a surgical eye lab. He also ordered rhesus monkeys to experiment on because their eyes are the closest to human eyes.* Small monkeys appear on the screen.

Glacier's focus was on intraocular implants which is replacing the lens of the eye. A diagram of an eye is shown. *First numbing drops are squirted in the eye. A small incision is made, the natural lens is removed, and a colored disk is inserted. To fully understand this surgery, you must learn the vital parts of the eye: cornea, lens, pupil, retina and optic nerve...."*

Every now and then I glance at Slate whose eyes are riveted on the screen. I can't tell if he's excited or frightened. If I were in his shoes, surely I'd be both. I try my best to stay awake but my eyelids refuse to cooperate; this part of the movie is very dull.

"Wake up, Jade." Slate tugs on my arm. "The guard asked if we want to go on an expedition and I do!"

"We're going on a trip? What?" I frown.

The guard starts to laugh but catches himself. "I asked if he wanted to visit a new exhibition. He seems interested."

"Can we, Jade? Can we?" Slate's grey eyes shine like a brand new coin from the Outside.

I wonder why the guard is acting so pleasant; it's a bit unnerving. However, I don't want to disappoint Slate, so I agree.

We gather our jackets and follow the guard into the stark white hallway. We make a quick left turn and then a right. The guard halts in front of a door labeled "Eye Exhibition." He stares into an iris scanner mounted on the wall. *Click.*

We enter a dimly lit, large room. The floor is bright white with the words "The eye is the window of the soul- Glacier Blue" painted in black letters. A replica of one of his eyes is below the quote.

"Let's play a game," the guard says. "Miss, go ahead and stand on the drawing of the eye."

"W-w-w-why?" I stutter.

"You'll see."

I contemplate darting out the door but realize I'd only be running into a hive of armed guards in the hallways. Not to mention the guard has his hand on Slate's shoulder. I reluctantly walk to the center of the room and stand directly on the eye.

A screen unfurls from the ceiling in front of me.

"A series of eyes are going to flash across the screen. The goal is to identify which eyes are yours. They'll be numbered and you'll have to remember your number."

The first pair of eyes appear on the screen but they're definitely not mine. Number two and three aren't either. I think four are too dark, five and six are too light. Number seven are a definite possibility, but so are ten and thirteen. By the seventeenth pair of eyes, I want to scream and stomp my feet, but just as I'm about to, the screen goes blank.

"Which number do you choose?" The guard asks.

I turn to face him. "N-n-n-number ten, no wait, number seven. W-w-what is the point of this, anyway?"

"Is seven your final answer?"

I chew on my bottom lip before I answer, "yes."

"That's incorrect, the correct answer is thirteen. Most participants think of this as a fun activity but the real reason the exhibit was created is for scientific research." The guard looks at Slate. "There aren't many gray-eyed Outsiders but there are a few. Would you like to play?"

"Yes!" Slate skips to the eye diagram. "Was it fun, Jade?"

"Sure," I lie. I return to the back of the room and stand next to the guard.

"Don't feel bad, most people don't guess correctly," he says.

"But shouldn't I be able to differentiate my eyes from strangers?" I ask.

He shrugs. "I wasn't able to either. I bet he'll be able to though, since there's only five slides."

Five pairs of gray colored eyes flash across the screen.

"Which ones are yours?" The guard asks.

"Number three!"

"You are correct."

"Can I play again?" Slate asks.

"Sorry, but that's the only game with gray eyes. However, I can tell you that people with gray eyes are typically wise and strong."

"That describes me," Slate says, flexing a muscle.

The guard and I grin. I'd ask him about green eyes but mine are artificial and I haven't had brown eyes since I was a baby. I can't match my eyes out of a line up, anyway.

That evening, I mention the eye exhibit to my parents. "There's a quote that says 'The eye is the window of the soul.' Isn't that a cool saying?"

"It is. Who came up with that?" My mother asks.

"Our founder," I reply.

My father snorts. "Is that what they're saying? Glacier Blue did not come up with that quote. In fact, no one knows for certain who said it; we only know it's an old English proverb."

My mother shakes her head. "That's plagiarism."

"Let's sneak in and paint over his name," I say.

"Or we could use paint thinner. I know I have a can around here somewhere," my father grins.

"Like father, like daughter," my mother says but she isn't smiling.

Chapter Nine

Excerpt from Grandmother Ruby's diary – October 29, 2011

When the elderly guard chastised me for being too early, I batted my eyelashes and apologized until he opened the back door to Samsara. He instructed me to head directly to the parlor, but that wasn't my intention. I had nearly an hour to snoop before I was expected there.

My first stop was the library, my favorite room at Samsara. There's something eerily fantastic about this library with its floor to ceiling shelves, peeling and pale yellow wallpaper and scuffed hardwood floor. I ran my fingertips along the dusty books. I plucked a random one from the shelf and flipped through it, taking several deep breaths. There's something intoxicating about the smell of old books.

For several minutes I leaned against the shelf and wondered what exactly I was looking for. Skimming each book in this library was futile. Just as I was about to leave, I heard someone sobbing. I followed the sound of heartbreak to the back of the room. A woman with long, dark hair was curled up in the corner. I tentatively asked if she was okay. Peaches lifted her head and nodded but her eyes were dull and lifeless, and tears ran down her round face. Before I had a chance to comfort her, or at least attempt to, she darted from the room. I considered following her but what could I possibly say or do to make her feel better? I wonder who or what caused her to be so upset?

With more questions than answers, I left the library but stopped abruptly in the Central Passageway when I heard Saffron's high pitched voice. She was arguing with someone over the phone about wanting the bastard out of her house and out of Nirvana.

I considered returning to the library but I was too curious to leave. Who did she want out of Nirvana? Was she referring to Bronze? Several minutes later she slammed down the phone. Before I had a chance to move, Saffron was in the hallway, glaring at me. Her golden eyes narrowed like a cat's but she didn't say a word; she just spun on her heel and left.

"What did you get yourself into, Grandmother?" I ask my empty dark room. As I'm turning the page to find out, I glance at the clock- nine thirty am. I have no choice but to shove the diary back into the pillowcase. I'm disappointed until I remember that Bronze has information for me. But a few hours later, when my parents and I are seated in the Center, he's nowhere to be found.

"Have you seen Bronze?" I whisper in Ty's ear.

He lowers his head and says, "Earlier this morning but not recently."

"Did you talk to him?"

Before Ty has a chance to respond, a woman sitting in front of us turns around and says, "Shhh! Our leaders are about to speak!"

"Sorry ma'am," Ty replies but as soon as she looks away he rolls his eyes.

As usual, our commune leaders are immaculately dressed. Obviously Rust's charcoal gray suit and Saffron's lime green dress were imported from the Outside.

"Good morning, everyone," Saffron says. "Rust and I have some personal news to share, both good and bad. I'd like to share the good news first." She laces her fingers through Rust's and beams. He's smiling too, but his smile doesn't reach his eyes.

She squeezes Rust's arm before she says, "My husband and I are having a baby." She pats her flat stomach. "I'm three months pregnant."

"She doesn't even look pregnant." A woman behind us mutters. "Not even a baby bump."

"You're just mad because you gained so much weight with Pumpkin," a man says.

"Am not," she replies, "and Saffron already has two children."

"That's a good point. Not fair, is it?" The man says.

According to commune law, the only way a family can have more than two children is if the mother or father is an only child. And Rust and Saffron have siblings. From Saffron's glowing reaction, she's keeping this child. I wonder how Bronze and Peaches feel about this. I crane my neck searching the first few rows but don't see them. Where is Bronze? He promised he'd be here. Maybe he skipped the Center meeting and he'll find me afterwards?

"This couldn't have come at a better time for us because..." Saffron pauses to dab her eyes with a tissue. "Our son Bronze has returned to the Outside, indefinitely."

Like a fist to the stomach, her words knock the wind out of me. I don't know any other Outsiders. I only know Bronze because he exports our wine. How else am I going to find out if my grandparents are still alive? I have trouble hearing anything else she says because commune members erupt in conversation.

Ty brushes his lips against my ear and whispers, "It's okay Jade. I'll tell you why later. Let's meet at the cabin as soon as lunch is over."

"But how do you know?" I frown.

He cups my chin. "Trust me."

I nod. "I do trust you."

"Excuse me," my mother says as she exits the aisle. Her hair is hiding her face like a curtain and she's covering her mouth with her hand. I excuse myself and follow her to the restroom. She props herself against the sink and stares in the mirror. The color of her skin nearly matches the mint green wallpaper.

"Mother, what's wrong?" I place my hand lightly on her back.

She shakes her head rigorously as if ridding away an awful thought. "Suddenly I was afraid that I was going to be sick. It must have been the waffles from breakfast. They were very rich." She smiles weakly. I know she's lying but I'm not sure why.

"Do you want to go home?"

"No, we don't have to. You and your father are probably hungry. I can make it through lunch, I think." She folds her arms low against her stomach and grimaces.

"Why don't you sit down and I'll be right back." I guide her to the little wooden bench.

My father and Ty are seated on a bench directly outside the restroom. When my father notices me, he bolts upright. "Is your mother okay?"

"She's not feeling well. Think the guards will allow us to leave?"

He crosses his arms and says, "Of course. When a commune member is sick, the guards have no right to force them to stay." I agree with him but I've heard otherwise. "And besides, the Center meeting is nearly over."

"Okay." I dart into the restroom. "You ready to go home?"

Relief floods my mother's face. "Yes."

She leans on me as we exit the restroom. In the hallway, my father takes over. He wraps his arms around her and she leans her head on his shoulder.

"I can carry you if you want. Like on our wedding night." He grins.

"You're ridiculous," she says. "Although that was a spectacular night."

I plug my ears. "Just what I don't want to hear," I reply. But they're too wrapped up in each other to notice.

"My parents say cheesy things like that, too. I'll pick you up when lunch is over, okay?" Ty says.

"Perfect. I'll see you then," I reply.

He leans down and kisses me on the forehead. His lips are incredibly soft. If I just tilt my head, perhaps our lips will meet...but he steps back too quickly.

"Jonquil, I hope you feel better," he says.

"Thank you, I'll be just fine. Nothing a cup of tea and a nap can't fix," she says.

Ty and my father shake hands and I watch as he strolls down the hall toward the Center.

When we reach the back door, two guards are standing on the porch. The female guard says, "The meeting isn't quite over and lunch hasn't been served. You know it's mandatory to remain until the end."

My father straightens his back and puffs up his chest. "My wife is ill, sick to her stomach. And my daughter isn't feeling well either," he lies.

The female guard looks at the male guard and he shrugs as if he could care less. Then she says, "Very well. Look into the eye scanner before you leave." *Click, click, click.*

I spend the hour before Ty arrives contemplating whether or not to share Grandmother Ruby's diary with him. On one hand, my grandmother specifically advised me not to share her diary with anyone. On the flip side, I could really use his help. I decide to bring the diary just in case.

On the way to the cabin, Ty asks, "How's your mother feeling?"

"She's resting, so she's bound to feel better. Maybe the heat made her sick." I pull my long auburn hair into a haphazard ponytail. "It's the worst Strawberry Spring."

"What's that?" He gently pushes my knee in order to shift gears. When I'm with Ty, I have a habit of sitting in the middle of the seat.

"You know how an 'Indian Summer' is a heat wave in autumn? Well, a 'Strawberry Spring' is a false spring in the winter."

"Who did you hear that from?" He grins.

"My mother. She probably made it up." I gaze out the truck window which is streaked with dirt. "I'm grateful for the early spring. I just hope winter doesn't come back with a vengeance. Do you think it will?"

"Nah, it's over."

"Let's keep our fingers crossed. Did anything happen at Center after we left?"

Ty looks at me. "Yes, but I hate to tell you about it."

"Who was sentenced? Will they be blinded or hanged?"

"Old man Folly will be hanged."

"For what?" I wince.

"Selling intraocular information to the Outside authorities."

I frown. "But that happens all the time."

"But this time it wasn't approved and Folly pocketed the money."

I rub my forehead. "That's horrible. I wish you wouldn't have told me. But then again, I would have found out. When will it take place?"

"Next Friday, after lunch. Publicly, of course."

I shudder. "I don't understand how anyone could watch something like that."

Ty reaches for my hand. "Me neither. I have some positive news, too. My father's feeling a lot better."

I caress his hand. "That's great news."

When Ty parks in front of the slave cabin, I immediately notice two rocking chairs on the little porch.

"Those chairs are so cute, where did you find them?"

"My mother went on one of her cleaning binges and threw them out. My father grabbed an axe and was about to chop them for kindling but I saved them."

"They fit this place. Its cooler now, let's sit outside." I sink into the rocking chair and gaze at the rich blue sky which reminds me of bluebell flowers. Ty is rocking back and forth with a peaceful smile on his face. Grandmother Ruby and Grandfather Navy used to sit side by side in rocking chairs, too. I wonder if Grandmother Goldenrod and Grandfather Rufous did the same. I bet they did. I move the chair so that I'm facing Ty. "So what did you find out? And when did you last see Bronze?" I ask excitedly.

"We met early this morning. He asked me to meet him at the edge of Nirvana."

"I'm confused. Why did he ask you to meet him? He told me that we'd talk at the Center. Why not talk to you there, too?"

A guilty look crosses his face. "I asked him to find information about my Uncle Hunter's disappearance. Don't get mad but I also asked him to come to me with info about your grandparents."

I fold my arms across my chest. "I'm a big girl, Ty. You don't have to protect me from anyone."

He throws his hands up in surrender. "I apologize. I just wanted to keep you out of it as much as possible. Because if someone finds out, especially Rust, we're in deep trouble."

I perch on the edge of the rocking chair, wringing my hands. "So what did you find out? Was it something bad?"

Ty scoots his chair closer to mine and brushes his fingers across my cheek. "No, nothing bad. Don't worry, I'll tell you everything." I stare into his tyrian colored eyes which instantly have a calming effect. When he follows his father's life path, his eyes will be red, my least favorite color.

"I can't imagine you with a different eye color," I say.

He tilts his head. "Funny, because I've been thinking the same thing about you." We sit still for a moment. I yearn to crawl into his lap and bury my head against his muscular shoulder.

Ty looks away, breaking the spell. "Bronze found out that your grandparents and my uncle live in a city called Main, which is only forty miles from here."

"So they're ok? What are they doing there? Do they live together?"

"Yes, they're doing well. Your grandparents own a bakery and my uncle works in construction. They don't live together but they live in the same apartment building."

"What's an apartment building?" I scrunch my nose.

"I asked Bronze that same question. He says it's a large building divided into sections where people live."

"Did he find out why they left? Does he know how they escaped unharmed?" I'm so excited I feel as if I could jump out of my skin.

Ty runs his fingers through his hair. "That's everything he told me. Oh and here are their addresses." He reaches into his pocket, pulls out a crumpled piece of notepaper, and hands it to me. *Rue and Goldie Martin, 107 18th Street, Main, VA, 10002; Hunter Davis, 99 18th Street, Main, VA, 10002.*

"How did you pay for this information?"

"I gave Bronze some of my best wood carvings. He should be able to sell them on the Outside."

My mouth drops open. "I can't believe you gave him those."

He shrugs his shoulders. "I couldn't think of anything else I owned of any worth."

I squeeze his calloused hands. "Thank you so much, Ty."

"You're welcome."

"I can't help but wonder what will happen to us if someone finds out we have this information? What will happen to our families?"

"Don't worry, no one knows. The only person who knows is Bronze and evidently he's left Nirvana for good. Strange he didn't mention anything to me about moving to the Outside. He must have left soon after we spoke."

I hesitate before I reach into my purse and pull out Grandmother Ruby's diary. "Ty, I know why he left and it wasn't by choice."

Chapter Ten

Excerpt from Grandmother Ruby's diary – November 7, 2011

This is the first day this week that I've felt strong enough to pick up a pen and actually write something. I'll have to write thank you notes to all of my friends and family to let them know how grateful I am for the gifts of homemade soup, fruit juice, and flowers. Carmine brought me bouquets of pale pink Sasanqua Camellias, winter roses. Jade took photographs of them; that way I'll never forget their beauty. I also asked her to photograph the deep red aster flowers that True brought me. When Jade asked who they were from, I told her I wasn't sure. I hid the note he wrote as well, calling me 'a ruby red star that shines just as brightly in the day as it does the night.' I didn't want Jade to think I had a romantic relationship with True. We became good friends since Navy passed away but Navy was my one true love.

After I shut the book, tears slide down my face like raindrops on a windshield. I wonder if she had stronger feelings for True then she claimed. My Grandmother Ruby was a complex woman, that's for sure. And I didn't know her as well as I thought. That's the part that hurt the most.

"I'm sorry for breaking my promise, Grandmother." I whisper even though once again I'm alone in my dark room. And yet, I know she'd understand why I confided in Ty. She would have confided in Grandfather Navy and possibly True. She'd forgive me.

Reading the remaining diary entries is going to break what's left of my heart. I don't feel strong enough to read them but I know eventually I will.

For now I lie on the floor and stare at the ceiling until my eyes become heavy. I wake to incessant knocking on the door. It's my father urging me to hurry up and get ready for the Center. This week went by so fast. When I step out of my dark room, I'm assaulted my sunlight.

This morning the most mundane chores feel monumental. Brushing my teeth and showering are exhausting. I don't think I truly understood what my father meant by the weight of sadness until now.

At breakfast, my mother asks several times what's wrong with me. I reply that I'm just tired which is partially true. I appreciate when my father tells her that we're all entitled to a quiet day. I go through the motions at the Center but I'm too wrapped up in my own thoughts to pay much attention to commune news.

At one point, I excuse myself and head to the restroom. I'm relieved that no one else is there. I enter a stall, sit on the toilet lid, bring my knees to my chest and cry. As I contemplate leaving the stall, washing my face and masking a smile; someone enters the restroom and locks the main door. Her high heels click against the tiles as she peeks under each stall. Curious, I remain where I am but lean forward in order to peer through the crack. I recognize her right away.

"Damn thing is so hot and itchy," Saffron says. She adjusts a small, flesh colored pillow strapped to her stomach. She stares into the mirror and at one point I'm convinced she knows I'm there. I hold my breath while she reapplies her hot pink lipstick and fluffs her long, blonde hair. Eventually she leaves and I exhale. What the heck is going on?

I wait in the stall until a group of giggling pre-teens enter the restroom. They barely pay any attention to me as I attempt to fix my eye makeup. When they leave, I tag along behind them. Fortunately, it's time for lunch so I follow them into the dining area.

When my mother asks where I've been I tell her I had an upset stomach. Sitting at the table is torture because all I want to do is gossip to Ty about Saffron's fake pregnancy. I wonder if anyone else knows. I'm sure Rust does. Aunt Scarlet probably knows too. Whose baby is it? Why is she claiming it as her own?

My head starts to throb so I rub peppermint scented lotion onto my temples but it doesn't help. I take deep breaths but still feel anxious. In fact, it feels like a heavy person is sitting on my chest.

After lunch, I search the crowd for Ty but Slate finds me first. He startles me by throwing his skinny arms around my waist.

"He's really taken a liking to you," Aunt Scarlet says with a fake plastic smile. She has dark rings under her eyes and for once her make up doesn't look perfect. I wonder what's wrong with her. I bet it has something to do with Saffron's phantom pregnancy. Aunt Scarlet probably wishes she had a chance to steal a baby. Then she and Saffron could fawn over their babies together.

"Scar- I mean Mom, can I go outside with Jade?" Slate asks.

"Of course. It's wonderful how close you are to your cousin," she says but her tone sounds disingenuous.

He grabs my hand and drags me to the exit. I can't help but grin. Maybe spending some time with Slate will calm my nerves. The Strawberry Spring must be keeping children indoors because there are only a dozen on the playground.

Slate hoists himself on a swing, clutches onto the chains and pumps his skinny legs. "You have to swing too!"

So I hop on a swing. As I sail through the air, the slight breeze feels refreshing. I close my eyes and lean my head back.

"Hey Jade."

"Hey Slate."

"Why do I see spots after I look at the sun?"

"I asked my father the same question when I was younger. First off, he warned me not to look directly at the sun because it can cause damage. He explained when we look at something really bright, like the sun, our eyes aren't used to it. Our retinas are especially sensitive to intense light and it takes them longer to react, causing images like spots to linger in our brain. Does that make any sense at all?"

"Not really but that's okay. Thanks for trying. Let's check out the tree house now!"

He climbs the tree house rope but I prefer utilizing the planks that are nailed into the tree trunk. At the top, we sit cross legged on the plywood and watch the handful of kids play chase below us.

"Have you made any good friends?" I ask.

"Yes," he smiles. "You, Naples, and Pearl."

"Of course we're your friends but what about the kids at school? No one's been mean to you, have they?" I'm with Slate at the school house every other day and it seems like he gets along well with everyone. But kids can be sneaky and mean and I won't allow him to be bullied. It's amazing how close I've gotten to this little boy in such a short period of time.

"No, they're nice to me. I miss my brother though. He was my best friend."

"I understand. I miss my Grandmother, too. And she was my best friend."

"Naples says that my brother is in here." He points to his heart. "And Mom and Dad are here, too. He says their memory will live on in me."

I wipe away tears that have pooled in the corner of my eyes. "He's right."

"That means your Grandmother is in your heart, too," he says. Just then, a butterfly lands on his arm. Its wings are a rich chocolate color with blue streaks. The butterfly remains for a moment but then gracefully flaps its wings and sets off into the world.

"Wow, that was so cool, wasn't it?" Slate's gray eyes are open wide.

"You're right, that was so cool." I laugh.

After a moment he asks, "Do you have a sister that doesn't live with you?"

I ruffle his white-blonde hair. "You know I don't have a sister, silly. Why would you ask that?"

"I met a girl that's a lot like you."

"Here in Nirvana? What's her name?"

"Peaches. She's going to have a baby but I'm not allowed to tell anyone." He wipes sweat from his brow. "C'mon, it's hot, let's go back inside." Slate attaches himself to the rope and quickly slides down the tree. "Are you coming?"

Somehow I find my voice. "In a minute. Go ahead in without me." He waves and runs off. Peering over the side of the tree house makes me dizzy. My heart is pounding and it feels like a heavy person is jumping on my chest. I breathe erratically and then everything fades to black.

When I open my eyes, I recognize my bedroom. Ty is sitting in my white desk chair. When he sees I'm awake, he scoots the chair closer to the bed.

"Ty? What happened?" My voice sounds groggy.

He plants a kiss on my forehead. "You fainted and fortunately didn't fall out of the tree house. What happened?"

"I felt like…" I pause to cough.

He brings a glass of water to my lips. "Take a drink first." The water feels cool as it travels down my scratchy throat.

"I felt like I was having a heart attack."

He smoothes hair from my forehead. "It's from all of the recent stress. Did Slate say something that upset you? He mentioned that you were talking about Grandmother Ruby."

I sit up and grab his hand. "That wasn't what upset me." I take a deep breath before I continue. "I found out more secrets."

Ty searches my eyes for answers. "Such as?"

"Saffron isn't pregnant!"

Ty wrinkles his forehead. "What are you talking about?"

"I saw her in the restroom with a small pillow strapped to her stomach. And that's not all. Guess what Slate told me? Peaches is pregnant! That must mean Saffron is taking her own daughter's baby!"

Ty releases my hand and paces around my bedroom. "No wonder you fainted." He runs his fingers through his hair.

"What should we do now?"

"I think the best thing to do is to stay out of it. It's their business and we have enough to worry about."

"But what if Peaches wants to keep her baby? Surely Bronze is the father and with him gone, who's going to help her?"

He sighs. "I don't know. This place is so messed up." He perches on the side of my bed. "Do you want to get out of here for awhile? Maybe go for a drive?"

"I'd love to. But let me take a quick shower first."

"While you're in the shower, I'll convince your parents fresh air will make you feel better." He winks.

"Good idea."

Ty won't tell me where we're going, it's a surprise. But there aren't many places to see in Nirvana, so it won't be much of one. Still, I'm happy when Ty parks his truck alongside Lady Lake. He laces his fingers through mine and we walk along the skinny dirt path to the water's edge.

"I should have brought my camera. It's so beautiful." The sky is riddled with streaks of purple and orange, the male crickets are rubbing their wings together, producing a dramatic chirping sound, and there's a clean, damp smell in the air.

I join Ty on a large, flat rock. "I already feel better. Nature has this calming effect, doesn't it? Especially at sunset. Gosh the sky is incredible. Don't you think?" I glance at Ty, expecting to see him smiling and peaceful but instead he's looking straight ahead with a serious look on his face. "What's wrong?" I ask.

"It's nothing."

"Tyrian, you know saying 'it's nothing' isn't going to work with me. I'll keep asking until you tell me." I place my hands on my hips.

"I can't tell what color the sky is," he says quietly.

"What? I don't understand."

He closes his eyes and hangs his head. "I'm color blind."

I grab his arm. "Why haven't you ever told me?"

"My parents made me promise to keep it a secret. In this commune, it's not exactly something to brag about."

"Can you see any color at all?"

"Most people who are color blind can still see at least certain colors but I'm one of the lucky ones that can only see in black, white, and shades of gray."

"But if you can't see color, why did you say you couldn't imagine my eyes a different shade?"

"Even though I can't decipher specific colors, I can tell your eyes are bright. I hope they'll always remain that way."

I blush. "Is color blindness genetic?"

"I'll never know whether it's genetic or if the doctor who performed my eye surgery screwed it up somehow."

"Thank goodness you're only color blind and not completely blind."

"That's exactly what I tell my parents. I don't understand why eye color is such a big deal in this commune. Who knows how many other surgeries have gone wrong. Sometimes I wonder if anyone has ever accidentally gone blind."

I shudder and wrap my arms tightly across my chest.

"I'm sorry, I didn't mean to stress you out even more. Let's act our age for once." He grins. He jumps up and grabs the tire swing. "Want to go for a ride?" He pushes the swing toward me.

"Sure." I climb on and hold onto the ropes tightly. He spins me around in a circle and I throw my head back and laugh. Eventually I yell, "Okay, that's enough, I surrender!" Ty's arms circle me as he grabs hold of the ropes. I feel his heart pulse and smell his musky cologne as he gently presses his chin on the top of my head. He sits on the opposite side of the swing and our knees touch. He caresses the side of my face, leans forward, and finally kisses me. And for that moment, all of the drama and heartache of the past few months washes away.

When we eventually break apart, Ty finds a blanket in his truck and spreads it alongside the lake. We lay side by side, gazing at the clear sky. It's as if all of the stars have faded away. I don't need a shooting star to wish on anyway because my wish has already come true.

But after Ty drops me off and I'm alone in my bedroom, all of the stress comes back ten fold. I have to collect my thoughts. I brew a cup of tea and head to my dark room. I tape a white sheet of poster board to the wall and locate a black marker. Then I begin to put the puzzle pieces together.

Chapter Eleven

Excerpt from Grandmother Ruby's diary – November 16, 2011

I was feeling better for a few days but this illness has come back with a vengeance. I've been to the hospital and they've run numerous tests. I just have to wait for the results to come in. I've been wearing sunglasses all of the time, even indoors, because lately my eyes are very light sensitive. I have other weird symptoms, too. My hands and feet have been cold and my hands often shake. My heart is beating erratically, also. All I can do is rest and try not to think about my mysterious disease. One bright spot has been True's company. And of course Jade's.

After adding my grandmother's new symptoms to the poster board, I chew on the end of a black marker, and just stare at the mess of information. I'm not sure how much more info I'll be able to decipher from the diary because at this point her handwriting is too light. It's as if she barely touched the paper with her pen; as if she accepted that she was fading away. She must have known, deep down in her heart, that she was dying from this mysterious disease. A chill runs from my heels to the base of my neck. Before I die, I hope it comes as a surprise. Perhaps when I'm an elderly woman, I'll lie down to sleep one night and just never wake up. With this macabre thought lingering in my mind, I lock my work shed and proceed to my house to get ready for work.

An hour later, Slate bounces out of Uncle Naples' truck and hugs me fiercely.

"I didn't mean to make you sick, Jade. I'm sorry." His gravel gray eyes are round like pebbles.

I sink to my knees so we're the same height. "You didn't make me sick, Slate. It was the heat."

"It's cool today, so you won't faint, right?" From his solemn expression, I can tell he must have been really worried about me.

"I won't faint, I promise." He clutches my hand and doesn't let go until we reach the school house.

All day I yearn to ask Slate questions about Peaches, and after school a golden opportunity arises when my mother decides to stay late to grade essays. Slate skips along the gravel path, swinging his back pack, as I stroll behind him.

Birds soar through the cerulean blue sky, at times resting on tree branches dressed in spring green leaves. A gentle breeze caresses my face as I take greedy breaths of the sweet scent of balsam.

"Hey, Slate, do you want to rest for a minute?" I sit Indian style in a patch of grass and he joins me. "Can I ask you a few questions?"

He nods his head as he rips blades of grass from the ground.

"Remember when you told me you met Peaches? Where were you?"

He furrows his brow. "We went to a house but I can't remember which street it was on."

"Can you tell me anything you remember? I want to help Peaches but first I need to know where she is."

"I was supposed to stay in the car. Scarlet—I mean Mom—told me she'd only be a minute. She just had to drop stuff off. But she took too long and I had to go to the bathroom. When I went inside I met Peaches. She's really nice and she looks sad, like you."

His last comment pierces my heart. "Were any other people there? Do you remember the color of the door?"

"No one else was there. The house was empty except for a table and a couch. Oh, and there was some other wooden furniture there, too. The door was blue. I can't remember anything else."

It sounds like Grandmother Ruby's house. "That's perfect. Thank you so much for telling me. I pinkie promise I won't tell anyone but Ty, okay?" We lock pinkie fingers.

"Okay. I don't want Mom to find out I told because she'll be really upset."

I place my fingers under his chin and gently lift it. "Is she nasty to you?"

"No, she's just strict. Naples says she means well but she isn't used to being around kids." He shrugs his thin shoulders.

"That makes sense. Since my mother and I are used to being around kids, and most of the time we even like them, would you like to eat dinner at our house?"

He laughs. "Can we stop by my house first? I have a surprise for you."

"What is it?"

"If I tell you, it won't be a surprise anymore."

"That's true. Let's take the short cut through the woods."

"I'll race you!"

I keep up with him for about a half mile before my chest starts to burn. "Slate, wait up!"

He immediately does an about-face. "Are you going to faint again?"

"No, I'm just out of shape, that's all."

"My Aunt Jen has a black and white fainting goat. His name's Billy."

"A goat that faints? That's weird," I say.

"Aunt Jen says that Billy faints when he's scared."

"Oh. When I'm scared, my face turns red and I stutter. What do you do when you're scared? I ask.

"I find a place to hide."

"That's a really smart thing to do, much better than fainting and stuttering." I giggle which causes Slate to giggle, too.

"There are some really good hiding places outside," he says. "Yesterday I hid in Pearl's dog house until the guard left. Mom called for me but I ignored her."

"A guard was at your house? Why?" I ask.

Slate shrugs. "I guess he's friends with Scar—I mean Mom."

"You can call her Scarlet around me. What did the guard look like?"

KRISTY FELTENBERGER GILLESPIE

"I couldn't tell because he was wearing a hat, sorry."

"That's okay, I was just curious."

"We're almost there, want to race?" Slate asks.

"Sure." I sprint after him until we reach the driveway. I want to keep my distance in case Scarlet is home.

"I beat you!" Slate exclaims before he darts into the house. In a minute he comes out carrying a plastic bag. Naples is right behind him.

"Hi, Jade. I can give you a lift if you'd like," Naples says.

"Or we can run the rest of the way," Slate says.

"I can tell from Jade's expression she'd rather not. I'll grab the truck keys," Naples says.

"Thanks, Uncle Naples," I say.

We pile into the truck and head towards my house. I know my parents won't mind if Slate joins us for dinner and I don't think they'd mind if Naples sans Scarlet joins us, too.

"Would you like to join us for dinner?" I ask.

"I'd like to but I'm grilling chicken for our salads tonight. It's the only thing Scarlet will eat." He pulls into the driveway. "Have fun, Slate. Give me a call when you're ready to come home."

"No worries, I'll bring him home. Thanks again for the lift," I say.

"Bye, Naples," Slate says.

Naples takes his time pulling out of the driveway. He probably doesn't want to spend time with Scarlet, either.

We enter through the kitchen and are welcomed with the smell of baked bread and tomato sauce. It's good to be home.

My mother is tearing lettuce for a salad.

"I hope its okay that I invited Slate to dinner," I say.

"Of course, the more the merrier. Wash up, the lasagna is almost ready."

We wash our hands in the powder room and join my parents at the table.

"Hey bud, how are you?" My father asks Slate.

"I'm good. How are you?"

"Relieved now that you're here; it's nice to have another guy around for company."

"What are Jade and I? Chopped liver?" My mother asks.

120 | P a g e

"No, you're great. I just wish we could have had a second child, a son."

My mother's eyes flash with what I assume is fury. "Or another daughter."

I place my hands on my hips. "Hey, am I not good enough?" I try to keep my tone light for Slate's sake; however, both of their comments sting.

"You're wonderful, Jade, I'm sorry," my mother says.

"I'm sorry, too," my father says.

"I'm not sorry, I'm hungry," Slate says which makes us all laugh.

I try my best to push their comments to the back of my mind but I know I'll dwell upon them later. Regardless, I slap a smile on my face and take a huge bite of vegetarian lasagna.

After dinner Slate insists we make a fire.

My father puffs out his chest and beats on it with his fists. "Men make fire, women and children clean up kitchen."

My mother takes a kitchen towel and whaps him on the behind. He grins and heads outside.

"My father was silly, too," Slate says.

"So that's where you get it?" I joke.

"Children clean up kitchen, women make hot chocolate," my mother says.

"Meh," I say.

After we finish, Slate grabs his plastic bag, and we walk outside. My father is poking and prodding a modest fire.

"Now what?" I ask.

"Now we have to find four long sticks. C'mon, Jade." He starts looking around the backyard. After we collect four sticks that Slate deems adequate, we return to our lawn chairs. Slate hands my mother and father sticks. Then he reaches into a plastic bag and pulls out a handful of white squares. "These are marshmallows."

"How did you get these?" I ask.

"Naples ordered them for me. We can put them in our hot chocolates, too."

"Are there any animal by-products in these?" My mother asks.

"Marshmallows aren't made from animals, they're made from sugar," Slate says.

"I'll take your word for it." My mother plops a marshmallow in each of our mugs.

"Now place one on the end of your stick and then roast it." He demonstrates. "Don't burn it!"

The fire crackles and hisses as we roast our marshmallows. When mine is nice and brown, I start to bite into it when Slate yells, "Don't eat it yet!" Then he hands me a piece of chocolate and two crackers. "Put your marshmallow and chocolate in the middle. Then smash it together. Now it's a S'more."

When I bite into the little sandwich, the gooey concoction is fabulous. My parents simultaneously say, "Yum."

While we roast our second marshmallows, my father asks where the name 's'mores' came from.

"Because everyone wants some more," Slate says.

After dessert, I drop Slate off at my aunt and uncle's house. I drive around Nirvana for twenty minutes before I find the courage to turn onto Sanctuary Street. I park the truck about a half mile from my grandparent's house and walk, because I don't want anyone to see our vehicle parked in the driveway. It's only eight-thirty pm but the house is pitch- black. I stand in front of the navy door and hold my fist inches away but I don't knock. I just stand frozen like an icicle, suspended in time.

What am I doing? Clearly no one's here. Why would Peaches be here anyway? As I'm about to turn on my heel in resignation, an unusual sound catches my attention. It sounds like metal clanking, like chains on a swing. Tentatively I follow the path to the backyard. I tangle with overgrown weeds and high grass, and swat at mosquitoes. Abruptly, the harsh metal clanking stops.

"Who's there?" A female voice calls.

"Jade," I reply. "Peaches?"

"Yes. Wait there, I'll come to you."

My skin feels like it's been bitten by a thousand mosquitoes. I alternate between scratching my arms and ankles.

"I was wondering when someone was going to look for me. Would you like to come in?"

"Yes, please. These mosquitoes are lethal." I slap my forearm.

I follow her into my late grandparent's house and instantly feel a familiar pang in my heart. As if reading my mind, she says, "It must be hard, being here."

"Very," I reply. She leads me into the kitchen and lights a candle. "Sorry I can't turn on a light. No one is supposed to know I'm here. Please have a seat. Would you like a glass of iced tea?"

"Please." There is literally nothing in the kitchen except a table, chairs, and some dishes in a drying rack. I watch as she prepares our drinks. Her movements are graceful, even though she's at least three months pregnant. I can't imagine how awful it would be to be pregnant at age sixteen. She joins me at the table and slides a glass of iced tea and a small dish of lemons in front of me.

"I have lemon but no sugar. My mother thinks sugar is bad for the baby. But I don't think a little sugar now and again is bad for anyone." She smiles which lights up her round face.

"If you'd like, I can bring you some sugar."

"I'd like that very much. Thank you."

It should feel awkward sitting across the table from a girl I barely know and yet it isn't uncomfortable at all. Peaches is such a sweetheart and I can't think of a single person who doesn't like her.

"So why are you here?" I ask.

"I could ask you the same question. Why do you think I'm here?" She asks softly.

I chew an ice cube before I answer. I don't want to come across as rude or intrusive. "I think you're here because your mother doesn't want anyone to know about the baby."

"Ding, ding, ding. You've won a prize!" She giggles. "Now, why are you here?"

"I heard about what happened to Bronze and I wanted to see if you needed help."

"He'll come back for me. He promised." She juts out her chin. She reminds me of Olive, one of my mother's students. Despite the fact she's pregnant, there's something innocent about her. I'm not sure what to say so I merely nod.

"We barely know each other, why do you want to help?" She tilts her head and studies me.

"Because if I were in your position, I'd hope someone would help me."

"You're nothing like your Aunt Scarlet. Ooops, I can't believe I said that." She clamps her hand over her mouth.

I laugh. "No worries. I take that as a compliment. Seriously though, is there anything that you need besides sugar? I'd stay longer but my parents will worry if I'm out too late."

"No, I've got everything I need here." She pats her stomach and grins.

"I'll see you tomorrow around eight?"

"Thank you, Jade. I'll see you then." She waves before she shuts the door.

I jog down several steps, feeling satisfied with the evening, when I hear people shouting, "Fire!" With outstretched arms, I move as quickly as possible through the backyard. It's difficult with weeds and thorns scratching my naked arms and legs. The sky is as black as tar and the stars only serve as a dim flashlight. When I finally reach the gravel road, commune members are gathered in groups, pointing toward the sky, which is streaked with brilliant orange and yellows mingling with smoke. So this is what a wild fire looks like. I stand, transfixed, until I hear a little girl cry, "Mommy!" I have to get home. I jog to the truck, hop in, and drive as fast as I dare through the windy, country roads. When I pull into our driveway, my parents are sitting on the porch swing, watching the night sky as intently as if it were a Nirvana produced TV show.

"Honey, where were you?" my mother asks.

"After I dropped Slate off, I went for a drive."

"We were worried. You could have called from Scarlet's house. Next time, please let us know that you'll be back late," my father says.

I sit on the front step and Licorice flops down next to me, resting his head on my thigh. "I'm sorry. I won't let it happen again." I take a deep breath. "So what exactly is on fire?"

"Thankfully, it doesn't look like any homes caught fire, just trees," my father says.

"What could have caused it?" I ask.

"Well, there wasn't any lightening. I'm assuming it was some careless teenagers, partying in the woods. No offense, Jade," my father says.

"None taken."

"It already looks like the fire is dying down. The firemen were on the scene quickly, as far as we could tell," my mother says. "Is the phone ringing? Jade, can you answer it, please?"

I dart inside and grab the kitchen phone. "Hello?"

"Jade, it's Ty." He sounds breathless.

"Hi. What's wrong?"

"You'll never believe what burned down."

"What?" My heart drops to the bottom of my stomach.

"Our cabin. It's gone, Jade."

I sink into a kitchen chair. "That's horrible. How did you find out?"

"My father's best friend is a fireman. He always tells us details most people don't get to hear."

"Does he think someone did it on purpose? Or maybe it was teenagers and it was an accident? We've found cigarette butts there before."

He sighs. "He's not sure. Could be either, really."

"I miss you. I wish you could come over."

"Me, too. And I'd totally sneak out if it weren't for the fact my father and I have a job at five am."

"It's getting late, so you better get some sleep. Thanks for letting me know."

"Are you working with your mother or father tomorrow?" He asks.

"My father, why?"

"How about I pick you up for lunch? Then we can drive to the cabin. Maybe something incriminating was left behind. Probably not but you never know."

"Don't pack your lunch, I'll make you one. See you tomorrow, Ty."

"Night, Jade."

That night, I toss and turn so much that Licorice sleeps in front of the bedroom door, as far away from me and my nightmares as possible. I can't blame him.

Chapter Twelve

Excerpt from Grandmother Ruby's diary – November 22, 2011

I've left numerous messages but still haven't heard back from anyone at the hospital. I worked there for forty years and know they aren't too busy to return a phone call. As soon as I feel a little better, I'm driving up there. I've asked Scarlet and Carmine to speak to the doctors but the doctors just tell them the results aren't in. I used to think Royal was too cynical but now I agree with him. If we lived on the Outside, perhaps we'd have superior health care.

I can picture her writing this. Most likely she was in bed propped against pillows, using the newborn light of morning. It was probably written before her first cup of coffee or tea. And before she meticulously applied red lipstick to what she called her 'naked lips.' I'm assuming she wrote in the early morning, before any friends or family visited. I stopped by every evening after work and I never noticed a diary or even a pen laying on the night stand but I did take note of the used tissues, herbal medicines, empty water glasses, and endless flowers scattered around her bedroom.

The flowers kept my mother busy. She was obsessed with picking through the vases, scrutinizing each flower, and throwing away the wilted ones. Grandmother and I would lock eyes, bite our lips, and then burst out laughing.

"What?" My mother said the first time we made fun of her. "Dead flowers don't conduct the right kind of energy."

"Then you might as well throw me away, too," Grandmother said, winking at me.

My mother looked startled. "Now Ruby, I—"

Then we would double over with laughter. After that, my mother would ignore us while she arranged the flowers.

And my father always seemed uncomfortable, stuck in grandmother's bedroom with the three of us, so he'd cut the grass, fix leaky faucets, re-paint the shutters, etc.

Thinking about my father reminds me that I'm working at the winery today. I peek out the tiny window in my work shed and sigh. The sky is overcast and the tree leaves are limp from last night's heavy rain. Ironically, it didn't rain until after the firemen exhausted the flames. Then it poured.

At the winery, I place a bell on the counter along with a sign that reads "Working in back. Please ring bell for service." My father and I spend the morning bottling Cabernet Franc. After he siphons the clear, red wine into bottles, I secure the cork. Even though the process is tedious, I enjoy my father's company.

"Take any impressive photos lately?" He asks.

"Impressive? No."

He cocks his head and stares intently at me. "You're still passionate about photography, right?"

I sigh. "I think so."

"If so, you have to feed your passion. That means you have to actually take pictures. And you have an eye, Jade. You notice things that virtually no one else does."

Heat spreads across my cheeks. I'm not used to hearing many compliments from him. "Thanks."

"You may take the afternoon off on one condition." He holds his right pointer finger up for emphasis.

"What's that?"

"Spend it taking pictures. Did you bring a camera with you?"

"Yes." My camera is such a part of me that I nearly bring it everywhere.

"Ding, ding." The shrill bell resonates.

"Saved by the bell." He smiles.

"It's lunch time so it's probably Ty. Thanks for giving me the afternoon off."

"You deserve it but I expect to see impressive photos within the next few days." He enunciates the word 'impressive.'

"I'll try." He gives me a stern look. "I mean I will." I'm so eager to see Ty I practically skip to the front room; therefore I'm startled when I notice Aunt Scarlet. She's drumming her fingers impatiently on the counter.

"Hello, Aunt Scarlet. Do you need to speak to my father or are you here to pick up wine?" I slip behind the counter.

"Neither." Her deep red eyes bore into mine. "Actually, I'm here to speak to you."

My stomach lurches like it does when my father drives too fast around bends in the road. Nonetheless, I paint a smile on my face. "Would you like to sit down on the couch?"

"That's not necessary. What I have to say will only take a minute." She chews on her cheek for a moment before she continues. "My main question is: why are you involving yourself in business that isn't yours?"

"W—w—what are you referring to?" I'm embarrassed by my stutter.

"Jade, don't play dumb. Why are you snooping around Nirvana?"

My mouth refuses to move, as if my lips are glued shut.

"Fine, I don't even need an answer. I'm here to advise you to stop. You have plenty on your plate already." She runs her hands down her sides, smoothing her charcoal gray dress. Then she takes her hands and rubs them together, as if dismissing our conversation.

When Ty walks through the door, I'm so relieved I nearly cry. "Good morning, ladies." Ty smiles, showcasing perfect teeth. He loops his arm around my lower back, squeezes my side, and kisses me on the forehead. "I hope I wasn't interrupting anything." He knows how much I dislike my aunt.

"No, we were finished with our girl talk. And Jade, you clearly have enough meat to fill your plate and I'd rate it Grade A. Have a great afternoon." She winks before sashaying out the door.

"Your aunt is strange. What was she talking about?"

I wrap my arms around his neck and pull him toward me. "I'm pretty sure she was calling you a steak." I rest my chin in the crook of his neck and breathe in his musky leather smell.

"What kind of steak? A filet mignon is my favorite cut, so would I most resemble that one? And why is your aunt comparing me to meat in the first place?"

"I wouldn't know. I'm a vegetarian, remember? Scarlet came here to tell me to stop snooping. She said I had enough on my plate and then you came through the door."

"Are you going to listen to her?"

I break away from him and gaze into his eyes. "What do you think?"

"I already know you're too stubborn to stop snooping. Let's eat and then drive to our cabin, at least what's left of it."

I ask my father if he'd like to eat with us but he declines. I unpack grapes, fresh bread, cheese, and other light fare. As we eat, I fill Ty in on my visit with Peaches. Of course, he advises me to be careful and I promise I will.

After lunch Ty drives through the unrelenting rain and parks in front of what now resembles a large fire pit. We stand under an umbrella, hold hands and simply stare at the remnants of the slave cabin. The faded purple flag is non existent. I feel empty like a bottle of wine after a party. I'm glad I forgot my camera.

"Do you think Scarlet did this?" I ask, horrified at the thought.

Ty squeezes my hand. "I sure hope not but who knows. Regardless of what happened, I'll miss this place."

"I will, too. We've had a lot of happy memories here."

"We'll make new happy memories." He tilts my chin and crushes his lips against mine. I drop the umbrella, wrap my hands around his neck and pull him closer. And in this moment, everything but the two of us disappears. There's no heartache, no charred cabin, and no mysteries. When we part I'm left breathless. Neither of us bothers to pick the umbrella up.

Ty says, "I'm so glad you feel the same way about me."

"Who says I do?" I bat my eyelashes dramatically.

"Even without words, your lips say everything. At least I think they do. Let me make sure." I fade into his twilight eyes as he leans in for another kiss.

"Well, are you right?"

"Of course." He wraps his arm around my shoulders.

"I've never kissed anyone in the rain before," I say.

"I thought I was your first kiss! Who have you kissed besides me?"

"You don't know him, he lives on the Outside," I joke.

"He better stay there if he knows what's good for him." He clenches his fist in mock anger.

"I don't want to but should we get back to work?"

"Yes, we should go." He nudges a piece of burnt wood with his boot. "I don't think we're going to find any clues here."

"Okay."

"You're even cute soaked. Unbelievable." He shakes his head.

"You're not bad yourself." Laughing, I grab the umbrella and leave the scorched cabin behind.

When I return to the winery, I wave hello to my father. Then I locate my camera and slip on yellow boots and a matching raincoat. I feel silly like a duck waddling through the mucky vineyard. And there aren't many pictures worth taking because without ripe, juicy grapes, the vines stand shriveled and naked. Regardless, I kneel in the mud, focus the lens of my camera, and snap pictures of anything that catches my eye. Some of the pictures might turn out decent including a crow perched on a wooden post, his striking coal black wings spread out, prepared at any moment to take flight. I turn my face to the sky and welcome the cold, refreshing raindrops.

A bolt of lightning flashes above the trees and that's when I notice two figures dressed head to toe in black. I can't tell if they're male or female because their ball caps are pulled down low. What are they doing in the woods during a storm? They're each holding something in their right hands. When they raise their arms, I realize they have knives. Instinctively, I raise my camera and peer through the lens. I can't see their faces any clearer but snap a picture anyway. I stand in the mud, frozen in place, until they race towards me. I feel like I'm going to throw up as I weave through the rows of vines. I don't look back until I'm a hundred yards from the winery. The figures have stopped chasing me. In fact they're just standing there. I sprint towards the door, fling it open and dash inside. I slam the door behind me which causes Licorice to bark incessantly.

"What's with slamming the door?" My father says as he enters the front room. When he sees that I'm pressed against the door and panting, he says, "What's wrong? Are you hurt?"

"T—t—two people were chasing me through the vineyard! They were wearing black clothes and they came from the woods! T—they had knives!"

"Why would they have knives?"

"I don't know but they did!"

"Calm down, you're safe now." He guides me toward the couch and turns the space heater on. "I'll be right back; I want to see if they're still out there." Then he strides toward the door. "I'll be right here on the porch."

I curl up into a ball and start to cry. All this time, I have tried so hard to be strong because like a tree branch, you have to bend with the wind or you'll break, but I'm at my breaking point.

After a few minutes my father returns. "I didn't see anyone. What did they look like?"

"I couldn't tell. I don't even know if they were men or women but they scared me to death."

"I can tell. Let's get you home." He wraps a blanket around my shoulders and quickly shuts the winery down for the evening. I'm not sure why my father is treating me nicer but I'm grateful.

At home, my mother can tell right away something's wrong. I sink into the bathtub under a mountain of bubbles, sip a cup of Carmine's funky tea, and fill my mother in on what happened. She perches on the edge of the toilet, wringing her hands. After I've finished, she gets up from the toilet and paces the small length of my bathroom.

"There's no way they wanted to hurt you, Jade. Everyone loves you. It must have been some kind of prank." She frowns. "A really messed up prank but a prank nonetheless. Yes, that's what it was." She nods her head like a rag doll. "Need anything else, sweetie? Another cup of tea?"

"No, I'm fine."

"Don't stay in the bathtub too long." She bends down to kiss my forehead before she leaves.

Sometimes I wish I was more like my mother. She lives in a world of make believe and denial. But that just isn't me.

I phone Ty next. When I tell him about the knives, he's enraged. "Who would do something like that? When I find out who did that to you…"

After he's calmed down, I ask him for a favor. "Can you please write a note addressed to Peaches explaining why I couldn't make it tonight? Also, can you tape it to a bag of sugar if your parents have an extra and drop it off at my grandparent's house, please?" After he promises to do so, I crawl into bed and immediately fall asleep. This time Licorice doesn't leave my side.

Chapter Thirteen

Excerpt from Grandmother Ruby's diary – December 3, 2011

When Dr. Tuscan, by far the most important physician in Nirvana, strode into my bedroom, I knew immediately there was no hope. He droned on and on but I concentrated on the crucial parts—Kidney cancer. Has spread everywhere. Few weeks to live. Room in hospice. The last thing he said was, 'Do you have any questions?'

When I die, will I be reunited with my one true love, my late husband Navy? Will I be able to watch over my friends and family? I have plenty of questions but he doesn't have the answers, so I obviously didn't ask.

I've made two monumental decisions. First, I'm going to write down everything disturbing I know about Nirvana. Second, before I die, I'm going to give this diary to Jade.

True knows a lot of the concealed things that occur in Nirvana and now so do I.

I sail the diary across my work shed. So far this diary has caused nothing but harm. I grab hold of the poster board and rip a third of the way through before I stop. Destroying the diary and poster board won't erase everything I've already found out. In order to feel any peace, I need answers to my questions. Why did Scarlet warn me? Did she burn down the slave cabin? Who was chasing me through the vineyard? Was it Scarlet and Saffron?

Since my mother gave me the day off to rest, I may actually finish this diary, once and for all. I double check that my work shed is locked, pick the diary up off the floor, and take a deep breath.

True knows a lot of the concealed things about Nirvana and now so do I. It took a lot of pleading on my part but True agreed to tell me everything unsettling that he knows about our commune, or as he calls it, our cult. I've asked him why he stays in Nirvana and he says that he has no where else to go. And besides, what if the rest of the world is no better?

Regardless, here is what True has told me...

After I finish Grandmother Ruby's diary, I rush outside and vomit in the grass. If the Outside is anything like Nirvana, there's no hope. I alternate between crying and vomiting until there's nothing emotionally and physically left. Stiffly, I return to my work shed and add the additional information to the poster board. There's nothing left to do but take a shower, brush my teeth, and wait for Ty who promised to stop by after work. I sit on the front porch swing but I don't swing. In fact, I don't do anything but sit there and stare straight ahead. Licorice lies by my feet the entire time. When my parents return home from work, they just think I'm still upset about what happened yesterday.

When Ty gets out of his truck, I race down the sidewalk and fling my arms around him. "I'm so glad to see you!"

"I was so worried about you last night. I stopped by your house but you were sleeping. I watched you sleep for awhile." He strokes my hair.

"You did? Why?" I mumble into his T-shirt.

"If I'm around, I can protect you."

I squeeze him tight before stepping back. "I finished the diary and wrote all of the key points down. It's in my work shed."

In the shed, I point to the bottom right hand side of the poster board. "Here's the most recent and worst information."

While he reads, Ty shakes his head in what I assume is disbelief. "Not that I don't believe your grandmother, but how do we know this True character is telling the truth?"

"We can visit him. He's a caretaker at the cemetery."

"Let's do that. Think it's too late now?"

"It's worth a shot. Plus I need to get out of here for a while."

After convincing my parents yet again a drive through the country will make me feel better, Ty and I head to the cemetery. "Where should I park?" He asks.

"He must live in one of the little cabins near the mausoleum which is in the center of the cemetery, so it doesn't really matter where you park."

"Okay." Ty pulls into the Blue Lot.

As we walk through the cemetery it starts to drizzle. The rain, coupled with the crows perched atop head stones, causes shivers to run down my spine.

"Is this a good idea?" I ask.

Ty shrugs. "I don't know but I'm not sure what else to do at this point. How are we supposed to know which cabin he lives in?"

"I have a feeling it's that one." I point to the last cabin on the right. I can vaguely make out a lit cigarette. As we approach, I recognize True.

"Jade? What are you doing at the cemetery this late? And who's your friend?" True descends the three front steps.

"True, this is my best friend, Ty. We'd like to talk to you if you have a minute."

"Nice to meet you, son," True says. They shake hands.

"Likewise, sir."

"Come on in." True coughs and flings his cigarette on the gravel. "It's not much but its home." We follow him inside. "Have a seat. Would you like something to drink? Hot tea, iced tea? Or a nice cold beer from the Outside?" He grins.

"Iced tea would be fine, thank you," I say.

"Same for me, please," Ty says.

His kitchen is small but tidy. The walls are painted yellow, the curtains are white with yellow flowers, and there's an arrangement of wild flowers in the center of the table. I wonder if Grandmother Ruby helped him decorate.

True places our iced teas on the table before he cracks open a beer.

"So you've finished the diary, then?" True asks.

My mouth drops open. "How did you know about the diary?"

"Why, it was my idea." He takes a long swig of beer. "I thought it might help."

"Did you know she wrote down everything damaging you told her about Nirvana?" I ask.

"Yes, I know. She asked if it was okay."

"But aren't you afraid an official will find out you've said these things?" I ask.

True scratches his chin which is covered in gray stubble. "Honestly? No. Ruby really wanted to know and she's more important to me than any official."

"So it's all true?" Ty asks.

"If she wrote down what I told her, then yes, it's all true," he says.

I take a deep breath before I say, "In her last entry, she mentioned something about poisoning. Her handwriting was so light it was hard to read. Did she mention anything about this to you?"

True's blue eyes darken. I remember hearing the color "true blue" is considered the purest color of blue.

"Ruby thought she may have been poisoned because some of her symptoms didn't line up with kidney cancer," True says.

"But she had a lot of symptoms that did," I say. "Vision problems, weight loss, back pain... what symptoms didn't make sense?"

"Shaky hands, respiratory issues, her emotions were out of whack, a number of things."

"But who would do such a thing?" I ask. "And why? My grandmother didn't have any enemies." I rest my head against my hands.

"I wouldn't rule anything out in this commune but the only people who were around Ruby were her friends and family. She was never alone."

"What about at night?" I ask.

True blushes. "I slept on the couch. Sometimes she'd wake up in the middle of the night and need something."

Tears slip down my face. "Thank you for taking such good care of her."

True hands me a handkerchief. "She took care of me too, honey." His voice catches.

I dry my eyes and ask, "What do you think we should do?"

"Well, you have two options." True finishes his beer and crushes it. "You can destroy the diary and pretend it never existed, which I would assume would be very difficult at this point. Or you can flee Nirvana with the diary and go to the Outside authorities. Not sure if they're any better but you never know."

"Just out of curiosity, what would you do?" Ty asks.

"If I were young like the two of you, I'd run from Nirvana and never look back," True says.

Cuckoo! A small bird pops out of the cuckoo clock on the wall. Nine o'clock pm.

"We better get going. Thank you so much for everything, True," I say.

"Good luck with whatever the two of you decide. I enjoyed your company," True says.

"It was nice meeting you, sir," Ty says.

"Wait here a second," True says. A minute later he hands us each a flashlight. "You'll need these."

"Thanks." We reply in unison.

True waves before closing his door.

I'm grateful for the flashlights because there's only a dim light emitting from the moon and stars. I try to focus on the strip of green grass but it's difficult to ignore the headstones on either side. If it weren't for Ty by my side, this would be an absolute nightmare.

"What should we do now?" I ask.

"I honestly have no idea. I'm having trouble wrapping my mind around this mess."

"Unfortunately we don't have much time to decide," I say.

"Well, True's right. We either forget about it or make a run for it. Those are the only options we have."

"But I don't want to choose either one. How can I just turn a blind eye to the horrible things I know? On the flip side, how can I abandon my family, my home, and everything I've ever known? And what if they catch me? I'm so sorry I dragged you into this mess!" Tears roll down my cheeks.

Ty stops and places a hand on my shoulder. "Jade, if you wouldn't have involved me, I would have been pissed."

"That doesn't make any sense. Why?"

"Because I love you." His twilight eyes pierce the center of my heart. I want to tell him I love him, too, but I'm speechless. "Nearly every night I dream about you. Often, you're a southern belle, seated in a carriage, and I'm a soldier on horseback. I watch as you disappear, headed northbound, as far away from the Civil War as possible. Before you go, you kiss a handkerchief and toss it out the carriage window. Before it touches the dirt road, I catch it. Strange, isn't it?"

"I—I—I think it's beautiful. And I love you, too." I drop my flashlight, wrap my arms around his back, and press my lips against his. After a long, lingering kiss, we walk quickly to the exit. When we reach the truck, Ty touches each tire.

"What are you doing?" I ask.

"Just wanted to make sure the tires weren't slashed."

My heart summersaults in my chest.

I cross my fingers that the engine starts. I'm euphoric when it does.

Chapter Fourteen

"Jade, will you be okay on your own for about an hour? I have a few shipments to drop off. Or you could always come with me, if you'd rather," my father says.

The thought of being alone anywhere scares me. "I'll help with deliveries."

"No problem. You ready?"

"Let me just grab my mug." Lately I'm addicted to Carmine's funky tea. On the way out, I flip over the "Closed" sign hanging on the door.

"C'mon boy, let's go," my father calls to Licorice. He leaps off the couch, eagerly wagging his tail. I'm envious of how simple his life is. No one is forcing him to choose a life path he doesn't want, or to change the color of his eyes in order to keep him in line or…a million other things. What am I going to do? If I remain in Nirvana, I'll have to undergo another eye color surgery which they may botch on purpose. That's what tends to happen to people who make waves in Nirvana. I shudder at the thought of being trapped in a chair, with sharp instruments closing in on my eyes. But if I leave Nirvana, I'll never see my mother and father again. I know without asking, they'd never come with me. Their home is here. And I can't involve them in this danger.

"Where's our first stop?" I ask.

"The cemetery, two cases. The caretakers sure like their wine." He grins.

If I would have known, I could have brought True's flashlights with me. But then wouldn't my father wonder why I had them in the first place? Oh well, next time. If I decide to leave Nirvana, I'd like to say goodbye to True. And I'd like to pay respect to Grandfather Navy and Grandmother Ruby one last time.

We park in the Blue Lot. My father loads the two cases of wine on the dolly and we walk along the same path that Ty and I took last night. I clip a leash to Licorice's collar so he doesn't relieve himself on anyone's grave. Dogs aren't technically allowed on the cemetery grounds but the caretakers don't mind as long as they're on a leash.

When we descend the hill, my father asks, "What in the world is going on?" There's an ambulance, multiple security trucks, and all of the caretakers are lined up wearing somber expressions.

An official immediately approaches. "Sir, you'll have to come back another time. This area is off limits."

"What happened?" My father asks.

"Sir, this is a private matter. Please go. And by the way, why do you have a dog on this property?"

My father throws his hands up in surrender. "I apologize, sir, we're leaving. It won't happen again. Let's go, Jade." My father turns the dolly and starts walking. I watch as two medical assistants wheel a stretcher from True's cabin. There's a sheet covering his body." Jade, we have to go now. Are you okay?"

I bend over and vomit.

My father takes Licorice's leash and holds my hair back while I vomit what little is in my stomach. When I'm finished he hands me a handkerchief and I wipe my mouth. The handkerchief reminds me of Ty's dream, but right now I'm anything but a southern belle.

"You poor kid. I knew you should have stayed home today. I'm taking you home now."

"But I don't want to be home alone." As tears form, I angrily wipe them away.

"You're safe at home, Jade. I'm not sure who those people were in the vineyard but I honestly don't see why they'd want to harm you. There's just no reason."

If you only knew, I think.

Once I'm home, I make sure all the doors and windows are locked. Licorice must sense that I'm scared, because he lies against my bedroom door. Even though I'm exhausted, I don't fall asleep. I just stare at the white ceiling.

That evening I call Ty.

"I have to talk to you and it's urgent," I say.

"Want me to pick you up?" He asks.

"No, I'd like to drive. I'll ask to borrow the truck and I'll be there in a few minutes."

As usual, my parents are sitting in the kitchen drinking tea. "May I borrow the truck? I'd really like to spend some time with Ty."

"If it's okay with your mother, its fine with me."

"Are you feeling better?" My mother asks.

"Yes, I feel fine."

"Are you sure? It looks like your hands are shaking?" She grabs hold of my hands. "And they're cold." She rubs my hands together.

"They're always cold. Cold hands, warm heart, remember?"

"That's true. But what's wrong with your nails?" She inspects each one. "There are white marks on them."

I slip my hands from her grasp. Sure enough there are little marks in the center of each of my nails. "I have no idea but I feel fine." I shrug.

"It could be a sign that there isn't enough potassium in your diet. We'll have to order bananas from the Outside."

"If I promise to eat more bananas, may I please go?"

She smiles. "Yes, but be careful."

"Wear your seatbelt," my father says.

When I reach the truck, I jump inside. I'm eager to spend some time with Ty. As I drive to his house, I forget about my discolored nails and my nauseated stomach. All I can think about are his beautiful purple eyes. When I pull into his driveway, he's waiting for me.

"So what's up?" Ty asks as he slides into the truck.

I wait until he shuts the door to say, "You're not going to believe this but True's dead."

"What are you talking about? We were just with him last night!" He runs his fingers through his thick hair. "How did you find out?"

"My father had some deliveries and I tagged along. Turns out the first stop was at the cemetery. The caretakers had ordered two cases of wine. When we got there, there was an ambulance and officials, and a stretcher coming out of True's cabin."

"Well, maybe he's still alive. Did you call the hospital to check?"

"The sheet was over his head, Ty."

Ty stares straight ahead as if he's in shock. "This is really bad, Jade. Really bad. We've got to come up with a plan."

I grab hold of his hands. "If I leave, will you come with me?"

"Of course I will. But how exactly are we going to do that?"

Feeling guilty, I look down at my lap. "I spoke with Ivory. In fact, I asked him how he tried to escape."

"And?"

"He promised to teach me how to disable the electric fence. He knows where the main power source is and everything."

"If Ivory knew what he was doing, why was he caught?"

"He ran out of time. We'd have to make sure we don't."

"Even if this plan works, what will we do once we're on the Outside? We don't have any money, or a truck, or anything. We've got to come up with a solid plan."

"Maybe we can borrow a truck."

"You mean steal one," he says.

"Technically, yes, but borrowing sounds better. And I want to ask Peaches if she wants to leave with us."

"But Peaches is pregnant."

"Exactly. But I'm certain she wants to keep her baby. If she stays here, Saffron will take it. We can't just leave her here."

"Anyone else you'd like to invite?"

I tilt my head. "Slate but I don't think I could take care of him."

"Jade, I was kidding. We'll be lucky if we can escape unscathed."

I place my hands firmly on the steering wheel. "I'm driving to Peaches. Do you want to come?"

He fastens his seatbelt.

I fiddle with the cassette player until "Paint it Black" by the Rolling Stones blares from the crummy speakers. Perfect song for this evening. We don't say a word as I drive along the only roads we've ever been on. I park in the same spot as I did the other night. We walk carefully through the backyard and climb the three steps to the back porch.

I knock several times but Peaches doesn't answer the door.

I feel panic stricken. "Ty, why isn't she answering the door? What if something bad happened to her?"

"Maybe you're just knocking too softly." He knocks louder.

In a moment, Peaches opens the door. Her hair is in disarray. "Sorry, I was lying down. Come on in." She smoothes her hair.

"I apologize for waking you." We follow her to the kitchen.

"No, I'm so glad that you're here. I feel like I'm going crazy from being stuck in this house," she says.

"I hope that you don't mind I brought my boyfriend, Ty. Have you been formally introduced?" This is the first time I've called Ty my boyfriend. I still can't seem to wrap my mind around it.

"We've met in passing but it's nice to see you again." A blush spreads across Peaches' round cheeks.

"Likewise." Ty offers his hand and they shake.

"Please have a seat. Iced tea? And thank you so much for dropping sugar off the other night. Much appreciated." She smiles.

We nod and sit down at the small wooden table.

"I've had enough of this chamomile tea, it makes me too sleepy." Peaches shoves a tin into a cupboard.

"My mom drinks that tea, too. Just curious, who brought that to you?" I ask.

"Your Aunt Scarlet. Funny she's the one who stops by every day. I suppose my mother can't be bothered." She places three iced teas on the table, along with sugar and lemons. "But my father visits every day."

I squeeze lemon into my glass. "I wonder why Scarlet checks on you every day?" I ask.

Peaches pulls her thick brown hair into a ponytail. "She's probably the only nurse who my mother trusts with her deep dark secret."

"That makes sense," I say.

"Have either of you heard anything from Bronze?" She asks.

We shake our heads.

She hangs her head. "He promised he'd come back for me."

Ty and I exchange glances. Our theory is that Bronze was murdered like True but we wouldn't dare tell Peaches that.

"Peaches, we have so much to tell you but so little time." I take a deep breath. I sure hope I can trust this girl. My sixth sense tells me I can. "Basically, my Grandmother Ruby found out a lot of horrific things that go on in Nirvana and she told me everything. Ty and I are planning an escape. We wanted to know if you'd like to come with us. I know we don't know each other very well but I was thinking about your situation." I ramble.

"I know a lot about the bad things that go on here." She nods. "I understand why you're leaving and I know some people have made it out of here safely. You just have to be careful. It means a lot that you'd think of me but I can't leave with you. I have to wait for Bronze. I know he loves me and he'll come back for me as soon as he can."

"Are you sure?" I ask gently.

"I'm sure. Because if I leave with you, how would Bronze ever find me?"

"Good question," Ty says. He's been so quiet throughout the conversation.

"Well, if you change your mind, you're welcome to come," I say.

"Where are you going to on the Outside?" She says.

"To a city called Main, it's about forty miles from here. Ty and I found out we have family there," I say.

"That's a good thing. When are you leaving?"

"As soon as possible but we have to figure some things out first," Ty says. He glances at the clock. "Unfortunately it's getting late. We really should be going." We stand up.

"Thank you so much for stopping by. Will you try and say goodbye before you leave?" Her eyes are so full of hope; it's heartbreaking.

"Of course." My voice catches. "I might be able to stop by a few more times. Is there anything else you need? My father has a ton of books, do you like to read?"

"No, thank you. I read really slowly, although I have read some great mysteries." She laughs. "Knitting keeps me busy. I'm making a pink blanket for the baby." She pats her stomach. "I just know I'm having a girl."

"It was nice seeing you, Peaches." Ty says as he walks to the door.

"Stop by anytime with Jade."

I'm surprised when Peaches flings her arms around me. "It's too bad we didn't go to school together. I just know we would have been great friends."

"Me too," I say.

Ty and I wave goodbye. As we head to the truck, tears well in my eyes. Its pathetic how much I've been crying lately; it's not like me at all.

"I feel so bad for her, Ty."

"I do too. It's a really sad situation. I'd bet my life Bronze isn't coming back."

"I can see why she'd want to wait for him. If I were in her situation, I would too."

"You'd wait for Bronze, huh?" Ty teases.

I roll my eyes. "Well now that I'm going to be an Outsider, I might as well date one."

"Well, you're stuck with me because I'll be right there with you." He leans down and kisses me and all of my tears dry up.

Chapter Fifteen

To my parents, this is just another family breakfast but for me, it's one day closer to my escape. We're seated at the kitchen table because it's raining too hard to sit outside.

"Do you know what day it is?" My father asks.

"It's the first of April," my mother says.

"Exactly. On the Outside, they call today 'April Fool's Day.'"

"Why?" She asks. "And where did you hear something like that?"

"I was flipping through an old encyclopedia and came across it. Around the world people play practical jokes on one another. No one's sure of where the idea originated."

My mother claps her hands together. "That sounds fun. Jade, we'll have to think of some jokes to play on our students." She beams.

I force a smile on my face. Now that I've made the decision to leave Nirvana, it's hard to be near my parents. I'm their only daughter, which means they'll never have grandchildren, they'll never retire, and there's a good chance they'll be shunned. How can I be so selfish?

On the other hand, if Ty and I speak to authorities on the Outside, maybe they'll help us. But other commune members have fled Nirvana and no one from the Outside has helped so far... But Ty and I will be different. Once we're situated on the Outside, we'll come back for our parents. And I'll come back for Slate. I have to think positive because if I don't, I won't find the courage to escape. I have to keep telling myself that there will be many more breakfasts with my parents on the Outside.

"In the encyclopedia, does it mention what kind of jokes people play?" I ask my father, which starts him on a tangent.

Throughout the morning, my mother and I play harmless jokes on the kids. In the afternoon, we explain 'April Fools Day.' We pass out construction paper and ask the students to draw fish, decorate them, and cut them out. We explain that in France and Italy, kids tape paper fish to each other's back and shout 'April Fish!' The kids have an absolute blast.

That evening, my parents and I are listening to music in the living room, when there's a knock on the door.

I jump from the couch. "I'll get the door. Maybe it's Ty." But when I fling open the door, it's Saffron and she looks... pissed. I yearn to slam the door in her face but instead I say, "Good evening, Saffron. Please come in."

She steps into the hall and says, "I'd like to speak to you and Jonquil."

"Why don't you have a seat at the table? I'll be right back." I say before I hurry into the living room. "Saffron's here and she wants to talk to us," I say to my mother.

"What? Oh, no." She places her head in her hands.

"What is it?" My father asks.

"I bet we're in trouble." She looks at my father. "We told the kids about 'April Fool's Day.'"

"Why that's harmless. Why would you be in trouble for that?" He frowns. "But come to think of it, in this commune, why wouldn't you?" He stands up. "Let's get this over with."

"She only asked to speak with us," I say.

"Well, if anyone should be punished it should be me. After all, I was the one who told you about it."

We walk to the kitchen single file. Saffron is seated at the table and tapping her long, bright pink fingernails. "Good evening," she says.

My parents say hello.

"Would you like something to drink?" My father asks.

"Ice water, please."

My mother and I join her at the table but she doesn't say anything until my father hands her the glass of iced water. She takes a long sip. Then she crushes an iced cube before she speaks. "Scarlet tells me Slate came home from school with paper fish all over his back. When she asked him about it, he carried on about some Outside holiday. Care to explain why you strayed so far from the curriculum?"

My mother straightens her spine and looks Saffron square in the eyes. "Our students work hard every day and once in awhile it's important to reward them with a fun activity."

"That's fine. However, teaching them about anything concerning the Outside must be cleared by Rust and I first."

"But I didn't think this activity would cause any problems…" My mother says but Saffron cuts her off.

"Exactly. You didn't think." Her tone is cold.

My father places his palms up. "Saffron, there's no reason for insults and I will not sit quietly while you're rude to my wife. I take full responsibility for today's activity. If there are negative consequences, they should be given to me."

"No need for any punishments. Just don't let it happen again." She slowly gets up from the table. "I really shouldn't have to deal with any stress right now." She places her hand on her stomach and strides out the door.

After she's gone, my mother says what we're all thinking. "What a miserable witch."

The next evening, I tell Peaches what happened. We're curled up on the couch in the living room.

"That sounds like my mother." She rolls her eyes. "I don't know what my father ever saw in her. He puts on a tough façade but underneath, he's a sweetheart." She smiles. "When I leave, he's the only person I'll miss. What about you?"

"I'm much closer to my mother than my father but I'll miss them both. And I'll miss Slate; he's become the brother I never had. Oh, and I'll miss you, too." I say.

"Don't miss me; I'll be right behind you. How's your plan coming along?"

I sigh. "Not that well. But we have to be out of here by July 7th. That's my birthday and I am not undergoing another eye procedure."

"My birthday is just two days after yours."

"Wow. Do you think our mother's shared a delivery room?" I ask.

Peaches shakes her head. "No, my mother gave birth in her bedroom because she wanted a quiet delivery. According to my father, she forced everyone around her to whisper. He says when she held me in her arms; it was the happiest day of her life. Evidently, she's changed her mind because I couldn't tell you the last time she's given me a hug. Or come to think of it, a compliment. My father says she was so disappointed when they couldn't have another child. Fortunately, a year after I was born, my parents adopted Bronze. But he was never close to our mother, either."

A chill runs through me. "I've heard whenever there's a car accident involving Outsiders, children are saved but adults aren't. In fact Grandmother Ruby mentioned it in her diary."

"I've heard that, too." Her voice is soft. "I don't like to think about things like that." She pauses before she says, "maybe I can steal money from my parents for you and Ty."

"I don't want you to get in trouble, it's not worth it."

"But I'll be right behind you, remember?" She grins.

The next morning, I wake up early in order to develop film before the Center meeting. Maybe the pictures I took in the vineyard are clearer than I thought. Maybe I'll be able to identify the people with the knives.

I squeal like a piglet when I notice a package on the porch outside of my work shed. It must be a gift from Ty because I can't think of another person who would surprise me with a gift. He's such a talented whittler that I bet it's a wooden figurine. I un-wrap several layers of rose colored tissue paper. When I uncover the gift, I gasp and nearly drop it. It's a homemade doll that is the exact replica of me except there are slashes where my eyes would be. Horrified, I release the doll and she bounces off the porch step. The wind carries the rose colored tissue paper into the sky. I watch as piece after piece gets tangled in tree branches. Who would send something like this? I yearn to get rid of it now. My hands are shaking as I gingerly pick up the doll and place it in the fire pit. I dump out the contents of my junk drawer to find a matchbook. I also have a small bottle of lighter fluid. As I hold the container over the doll, I have a change of heart. As much as I yearn to destroy this monstrosity, perhaps it can be used as evidence. But what if whoever made it works closely with the authorities? I won't go to the commune guards with anything but perhaps I can bring evidence to the Outside. I remove it from the fire pit and carry it by its black plastic shoes into my work shed. Then I toss it into the bottom of the closet and slam the door. I have got to get out of this place.

When I enter the kitchen, my parents are sitting at the table, drinking coffee.

"You look like you've just seen a ghost, Jade. Are you okay?" My mother asks.

I join them at the table. "I'm fine. Just feeling a little lightheaded from the chemicals."

My father smiles. "Developing some impressive photos, right?"

I nod my head. "Exactly."

"Are you up for work today?" My father asks, cocking his head. "If not, I understand. And we're in a good spot, now that bottling is finished. I should be fine on my own."

The right thing to do is work alongside my father and mother everyday until Ty and I flee. But the selfish part of me yearns to visit the cemetery. Who knows when I'll have the chance before it's time to leave Nirvana?

"If it's okay, I'd like to visit the cemetery today."

My parents exchange brief looks before my father says, "I want you to do whatever will make you feel better. Why don't you take the truck? Drop me off at work and then it's yours."

Typically I'd enjoy the long walk to the cemetery but not with all of the bizarre things that have been going on. "That sounds great, thanks."

"On another note," my mother says gently, "have you decided which life path you'd prefer? Not that we're trying to rush you. It's just that we're curious, me especially." She laughs nervously as she places her hand over mine. Her yellow eyes hold as much hope as sunrise.

Yes, but you're going to disown me for it, I think. "Not yet. I'm sorry."

"No reason to be sorry. You take your time, it's your decision. We're proud of you, regardless." My father says. My mother blinks rapidly, as if holding back a flood of tears.

The familiar pang of anxiety runs through me. When the time comes, am I really strong enough to leave my parents, my home, everything that's familiar? Or will I watch Ty walk away from me forever? Either way what's left of my heart will break.

Two hours later, I'm kneeling in front of Grandmother Ruby's grave. Clouds intermittently block the sun, casting ominous shadows. There's a women, leaning on her cane and wiping her eyes with a handkerchief, and a male caretaker pulling weeds, but they're both some distance away. I'm grateful for the solitude.

"Roses still aren't in season, Grandmother, but I brought wildflowers." I prop them against her headstone. "They're pretty, aren't they? I picked them from the meadow outside the cemetery. There are daisies, bluebells, dandelions…and a few more that I don't recognize. You'd know the names of them, I'm sure. Most people don't consider dandelions to be anything but weeds." I pluck one from the bunch. "Remember how many wishes we'd make with dandelions? That seems like a long time ago…" I toss it and trace the etching on her headstone.

"It's been really hard without you here. I miss you so much." I bow my head. "I thought your diary would give me all of the answers but it's created a lot more questions. But I'm honored that you trusted me enough to give me your diary. That must have been a hard decision. And when it comes down to it, I'd rather know the truth. And I'd rather be true to myself. Grandmother, the truth is I don't want to follow my mother or my father's life path. I want to create my own." The clouds part so I tilt my face to the sun. "I want to explore the Outside…take pictures of the ocean, eat dessert for breakfast, travel… According to Bronze the Outside isn't a bad place. He said Grandmother Goldenrod and Grandfather Rufous are happy there. My plan is to find them, somehow expose Nirvana to the Outside authorities, and come back for my parents and of course, Slate. Is that the right thing to do?" I close my eyes and see an image of Grandmother Ruby. She's speaking to me but I can't hear what she's saying. I'm distracted by the red glow that surrounds her. Suddenly tired, I lie on a grassy area next to her grave, and fall asleep. I wake to someone shaking me gently and calling my name. Groggily, I sit up and look up. I have to shield my eyes from the sun.

"Here, I'll help you up." Rust offers his hands. I place mine in his and he lifts me as if I'm as light as a wildflower. "How are you doing, Jade?" A look of concern washes over his handsome face.

"I've been better."

"When you lose someone you love, the pain remains. Sometimes you fool yourself into thinking you've recovered but then you smell something or see something that reminds you of that person and suddenly the pain is back with a vengeance. It's like the childhood bully who leaves you alone for a few days. Just when you've relaxed and convinced yourself he or she has moved on to someone else, the bully jumps out from behind a tree, with their tongue sticking out, and you realize you're no further ahead." He runs his fingers through his hair, looking embarrassed. "Sorry, I don't know why I said all of that."

"I think what you said is perfect." Heat spreads over my neck and face.

Rust smiles. "Are you heading out?"

"I'd like to visit my Grandfather Navy's grave before I go."

"If it's okay, I'll walk to the Blue Lot with you since I'm parked there."

I nod. We walk side by side along the wooded trail. Even though my father warned me to stay away from Rust, I feel comfortable next to him. Safe, too. Ty makes me feel the same way.

"If you don't mind me asking, who did you visit today?" I ask.

"I paid respect to my grandparents, my parents, and my brother. Of course I miss all of them but I especially miss my brother." He kicks a rock which skitters and hits a tree trunk.

"May I ask what happened?" It must have happened a long time ago because I have never heard about it.

"My brother's given name was Heliotrope but he despised it. The only person who was allowed to call him that was our mother and only when she was angry with him. Therefore, we all called him Lio. I never once teased him about his name because he was older than me and much larger." He chuckles.

"Just curious, what was your given name?"

"Tyrian, but like your friend, I went by Ty." My heart does flip flops at the sound of Ty's name. I just saw him last night and yet I miss him. "Anyway, Lio, a bunch of his friends and I were at the lake. I had just turned eight and Lio was twelve. He always let me tag along wherever he went; he was that kind of brother. As usual, Lio and his friends were daring each other to do silly things like 'I dare you to climb a tree naked' and 'I dare you to hold your breath underwater for two minutes.'" He sighs. "My brother, being the leader, felt the need to up the ante. He pointed to a massive oak tree and asked his friends to take turns seeing who could climb the highest. His friends laughed at him because climbing trees was nothing new to them. But they stopped laughing when Lio clarified his dare. 'After that you have to crawl onto a branch and jump into the lake.' We were always jumping into the lake but always from the safety of the ground. One by one, Lio's friends climbed the tree. And each time they climbed higher and higher. Lio of course climbed the highest and he didn't hesitate before jumping head first into the lake." I braced myself for what Rust was about to say. "When Lio didn't pop up, we panicked. Several of his friends jumped in and swam toward the spot where he landed. But before they could reach him, he popped up laughing which caused us to laugh in relief. Then one of his friends said, 'Hey, Ty, it's your turn to jump.' Immediately Lio said, 'He's only eight, leave him alone.' But I of course had something to prove. So I marched to that tree as if it were the last thing I'd ever do." He pauses, as if reliving the moment. I glance at the sky. The sun is completely obstructed by the clouds.

"Even though I was scared enough to pee myself, I climbed that tree. I didn't climb nearly as high as the others but I was proud of myself. I gingerly crawled onto the branch and when I couldn't hold on any longer, I let go. I hit the water so hard it knocked the wind out of me. I sank to the bottom of the lake. Lio of course dove in to rescue me. But when he grabbed me, I panicked and started thrashing. I must have slipped out of his grasp because I remember kicking him in the head. I reached the surface but Lio didn't."

"I'm so sorry."

"Me too. I've never really forgiven myself. Lio should have been the leader of Nirvana, not me." He glances at me. "I apologize if I've made you uncomfortable. I haven't spoken to many people about it. In fact, besides my parents, Saffron, and my daughter, I've only told that story to your mother, and now you. How is your mother, by the way?"

"She's doing well. Were you close friends, growing up?" I ask.

Rust smiles, but it looks forced. "Yes, we were very close. Like you and Ty actually. But that was another life time ago."

Should I ask him what happened to their friendship? Do I want to know or will it unearth more questions? As I'm contemplating this, we arrive at the Blue Lot.

"It was nice talking with you, Jade. You remind me so much of your father." I remind him of my father? But they despise each other. When I frown, he says, "I meant that as a compliment. Please tell your mother I said hello. Be sure to take care of yourself and if anyone bothers you, let me know, okay?" He places his hand on my shoulder. Why would he say that? Does he know about Saffron's visit to our house? He squeeze my shoulder before he turns and strides toward his truck. My head is spinning as I walk to Grandfather Navy's headstone. Before I have a chance to kneel, I notice Saffron. Her pretty face is twisted in a hateful scowl and she's staring right at me.

Chapter Sixteen

"What were you speaking with my husband about?" Saffron's yellow eyes may as well be red, they're so treacherous. Her hands are on her narrow hips and the small faux baby bump is pressing against her tight pink dress.

"W—W—we were just talking in general." As much as I hate to admit it, I'm intimidated by her.

"I doubt that. I thought I made it clear to your parents that I don't want you to speak to my husband but evidently, I didn't. So I'm making it crystal clear to you now. Stay away from my husband. You have absolutely noting to say to him. Do you understand?' She enunciates the last sentence as if I'm a child. I yearn to reach over and slap her but of course I don't.

With resignation, I say, "I understand."

"Terrific." She smiles so wide I can see her gums. "Do take care of yourself." I watch her amble through the grass. For once she's ungraceful because with every step, her pink high heels sink into the grass.

She must be nuts. Why else would she have such a problem with Rust and I speaking to each other? Is it because Rust and my mother were so close at one time? I try my best to shake thoughts of Saffron out of my head as I pay my respect to Grandfather Navy. I don't stay nearly as long because my stomach is growling. It's well past lunch time. However, before I leave the Blue Lot, I visit True's grave. Someone had placed a bouquet of white flowers on his grave. I'm not sure the name of the flowers but they're beautiful. The only thing I say is, "I'm sorry I pulled you into this mess. May you rest in peace."

In the truck I eat a tomato and mayonnaise sandwich and an apple. Then I drive to the winery because I don't want to be home alone. When I reach the vineyard, my father decides to close up shop which is a nice surprise. We spend the afternoon making vegetable soup and chocolate chip cookies. When my mother gets home from work, she's so pleased she cries. I try really hard to sit back and enjoy our family dinner, but all I can think about is how miserable I'm going to make my parents. Within a few months I'll be gone and they'll have to bear the consequences. With every bite of soup, I have to take a drink of water to help push it down.

After dinner, I swing by Ty's house. I'm disappointed when his mother tells me he's working late. I figure since I have the truck, I may as well check on Peaches. When she answers the door, she looks terrible. Her hair is disheveled, her cheeks are streaked with tears, and her cotton dress is wrinkled.

"Peaches, what's wrong?" I follow her to the couch and sit down beside her.

"Something dreadful must have happened to Bronze. It's been weeks and I haven't heard anything from him. I kept telling myself that he was just having trouble reaching me but he's used to sneaking around and he's good at it. That's how we were able to spend as much time together as we did." Even though it's dark I can tell her cheeks are red. "Jade, we have to get out of here!" She starts to sob, hysterical tears that rack her body. I wrap my arms around her and wait until her tears subside.

"I agree with you. But first I have to find out who's been terrorizing me. I think it might be your mother, with the help of my Aunt Scarlet, of course."

Her eyes grow wide. "What has she done now?" I inform Peaches about the homemade doll with the missing eyes and the incident at the cemetery.

"Do you think she knows we're planning to escape? But if she did, wouldn't she try to scare me, too? Because I haven't received any dolls or anything."

"I don't think she knows our plans. I don't think she'd try to scare you because she's probably afraid you'd lose the baby," I say gently. "By the way, did you know you have a terrible case of mono? So terrible you can't get out of bed, feed yourself, nor have visitors?"

"Is that what she's telling people?" Peaches rolls her eyes. "I'll miss my father but I will never miss *her*. So when are we leaving? I figure I can sneak into Samsara during the Center when every one is preoccupied, open my father's safe, and steal most of the money."

"But how would you get past the guards and the iris scan?"

"I've lived there my whole life; I know ways to sneak in. And I know ways to sneak out," she says proudly. "Bronze and I used to do it all the time. Though without Bronze we'll have to bribe a guard or an Outsider. I miss Bronze so incredibly much." Her face crumples.

"I just need a little more time before we leave. I need to find out if my grandmother was in fact, poisoned." I stand and pace the length of the living room.

"How are you going to do that? And who do you think would do such a thing?"

"I'm planning on sneaking into a few people's homes. If my grandmother was poisoned with Arsenic, there's a chance that there's a bottle left behind. There are two people I think could have done something like this. Actually I think they did it together. My Aunt Scarlet." I hesitate. "And I hate to say this, but your mother."

Peaches vehemently shakes her head. "I know my mother is a witch but I don't think she's capable of murdering someone."

"I feel the same way about my aunt but I don't know who else would do such a thing." I collapse on the couch and massage my forehead.

"In murder mysteries, it's always the person you least expect it to be," Peaches says.

"I don't read much but I'll take your word for it."

"Like I've mentioned before, I don't read much either. It's such a struggle for me."

"That's another thing we have in common," I reply.

"I wish we could have been friends under different circumstances," she says. "I bet I would have liked going to school with other kids. But my mother wouldn't hear of it." She stares off into space for a moment. "Hey, do you want me to sneak into my parent's bedroom and search for Arsenic?"

"Would you? That would help so much."

"I'll just have to come up with a reason to go home. I know." Her eyes light up. "Tomorrow I'll ask Daddy to pick me up for dinner. I'll tell him I'm going stir crazy and just have to get out of here, which is actually the truth."

"And I'll sneak into Aunt Scarlet's home tomorrow while she's at work."

We hug each other tightly before I depart.

The next morning, my mother is visibly irritated when I ask for the day off. "Jade, you've been missing an abundance of work lately. Someday when I retire, you won't be able to do that. That is if you pick teaching as your life path. But the same rule applies if you choose winemaking. It may be hard to believe but some day your father will want to retire, too."

"It's just that I didn't get a chance to visit Grandfather Navy's grave yesterday. I had to leave because I had a stomachache. I think I'll feel better once I visit him. It's been so long. And my stomach is still queasy today."

"I noticed you didn't eat much dinner last night. You must have been sick because that vegetable soup was delicious. Stay home today but that's it and I mean it."

"I promise, I'll be back to work for good tomorrow."

Her yellow eyes soften like butter left out in the sun. "Since you aren't feeling well, I'll ask Royal if you can take the truck."

"Thank you." I throw my arms around my mother's waist and squeeze her as if it's the last time I'll ever get the chance.

After dropping my father off at the winery, I drive to Aunt Scarlet's house. I make sure to park a half mile down the street. Slate mentioned they keep an extra key in the bird feeder so I plunge my hand into the bird seed and root around until I find it. I quickly unlock the bright red door. A large ball of white fur immediately lunges at me. "I've missed you, too, Pearl," I say, petting her.

I start my search in the master bathroom. I open both medicine cabinets which are stuffed with a plethora of herbs but no Arsenic. There's no poison in the drawers either. Satisfied there's nothing in the bathroom, I rummage through the master bedroom. I feel a twinge of guilt but continue. Not only am I looking for Arsenic, but anything that might give me a clue that Aunt Scarlet is the one terrorizing me. But I don't find a black ball cap, or material to make a doll, or anything incriminating at all. I'm careful to straighten everything I touch. When I'm finished in the master bedroom, I investigate the remaining rooms and find nothing. Its possible Aunt Scarlet poisoned Grandmother Ruby with Arsenic and then got rid of the evidence. But if my grandmother was poisoned, and it wasn't Aunt Scarlet, who was it? And if Aunt Scarlet isn't the one who's terrorizing me, who is it? There were two people in the vineyard and I assumed one of them was my aunt.

I wonder if Peaches will eat dinner at Samsara this evening and if she'll find something. Most likely she'll spend the night so I won't be able to talk to her until tomorrow evening. Unless she calls me from Samsara but that's a risk I don't think she'd take.

I glance at the clock and can't believe it's nearly noon. Ty's stopping by my house for lunch so I've got to go. Pearl whines when I leave which breaks my heart because she was my grandmother's dog. If it weren't for the one dog per family rule, we would have taken Pearl home. I know for a fact my aunt doesn't like dogs but fortunately my uncle and Slate do. "You're in good hands, girl." I pull several treats from my pocket and place them in her food dish. She instantly forgets about me.

Ty and I pull into the driveway simultaneously.

"Hey stranger," Ty says. "I feel like I haven't seen you in forever." He props his sunglasses on top of his head. When he smiles, the corner of his eyes crinkle.

"Gosh, I've missed you." I wrap my arms around his trim waist and lay my head against his broad chest. He rests his chin on the top of my head. When I hear his stomach rumble, I break our embrace. "Let's eat and I'll fill you in on what's happened."

"There's more? I can't imagine what you've been going through."

After I've updated Ty, I say, "Sometimes I wish I had destroyed my grandmother's diary. My life was so simple then."

"But do you really want to live in a place that's so twisted? Obviously my Uncle Hunter and your grandparents didn't. Don't you feel trapped and suffocated by all these rules and regulations?"

I sigh. "Yes. I'm just scared."

He reaches across the table and cups my chin. "Don't be."

"I know, I need to man up like my father says. Well actually, woman up." I tap my fingers on the kitchen table. "One thing I have to do is visit Ivory. It's now or never, right?"

Ty nods. "I wish I could come with you but I have to get back to work. Be careful."

"I'll try not to get electrocuted."

"You're a nut," Ty says before he kisses me.

"Takes one to know one," I say.

He rolls his eyes and smiles. "See you later."

"Bye."

Before he climbs in his truck, he says, "seriously, Jade, be careful."

"I will, I promise."

Before I leave, I tidy up the kitchen and fill a tote with four wine bottles. As I drive to the blind camp, I relish the warmth from the sun on my left arm. Maybe I can convince my father to cut the roof off of his truck, like some of the guys have done. That way my right arm would match my tanned left arm. Or maybe I'll purchase a roofless car on the Outside; I think they're called Jeeps. When I arrive at camp, I notice most people are gardening. Ivory is crouched down between Magnolia and Antique.

"Hi, everyone." I say.

Antique and Magnolia turn and smile. Ivory stands and wipes his hands on his pants. "Are my hands clean enough to shake? I've been digging in the dirt all morning."

I laugh. "They're clean enough."

"Oh yeah," he says. Instead of shaking my hand, Ivory smears dirt on the left side of my face.

"I'll make sure that you don't drink any of the wine I brought," I joke.

"Well in that case, I better behave myself." He pulls out a handkerchief from his pocket and wipes my face.

"You, behave yourself? Fat chance," Magnolia says with a snort. "Help me up. It's wine-thirty," she says.

Ivory offers one hand to Magnolia and the other to Antique.

"For you it's always wine o'clock," Antique says.

"Jade, can you believe I have to deal with these two every day?" She smiles.

"This should help take the edge off, at least that's what my father always says. It's all Chardonnay; I figured that white wine would be more refreshing on a day like today." I loop the wine tote around Magnolia's arm.

"You're a life saver," she says. "Would you kids like to join Antique and I?"

"No, thanks," Ivory and I reply in unison.

"Suit yourselves," Antique says.

I wait until they're out of ear shot before I say, "Do you have time to teach me how to disable the fence?"

"Let me check my watch." He pretends to glance at his bare wrist. "I think I can squeeze in a few hours in my hectic day."

"You're something else," I say.

"That's what all the girls say." He smiles sadly.

I clap my hands together. "So, should I drive to the fence or should we walk?"

Ivory leans on his cane. "I'd like to choose the lazy option."

"Me too, actually."

"I just have to grab a screwdriver and then I'll meet you in the truck," he says.

A minute later, he climbs into the truck. "So when are you planning on leaving?" He asks.

"Sometime before my birthday because the thought of going through another eye surgery freaks me out."

"Is anyone going with you?"

"Ty's coming and maybe Peaches."

"You and Ty should be fine but they'll never let Peaches go; Rust's heart would break and Saffron's pride would shatter."

"Peaches says she has a plan. In fact, she used to sneak out all the time with Bronze."

"You know I'll do my best to help you."

"You're a great friend, Ivory."

"Ditto."

"Alright, we're here." I park the truck and we get out. The fence looms ahead of us like a metallic monster. "It looks really intimidating."

"It's actually not that complicated."

I walk alongside Ivory, every now and then guiding him away from thorny brush.

"Then why don't more people leave Nirvana?" I ask.

"I think most people are scared of the unknown. We're outliers, Jade."

I wrinkle my forehead. "What's an outlier?"

Ivory bites his bottom lip. "Imagine a bell shaped graph; the majority of commune members fall in the middle of the graph, beneath the bell. The rest of us fall outside the norm and are considered outliers. Does that make sense?"

I nod. "I wonder why we're different. Do you think it's a good or a bad thing?"

"Evidently we carry a rebel gene. I'm not sure it's a good or bad thing." A serious expression crosses his face. "For you I hope it's a good thing."

"Me, too," I whisper.

He pauses. "There should be a fence charger nearby; in fact there's one every mile."

I notice a gray box attached to the fence. "There's one over here." We walk a few feet to the left. Ivory leans his left hand on his cane and pulls a screwdriver from his back pocket with his right.

"Like I said, it's not complicated; however, once you disable the fence, you'll only have two minutes before the alarm sounds at the main entrance."

I exhale sharply. "Only two minutes?"

"That's it. You ready to learn?"

My heart slams against my chest. "I'm ready."

Chapter Seventeen

Nervously, I knock on my late grandparent's back door. I wait a moment until I knock again. When Peaches doesn't answer, I start to worry. Is she still at Samsara? Have Rust and Saffron persuaded her to stay there? Or worse, has something bad happened to her? Not knowing what else to do, I turn and step down from the porch.

"Hi, Jade. Sorry I didn't answer right away, I was in the little girl's room. My baby enjoys pressing on my bladder." She fondly rubs her stomach.

With a sigh of relief, I retrace my steps. "I started to panic when you didn't answer. I'm such a basket case these days." I trail Peaches into the kitchen and collapse into a chair.

"With everything that's happened to you, who wouldn't be?" She places a small plate of lemons in the center of the table, next to a bowl of sugar. Then she hands me a glass of iced tea before she sits across from me.

"Thanks. I couldn't wait to talk to you. I found absolutely nothing incriminating at my aunt's house. What about you?"

"I wanted to call you last night from Samsara but I thought it would be too risky. Let me start from the beginning. When my father stopped by yesterday, I explained how much I missed him, which is true, and my mother, which is a lie, and asked if I could come over for dinner. He was thrilled and asked why I didn't just move back home. However, he knows how much stress my mother causes me, which would be detrimental to my baby. I had to sneak into his truck and into the back door of Samsara which is ridiculous. But then again, my mother wants to steal my baby which is the definition of ridiculousness." She takes a deep breath and exhales slowly. "My mother was surprised and probably unhappy to see me. Of course, she plastered a fake smile on her face. I wanted to throw up when I saw the pillow strapped to her stomach. We ate an early dinner because my parents had to attend a function on the Outside. I'm assuming it had to do with an oil company. They're probably trading intraocular information for oil." Her orange colored eyes narrow. "I couldn't believe my luck, I was free to search our living quarters. And Jade, I did find something."

"W—w—what did you find?"

"In my mother's closet, a black ball cap, pants and a shirt were stuffed in the corner which all but proves she was chasing you through the vineyard."

"Was that it?"

Peaches places her hand protectively on her stomach. "I also found various sizes of round pillows. It makes me sick that she thinks that I'm going to hand over my baby to her without anyone finding out. She's in for a shock."

"That's awful, I'm so sorry you had to see that."

"It's okay because this baby isn't going anywhere. Anyway, if your Aunt Scarlet wasn't with my mother, who was?"

I rise from the table and pace the length of the kitchen. "And who made the doll? Is your mother close friends with anyone besides my aunt?"

"Actually for the past few months she has been spending time with an older lady, someone around my grandmother's age. But surely a grandmother wouldn't try to scare you to death like that."

"Anymore, I wouldn't be surprised by anything. What's this woman's name?" I ask.

Peaches chews on her cheek. "I'm lousy with remembering names but I'm pretty sure it's Carmine. And she has red eyes, so that makes sense. Yes, that's her name."

Immediately, I stop pacing. "Is she short and slightly overweight? With plain features?"

"Yes, that sounds right. Do you know her?"

I sink into a chair before I say, "Yes. Carmine was my grandmother's best friend."

An hour later it's getting late so I head home. It's plausible but hard to believe Carmine is Saffron's accomplice. I'll be devastated if it turns out to be her because she's been so kind to me and my family over the years. In fact, I still sleep with the lavender blanket she knitted for my sixth birthday. And even though I've always been a tom boy, I appreciate the homemade dolls she's made for me. The dolls! I smack myself on the forehead. How could I be so dense?

As soon as I step foot into my bedroom, I grab a doll from the shelf. She has black hair and purple eyes which match her dress. Then I march to my work shed and pull the doll with slashes in place of eyes from the closet. When I compare the two, there's no doubt the same person made them.

That Thursday evening, I drive to Tranquility Terrace where Carmine lives. I park my father's work truck a half mile down the road and walk quickly along the gravel road. I assume Carmine will be at Samsara playing cards. I also assume she still keeps an extra key under the doormat. I sigh with relief when I lift the red mat and find a single silver key. Carmine's toy poodle, Creamy, barks her little head off the moment I open the door. Fortunately I'm prepared and pull a few dog biscuits from my pocket. She immediately quiets down and devours the treats. Feeling paranoid, I replace the key under the mat and lock the door.

I figure the best place to start is in her bedroom. I'm not surprised when I discover a black ball cap, pants, and a shirt folded neatly on a closet shelf. My stomach sinks when I hear the sound of the front door opening. My eyes dart around the room when I hear the sound of footsteps trudging down the hall. I slip into the closet and pray she doesn't open it. I feel like a rabbit caught in a metal trap at the mercy of a hunter.

"Hello, Creamy," she says. "No, I'm not back for good, sugar. I just forgot my reading glasses. I can't play bridge without them."

I peer through the slits as she picks up a pair of glasses and a leather book from the nightstand. It resembles Grandmother Ruby's diary but it's brown. After dropping the items in her purse, she pauses in front of the closet. If she opens the door, I'll push past her and run. That's my only option.

"Should I bring a sweater? Sometimes it's cold at Samsara." She taps her fingers against the door. "No, I should be fine." Then she smiles sardonically and marches out of the bedroom.

I don't move until I hear the front door slam. If she didn't know I was there, why did she smile like that? She must have known. She didn't open the door because then the game would be over. She wouldn't be the cat anymore, or I the mouse. She clearly enjoys toying with me. I wish I could say I wasn't freaked out but I was. The logical part of my brain told me to continue my search. There could very well be Arsenic poisoning somewhere in this house. But the emotional side of my brain won out. As soon as my feet hit the porch, I was off running.

Once I reach the truck, I lock the doors and rest my head in my hands. Eventually my breath returns to normal but my thoughts dash through my mind like lighting across the sky. And I'm left with an abundance of questions. Did Carmine and Saffron murder True? Did they poison my grandmother? If the answers are yes then they must be severely punished. But what proof do I have? Even if I would have found Arsenic poisoning in Carmine's house, it wouldn't prove anything to anyone but me. What else can I do? As I stare out the window at the tree trunks, I'm reminded of the brown leather book Carmine dropped into her purse. Is it a diary? It's worth finding out. But how do I get a hold of the book without sneaking back into her home? Because I am not doing that again. I feel like I'm going to be sick, so I climb out of the truck. I crouch by the side of the road and dry heave. Eventually, I return to the truck and drive towards Peaches house. Lately, I've been sick to my stomach nearly every day. Is stress causing this? Or is something physically wrong? When I describe my symptoms to Peaches, she frowns.

"Gosh, it sounds like morning sickness except yours lasts all day. You don't think that you're…"

I cut her off before she says the word. "No, of course not." I immediately feel rotten for snapping at her. "I'm sorry. I haven't been myself lately. Do you think its stress?"

"It definitely could be. You should get checked out."

I shrug. "Maybe."

"I'll make you a cup of peppermint tea. That should soothe your stomach." She gets up from the table and picks up a tea kettle. "So did you find anything at Carmines' house?"

I fill her in on what happened. "So now I just have to figure out a way to borrow her diary without breaking into her house."

I'm impressed when Peaches immediately comes up with a solution. "There's a young nurse who owes me a few favors." She opens a drawer and pulls out a pen and note pad. She writes down a four digit phone number. "Here's her number. When you call, ask her to lift the diary from Carmine's purse during the physical. Then she can sneak it to you."

"What's her name?"

Peaches bites her lower lip and rolls her eyes upward. "What is her name? Her eyes are the color of clay and her name is odd..."

"Is it Terracotta?"

Peaches grins. "That's it."

"But they're both nurses. What if Terracotta feels loyalty for Carmine and refuses to do it? And how can we insure that Terracotta serves as Carmine's nurse?"

"Believe me, Terracotta will do it. And nurses have ways of picking and choosing their patients." Peaches says with confidence.

I bite my lower lip. "Are you sure this is a good idea?"

Peaches places her hands lightly on my shoulders. "Trust me on this."

I gaze into her orange colored eyes. They remind me of warm pumpkin pie "Okay."

The next morning, from a safe distance, I watch Carmine enter Room 3. After the door closes, I slowly move closer. Like clockwork, a few minutes later, Terracotta says to me, "Miss, you forgot your sweater." She hands me a folded green sweater.

"Thank you," I say. I scurry down the hall where Ty is waiting. After the exchange, he tucks the diary beneath his belt.

He runs his hands through his hair. "Do you really think she'll call you out and blame you for stealing it?"

"I really do. But I don't think she'd do it in front of any witnesses, so that's something." I shrug. "And I'm not as nervous as I thought I'd be."

"Babe, let's go." He loops his arm through mine as we descend the long stair case to the Center meeting. In the Central Passageway, he squeezes my shoulders and whispers, "You're stronger than you think." Reluctantly, we break apart to sit with our respective families. My eyes are riveted on the oak wall clock. At five minutes till twelve, Carmine squeezes next to me on the bench.

"Good afternoon, Jonquil, Royal, Jade," she says. After my parents say hello, Carmine hisses in my ear. "I need to speak to you in the hallway right now, missy."

"I think I'll excuse myself to use the restroom too," I reply, loud enough for my parents to hear.

"Make it quick," my father says, pointing to the clock.

In the hall, she points to the bench. "Sit," she says this as if commanding her dog. But I stand my ground. I will not allow this woman to have the upper hand. Her dried blood colored eyes flash. "Give me your purse." She places her palm inches from my face.

"Why?" I'm amazed when I don't stutter.

"Don't play with me. I know you were in my house the other day snooping around for who knows what. Purse."

I hold my purse protectively against my chest. "I don't have anything that belongs to you."

"Yes, you do." She enunciates each word before she snatches the purse from me, scratching my cheek with her long nails.

"Ouch." I place my palm against my cheek. Before I have a chance to stop her, she dumps the contents of my purse on the ground. Lip gloss, a hair brush and feminine products decorate the floor. When she stands, her face is flushed and she's breathing heavy. "Let me see your sweater." I don't mind handing her the bulky green sweater because it's not even mine. She pulls the pockets out but finds nothing but lint. "Where is my diary?" She sneers.

Cobalt, our funeral director, shuffles by us on his way to the restroom. Carmine smiles broadly. He barely glances at us as he pushes open the door.

"I don't have your diary." I say. On the outside I may look poised but on the inside I'm shaking like a leaf on an incredibly breezy day.

"You don't want to mess with me, missy." She looks like she just sucked a lemon, her face is so twisted. "I admit, yes, I left the doll on your doorstep and chased you through the vineyard. It served as a warning but it clearly didn't work. You continue to stick your nose in places you have no business being in. I'll just have to up the ante, won't I? You better sleep with one eye open, Jade." She raises her hand as if she's going to slap me but reconsiders when Cobalt exits the restroom. The final warning bell dings. Carmine turns on her heel and follows Cobalt into the Center. I crouch in order to pick up the contents of my purse before joining the others. Fortunately, Carmine has found a new seat. Regardless I can't concentrate on anything Rust and Saffron are saying because I'm obsessed with the question "what next?"

Several hours later, I'm lying on the floor of my work shed with my eyes wide open when Ty arrives.

"Hey, are you okay?" He lifts my head gently in order to slide a throw pillow underneath. He lies on his side and pulls my back against his chest. I melt like vanilla ice cream into his strong arms. "So what happened back there?"

"In a nut shell, Carmine searched my purse and sweater pockets, scratched my cheek, and threatened me. Ty, it was awful. She also admitted making the horrific doll and chasing me through the vineyard."

"Did she mention why? She was so close to your grandmother, they were practically sisters. I can't imagine why she'd want to hurt you. She must have snapped."

"Carmine claimed she was warning me to keep my nose out of other people's business. She also threatened to up the ante if I didn't listen. She's such a witch."

"I think calling her a witch is putting it mildly but let's see what kind of spells she has written down in here." He holds up the brown leather book. "I'll read it out loud if you'd like." Ty knows how much I struggle with reading.

"Yes, please."

I halfheartedly wiggle out of his embrace. He sits up and places a pillow on his lap so that I can rest my head against it. Ty holds the book in his right hand and strokes my hair with his left. "Fortunately there aren't all that many entries or else we'd be here all night. Not that I mind spending that much time with you." He grins and I reach up and lightly pinch his cheek. "The negative thing is there aren't any dates. Plus her name isn't on it. If there is anything incriminating, how could we prove to Outside authorities that it's hers? But let's cross that bridge when we come to it. Okay, here goes.

That woman gets everything and she always has. I hate her for it. Foolishly, I thought by being close to her, her beauty and charm would rub off on me. Since that's not going to happen, perhaps I can rub some of my ugliness and venom onto her. Perhaps I can destroy her.

The entire diary is filled with similar entries. Carmine doesn't mention my Grandmother by name but it's so obvious.

"I can't believe how deep her hatred was for my Grandmother. I thought they were best friends." I shudder. "How can someone be that deceptive?"

"She must be mentally ill."

"She must. How am I going to give her diary back now?"

"I'd hold onto it. You never know, you may be able to use it as evidence on the Outside."

"But what if she breaks into my work shed and steals the diary back? What if she hurts someone else in the process? Maybe you can take the doll and diary and keep it at your house for the time being but I may decide to give the diary back."

"That's a good idea. Do you think if I broke into her house I'd be able to find anything else?" He asks.

"No, I don't want you to do that. It's too dangerous. We'll just have to think of something. Let's go see Peaches. We have to plan a specific day to get out of here."

Chapter Eighteen

That night, insomnia takes hold and there's no amount of warm milk, chamomile tea or lullabies to break its clutches. I can't sleep because we've chosen a date to flee Nirvana; May 12, which is three weeks from now. Twenty-one more days until I'm free from choosing a life path, undergoing an eye color surgery, obeying ridiculous rules…On one hand I'm petrified, on the other, thrilled. That is, if they don't catch us.

In the meantime, I'm bracing myself for Carmines visit. She must know I have her diary and she knew I was in her closet that day. Since it isn't much in the way of evidence, I'm giving it back. Hopefully she'll take it as a sign of resignation. Peaches says in mystery novels, the bad guy always spills their guts at the end. Hopefully, Carmine will do the same because I'm going to tape record our conversation. Peaches says that's a common device in mysteries, too.

The next morning, I look awful. There are dark circles under my eyes and my skin is pale. The scattered, hazy sky matches my indecisive mind.

After tucking Carmine's diary and the tape recorder into my purse, I join my father and Licorice in the truck. Even though I'm close with my mother, I enjoy the tranquil mornings with my father. On the other hand, by afternoon I'll miss my mother's endless chatter.

At the winery, Licorice spreads out on the couch and instantly falls asleep. I take a seat at the counter, rest my chin in my hands and wait for Carmine's inevitable arrival. I gaze at the vines with their tiny green grapes which remind me of renewal and hope. I could use some of both right now.

It doesn't take long before Carmine's beat up truck pulls along side my father's. I pull the tape recorder from my purse, set it under the counter, and push the "record" button. Carmine waddles up to the counter with a gleam in her dried blood red eyes. She hoists herself onto a stool.

"I'd like a glass of Chardonnay and my diary, please." She enunciates the word please.

Inwardly, I'm smiling because this is exactly what I wanted her to say. Because once she starts drinking, she'll start talking. Alcohol is a liquid truth serum. I give her a heavy pour of Chardonnay and slide the glass in front of her. While she takes a healthy sip, I find her diary and place it on the counter.

"Good girl. Thought I'd have to wrestle you for it. And believe me, I'd win." She flexes her bulbous bicep and grins. "Now what made you snoop in my house, anyway?"

I look her straight in the eye and say, "I had a hunch you chased me through the vineyard and left me a gift but I had to find out for myself." I'm so proud of myself for not stuttering.

"If you'd mind your own business, girl, I wouldn't have to scare you." She takes a gulp of wine. "You need to follow the rules which include not sneaking into other people's homes. You could get in trouble for that."

"You could get in trouble for what you did, too."

"Exactly, so we're even. Pour me another glass, this is tasty."

I dispense another heavy pour and wonder why my glamorous grandmother was ever friends with someone the polar opposite.

"With these pours, you'll make an excellent vintner. Have you decided on this life path?"

The last thing I want to do is make small talk with this crazy woman but I have to in order to keep her talking.

"I'm still not sure. Both have their positives and negatives."

"Too bad nursing wasn't on the table. Ruby and I really enjoyed it." The sound of my grandmother's name causes chills to run up and down my spine. "You know, we were best friends through grade school. Back then it didn't matter as much that I was chubby and homely while Ruby was svelte and gorgeous. But by the Academy, it was crystal clear who all the boys were after." She pauses to swig more wine. She drinks wine like water which could work to my advantage. "You know, I had a crush on Navy. We even fooled around a few times." The thought of my grandfather and Carmine intimate makes me sick. "But that was before Ruby showed interest in him. After that, Navy wanted nothing to do with me. The exact same thing happened with True and I loved that man. After my husband and True's wife passed, we clung to each other like ivy on a tree. That is until your grandfather died. Afterwards, True dumped me and crawled after Ruby like a dog with its tail between its legs. He broke my heart." She hangs her head for a moment. I can't help but think of the word *motive*.

"But if you were so jealous of my grandmother, why remain friends?"

"There were some positives. For one, since everyone loved Ruby, I was treated quite well by association. Plus, she was such a hard worker, always picking up my slack."

"But you were as close as sisters. At least it seemed that way."

"I'm a good actress, Jade, that's all." She throws her hands up.

"I thought I heard a familiar voice. Carmine, how are you?" My father strides to the counter and kisses her on each cheek. Observing him that close to the enemy makes me sick. I reach under the counter and click the *stop* button on the recorder before sliding it into my jean pocket.

"Excuse me, I have to use the restroom," I say. In the restroom, I collapse on the little bench, hug my knees to my chest and rest my head. She didn't admit to anything but my sixth sense tells me she did it; she poisoned my Grandmother Ruby.

That evening, I relay the information to Ty via the phone. "I always wondered about their friendship. Very yin and yang," he says.

"What does yin and yang mean?' I scrunch my nose.

"I actually read about this concept in one of your books." I can picture him grinning on the other line. "Yin and yang mean shadow and light, polar opposites."

"That describes them perfectly. Suffice it to say, my grandmother is light but I'd label Carmine darkness," I reply bitterly.

"One can't exist without the other, Jade," Ty replies gently.

When I don't respond, he says, "I'm sorry I brought it up, it was stupid of me."

"No, it's an interesting concept; I'm just really emotional right now. What kind of person pretends to be your best friend for fifty years and then intentionally poisons you? She's evil!"

"That's beyond evil. You know I would never hurt you, right? I love you."

"I know that. And I would never hurt you because I love you, with my whole heart."

After we reluctantly hang up, I borrow the truck to visit Peaches.

"I'm so glad to see you, Jade! It's so lonely here. Maybe if we're quiet we can sit outside since it's such a nice evening." She leans against the screen door and gazes wistfully toward the sky where stars are sprinkled like a trail of hope.

I smack a mosquito against my forearm. "It's a beautiful night except for these blood suckers."

"No worries. I have insect repellent." We take turns spraying each other before settling on the back porch steps.

"Do you want to hear the tape?" I place the recorder between us.

She rests against the railing and places her hand protectively on her stomach. "Yes."

I push *play* and listen to Carmine's jealousy seep through the tiny speakers like venom.

After our conversation ends, Peaches shudders. "Wow, that's unreal...and horrible."

"As awful as it is, it's not enough to prove anything. She didn't confess." I sigh.

"But it proves a motive—Jade, did you hear something?" Her eyes dart to the yard overgrown with weeds and ancient oak trees.

I strain my ears and hear a rustling. "Maybe it's a rabbit or a deer. The woods are filled with both."

"I don't think so," her voice trembles. "It sounds more like a person or a black bear. We should head inside."

I shove the recorder in my jeans pocket as we stand. I pray it isn't Saffron; next to Carmine, she's the last person I want to see. Aunt Scarlet is a close third.

Instead, a robust male voice says, "Hi girls." I know immediately it's Rust.

"Daddy?" Peaches mouth forms the shape of an "O."

"May I come in?" His speech sounds slurred.

"Of course." She holds the screen door open.

I stand frozen on the porch. Clearly, we're in trouble. No one is supposed to know where Peaches is and my parents think I'm at Ty's house. They're going to be so upset when they discover what I've been up to. In spite of this, I make a last ditch effort to leave by saying, "I should be going."

"No, please stay," Rust says. He grips the porch rail for support.

We settle at the kitchen table. The glow from the candle reflects Rust's handsome, rugged features. His dark hair is tousled and he's in need of a shave. I've never seen him looking so...unpolished. It's unnerving.

"I didn't know y'all knew each other." He gestures to Peaches and I. "But I figured it was inevitable." Peaches and I share a confused look.

"Daddy, have you been drinking?"

"Yeah." He scratches his chin. "Is it that evident? I rarely drink but when I do, I usually embarrass myself." He hangs his head. "I shouldn't have stepped in." He rises from the table.

"I don't want you to leave, I'm just worried. How much have you had to drink?"

"Quite a bit. I shouldn't have driven here."

"I'll get you some water," she says. But before she stands, Rust places his hand over hers.

"No, I'm fine. Please sit down." He looks from Peaches to me. His eyes look bloodshot. "It's important I speak to both of you before you embark on your uh, journey."

"How did you know?" Peaches whispers.

"I know you well, sweetheart." His lips turn up slightly in a heartbreaking smile.

"Are you going to try and stop us?" she asks.

"No, I'm not." He shakes his head resolutely. "What your mother is doing aint right. It's one hundred percent wrong. That's your baby, not hers. I've explained this to her, but she won't hear of it. In fact, any time I bring it up, she flies of the handle." A brief silence follows.

My stomach is in knots and the suspense is making it worse so I ask, "What did you need to speak to us about?"

"It's something I've wanted to disclose for years but I've procrastinated for a number of reasons. Regardless, my consciousness won't allow me to remain silent. It's time to tell the truth." How much has he had to drink? It must have been a lot.

Peaches leans across the table to hold my hand. We both know whatever he's about to reveal will change our lives forever.

He turns to me and I can't help but gaze into his blazing rust colored eyes. "Jade, your mother and I attended school together, so our friendship goes way back. So you've gotta believe I never meant to hurt her, okay?"

"Okay."

"So I fell in love with her the moment we met. Well, as much as a five-year-old is capable of romantic love." He grins at the memory. "It was clear that Royal was head over heels for Jonquil, too. There was always a tension in the air whenever the three of us were together. But I just knew she felt the same way about me and that her feelings for Royal were strictly uh, what's the word, platonic. The summer we turned fourteen, the three of us spent nearly every day together. It wasn't that Royal and I were fond of each other, not at all. Deep down we were probably both afraid to leave her alone with the other. Every morning I hoped that would be the day Royal would suffer from food poisoning, chicken pox, the flu…basically anything that would put him out of commission for awhile. It sounds awful now but back then I yearned to spend time with Jonquil minus Royal." He hiccups. "I think I'd like a glass of water. I'll bring you glasses, too." He stumbles but catches himself and leans against the counter.

"This explains the odd tension between your father and mine." I whisper to Peaches. "I figured something like this happened."

"But there must be more to the story, don't you think?" She crinkles her forehead.

"Unfortunately, yes." I squeeze her hand.

"Here you are." He hands us each a glass of water. "Now where did I leave off?"

"You wished my father ill." There's an unintentional edge to my voice.

"Unfortunately...so Royal comes down with the summer flu. Jonquil and I spend the day swimming at Lady Lake. She was wearing an orange bikini from the Outside and it matched her eyes perfectly. She was so pretty, still is pretty, I mean. You know what I mean." He throws his hands up. "We stayed at the lake until twilight and that's when I kissed her. After that, it was clear we were a couple. Royal was devastated but he accepted Jonquil's choice. When we were sixteen, I proposed to Jonquil at the lake. We planned to marry immediately after our eye color procedures. But then I went and screwed it all up. I felt pressure to take over as commune leader, to marry and have children and yet I was only sixteen years old. I contemplated fleeing Nirvana but Jonquil wouldn't hear of it. I asked my father if he'd continue as commune leader for a few more years but he was convinced I needed to start as soon as possible. I even gently asked Jonquil if we could postpone the wedding but she refused. For a while I was in a really bad place." Rust pauses to take a long drink of water.

"One evening I was walking aimlessly along the lake, feeling sorry for myself, when I found Saffron swaying on a hammock. I had been drinking, like I've been tonight. I'm not using drinking as an excuse though. I'll never forgive myself for what went on that night. The next morning I broke down and told Jonquil what happened. She never forgave me. Instead, she moved on to Royal and I settled for Saffron. Some time after Saffron and I married, we tried to have a baby to no avail. She grew bitter and pushed me away. I was taking a walk one day in the Secret Grove and found Jonquil crying. She told me Royal didn't pay any attention to her." He looks off into space as if seeing a ghost. "We were intimate that night but swore it would never happen again and it hasn't and it won't. Then Jonquil discovered she was pregnant with my child." He hangs his head.

Peaches squeezes my hand so hard it hurts.

"We agreed the best thing would be for her to raise the child and we wouldn't tell Saffron or Royal about our indiscretion. But on her next check up, Jonquil found out we were having twins. She stopped by my office to tell me right away. What we didn't know was that Saffron was hiding behind the drapes. After Jonquil's news, Saffron sprang from her hiding place like a mad woman. I had to literally hold her down until Jonquil left. A few days later, I invited Royal and Jonquil to Samsara to meet with Saffron and I. The four of us agreed to split the twins up. Jonquil was a mess but Saffron and Royal wore her down until she crumbled."

"W-w-why would my father do that to her?" I feel a sick pang in my gut.

"I hate to say this but I think he was trying to punish her. You have to keep in mind that Royal hated me and he knew Jonquil loved me."

"Well, he succeeded in hurting her. I always thought she was happy but...how did you decide who kept who?" I whisper.

"Jonquil kept the first baby and I kept the second. You were born two minutes before Peaches."

"Oh my gosh, we're sisters." Peaches eyes are as round as pumpkins. She opens her arms and we embrace.

Instead of tears, anger wells inside of me. I feel a surge of adrenaline deep in my stomach, almost as if I could throw up electricity. My life has been a lie. Who I thought was my father isn't. I thought I was an only child but I'm not. It's unreal.

When Peaches and I break apart, I turn to Rust. "It's strange that neither Saffron nor my father could have children of their own."

Rust rubs his forehead. "That's not necessarily true, Jade."

"What exactly do you mean?" I ask.

"I know you're familiar with our commune law which states a woman may only give birth to two children. After you and Peaches were born, Jonquil was required to have her tubes tied."

"Even though one of her babies was taken from her? How could you do that to her? How could you do that to us?" Peaches looks panic stricken.

"It was a mistake and I'm so sorry. If I could turn back time, honey, I would in a heartbeat."

Peaches bolts from the table, covering her mouth with her hand. I turn to Rust and say, "I think it's time for you to go." Then I follow my sister to the bathroom.

If I had any reservations about leaving Nirvana, I don't now.

When I return home that evening, I can't bear to look at my mother and who I thought was my father. No wonder Royal and I have never been close. I'm someone else's child and serve as a constant reminder of my mother's affair. When my mother tries to talk to me, I feign exhaustion and crawl into bed.

The next morning, I phone Ty and ask him to meet me at the lake that afternoon. At work I spend the day counting down the minutes until it ends. Afterwards, In order to clear my head, I walk the few miles to Lady Lake.

I think about my father's story; or who I thought was my father. Now he's a fake-father. His story makes more sense now. Clearly my fake-father is Azul and my mother is Rosado. Rosado's dead baby girl must be Peaches, because even though Peaches didn't die; she was taken, which broke our mother's heart. Obviously Morado, Rosado's lost love, is Rust. However, my mother has never been committed to the mental ward, at least I don't think so. Perhaps I should read more of my fake-father's stories.

I feel betrayed. I feel angry. I feel like screaming. The only thing that helps is chucking rocks into the lake and watching the ripple effect. I'm so absorbed in this activity I don't notice Ty until he wraps his arms around me and leads me to a grassy area. Then he pulls me between his legs and rests his chin on my shoulder. He doesn't say anything, just kisses my neck softly until I allow myself to relax. After repeating Rust's confession, Ty says, "That's unbelievable. I'm speechless."

"How do you think I feel? Ty, I have to leave Nirvana as soon as possible. There's no way I can live a lie for three more weeks."

"We'll have to ask Peaches if she's ready. She's the one who has to steal Rust's truck and his money."

"The way I see it, it's not stealing. After all, Peaches and I are the descendants of the original commune leaders, Hazel and Glacier." I shake my head. "Imagine if I had been born second…

thank goodness I wasn't. Poor Peaches. Let's go to her now so we can revise our plan."

"Okay."

But as soon as I stand up, I feel a wave of nausea. I immediately throw up into a patch of weeds. Ty holds my hair back and after I'm through, he hands me a bottle of water so that I can rinse out my mouth.

"Jade, you have to see a nurse about this. Promise you will."

I cross my fingers behind my back and say, "I promise. I just don't know why I've been so sick…Oh my gosh, Ty, do you think I'm being poisoned?!"

"What?" A look of horror crosses his face.

"My grandmother was poisoned, True was murdered; why wouldn't they poison me?" I stare at my fingernails. "Do you think this is a symptom?"

"Your hands? But they look fine."

"Look at my nails. I have white marks on each of them." My hands are shaking.

Ty grabs hold of my hands. "As soon as we leave Nirvana, we'll go to a hospital on the Outside, okay?"

I nod. "Okay."

On our way to Peaches' house, I wonder who is poisoning me and how? It would be easy to do so at the Center since we're given plated meals. But otherwise, I eat all of my food at home and I refuse to believe my mother or Royal would do such a thing. But who knows how jaded Royal is? And then the answer hits me like a blow to the stomach.

"It's Carmine." I say flatly.

"What's Carmine?" Ty asks.

"Ty, it's the funky tea that Carmine made. It must be."

"You think she laced the tea?"

"I know she did."

Ty wraps his arm around me. "Don't worry Jade, she'll be punished for what she's done. Don't get rid of the tea, keep it as evidence."

"Okay." I clutch my stomach. How did my life end up like this? A few months ago everything was fine. It's unreal.

"Should I pull over?" Ty asks.

"No, I'm okay."

Fifteen minutes later, we're standing on the back porch knocking, but no one is answering.

Ty jimmies the lock on the window, pushes it open, and hoists me up. I check every room, even every closet, but she's not there. And none of her belongings are either. When I stick my head out the window, Ty looks at me expectantly.

"She's gone. I think they forced her to move back to Samsara. Saffron isn't stupid, she must have found out what was going on."

"Now what?"

"Now we figure out a way to help her escape from Samsara."

Chapter Nineteen

Friday at the Center meeting, my hands are shaking incorrigibly so I slip them beneath my thighs. Even though I'm beginning to doubt the plan Ty and I devised; I must carry on for the sake of everyone I love. I glance at my mother and fake-father and take a mental snap shot for it very well be the last time I see them. As my beautiful mother stares at Rust, her yellow colored eyes shine as bright as the sun. Clearly, part of her heart remains with him. Royal glares at Rust. His eyes remind me of ice freezing Lady Lake. Rust flourishes on stage, commanding attention with his rapturous red eyes. Next, my eyes rove until I spot Slate. He's leaning his head on Naples' shoulder and his steel gray eyes are fighting the urge to sleep. I'm certain Naples will care for Slate until I return for him. If I thought I could care for him, I'd take him but with Peaches and her baby on the way, it's just too much.

Last, I lock eyes with Ty who winks at me and mouths, "I love you." I wink and mouth "ditto." I watch as he discreetly departs the meeting. I count to the number sixty twice before I excuse myself, too. I shove my shaking hands into the pockets of my jean jacket and take a deep breath. Then I slink along the hall toward the family living quarters. A guard stands with his legs spread and his arms on his hips in front of the double wooden doors.

On cue, Ty clutches his stomach and says, "I'm going to vomit."

The guard disregards his post to come to Ty's aid. "I'll help you to the restroom, son."

"What I really need is fresh air." Ty groans.

The guard looks up and down the hallway. He doesn't see me because I'm hiding behind a suede curtain.

"Let's go." The guard follows Ty onto the back porch.

I shove the double doors open, and tip toe down the family hall. In passing, Peaches mentioned her bedroom was the last door on the left. I turn the door knob which is not surprisingly locked. I pull a paper clip and tension wrench from my back pocket. I straighten the paper clip and bend it slightly at the top. Next, I insert the tension wrench into the lower part of the keyhole and insert the paper clip into the top section. I move the paper clip until all five pins unlock. I turn the wrench and the door pops open. Ivory taught me how to pick a lock just in case.

"I just knew you'd find me!" Peaches flings her arms around me, practically knocking me over.

"I couldn't leave my sister behind." Saying the word *sister* sounds so foreign. If only our parents had done the right thing, it wouldn't. When she releases me, I push the door closed and lock it.

"How are we going to get out of here? Is the window locked?" I pace through Peaches frilly pink bedroom.

"The window is locked from the outside but I have a plan." She rifles through her closet and pulls out an oversized sweatshirt and two baseball caps. "I figure this sweatshirt will help disguise my belly." She smells the sleeve before she says, "This was Bronze's sweatshirt." The word *was* stands out. Perhaps she's accepted the cold possibility that Bronze may be dead. Next, she tosses a ball cap to me. After twisting our hair into buns and pulling the ball caps low on our foreheads, we're passable as boys.

"So what's the plan on your end?" She asks.

I check my watch. "Right about now Ty should be setting fire to the old kitchen yard."

She wrings her hands. "Fire? But there will be chaos...but that's what we want, don't we?"

"Absolutely. Once we leave your room, we'll have to break into your father's office."

"No need to break in." She grins, pulling a key ring from her pocket. "My, or should I say our father gave it to me as a peace offering."

"Excellent, now…" I'm interrupted by the frantic sounds of people screaming. "Fire!" It must be spreading faster than Ty and I factored. Within seconds, a male voice is pounding on the door, and yelling "I'll get you out, Miss Peaches! I'll find an axe!" We listen as his footsteps race down the hall.

"We've got to go, now. I thought we'd have time for you to pack. I'm sorry," I say.

Peaches opens the drawer of the night table and pulls out a picture of Bronze. "This is all I need." She folds it and shoves it in her pants pocket.

We lock her bedroom door before darting into Rust's office. The safe is situated behind the ornately carved oak desk. Peaches punches in the eight digit code and the door springs open. She pulls out a manila envelope with *Jade and Peaches* scrawled on it. She pulls out a stack of money, a map, and another key. She shoves the envelope in her sweatshirt pocket.

She holds the key up and smiles triumphantly. "This is the key to Daddy's old truck!"

"Really? But Ty borrowed a truck for us. It doesn't matter - let's get out of here."

We creep into the family hallway. The double wooden doors block our view from the Central Passageway but we can hear people yelling and cussing at one another.

"Follow me." She clasps my hand and drags me into what appears to be a linen closet. She opens a trap door and we slowly descend the narrow staircase which leads to a canning cellar. Small windows smeared with dirt allow select rays of sunlight to shine through. She grabs two flashlights from the counter and hands me one. Then using one of the keys Rust gave her, she opens a wooden door. The glow from the flashlight reveals a tunnel of sorts.

"What is this?" I ask.

"It's a slave tunnel, can you believe it? I've lived here my whole life and didn't know about it till Daddy told me."

"Why is he helping us?"

"He said he couldn't save Lio but he could save us."

"But this isn't the plan! Ty's waiting for us in a truck he borrowed. He paid off several Outsiders who promise to let us go. They were friends of Bronze," I say softly.

"But Daddy's truck is parked outside Nirvana, where the tunnel ends. Won't that be safer?"

"I don't know." I chew on my lip.

"Jade, we don't have time to talk about this."

"You're right. I need to get Ty."

I follow Peaches across the cellar and up a ladder which is wide enough for the two of us. She tentatively opens the cellar door. We immediately start to cough and my eyes water from the smoke billowing from the dining hall. People continue to stream from Samsara and race for their vehicles. Others mill around watching the fire as if it were a movie.

"Wait here," I say. I dash to a black truck covered in mud and slide in. I grab my backpack from the seat and take deep breaths. Where's Ty? Why has the fire spread so quickly? This wasn't the plan. I root through the glove compartment and find a napkin and a pencil. I scribble the words "Change of plans, meet at fence" and lay it on the seat. I pray that he's okay. Then I leap from the truck and race back to the cellar. I slip inside and Peaches quickly closes the door.

"Where's Ty?" She asks.

"I don't know. I left him a note. Peaches, we've got to go!"

We turn our flashlights on and enter the tunnel. Without our flashlights, it would be pitch black. I run my hand along the wall as we walk. It feels cool and rough. "Is this red clay?"

Peaches shines her flashlight on the wall. "Looks like it."

"How far is this tunnel?"

"Daddy says it's a mile to the Outside."

"Do you think you can run?"

"Yes." She places her hand protectively on her stomach before we take off. We don't talk as we run. Every so often I glance at Peaches to make sure that she's okay. She's breathing heavy but she's keeping up with me. After approximately ten minutes, we slow down when we come to a narrow ladder.

"Oh my gosh," I say.

"Are you ready?" Peaches asks.

"Yes."

She climbs the ladder first. She unlocks the trap door and sunlight streams in. I follow my sister out of the tunnel, out of Nirvana.

"Look, Jade."

I turn to see the massive electrical fence. But this time we're on the Outside.

And as promised, a rusty green truck is parked nearby.

"Let's wait for Ty inside the truck," Peaches says.

"Good idea."

Inside the truck, Peaches starts the engine. She sighs in what must be relief. "I had to make sure it would start," she says before she turns it off.

"Do you have any regrets?" I ask.

"None," she says quickly. "Do you?"

I think about my parents who have done nothing but lie to me and the commune with its rules, regulations, and deceit. I also think of the impending eye color procedure and forced life paths. "No," I reply. But deep down, I'll miss parts of Nirvana, my home for nearly seventeen years. And the memories of my parents will remain locked in my heart forever.

"What's in your book bag?" She asks.

I tick the items off on my fingers, "Grandmother Ruby's diary, the recording of my conversation with Carmine, the homemade horror doll and poison tea from Carmine, and my camera." I don't mention the photo book filled with pictures of my parents, Licorice, Slate, and Ty. When I realize I may never see Licorice again, tears spill down my face.

"It's going to be okay," my sister says, rubbing my back. "Let's talk about happy things like all of the cake and ice cream we're going to eat on the Outside." She sounds so much like our mother I can't help but smile. Growing up with Peaches would have been so much fun.

I try my best to relax but after twenty minutes, I start to panic. My heart leaps when I see Ty's truck in the distance. I jump out and wait outside the fence which is littered in signs like "Keep Out," "Private Property," and "Danger."

"What took you so long?" I ask as he approaches. Before he has a chance to respond, I ramble, "I'll have to explain to you how to deactivate the fence but if I can do it, then you definitely can; and a screwdriver will fit through the opening." I pull a screwdriver from my back pocket and prepare to slide it through a small opening in the fence. However, something in his expression makes me stop.

"Ty, what's wrong?"

"In the midst of everything, my father had a heart attack. I can't help but blame myself. Jade, I can't leave my family right now. I can't come with you." Tears fill his twilight eyes.

"I can't leave without you!" I cry.

"You have to for your sister and her baby. I'll join you as soon as I can."

"Do you promise?"

"I promise." He steps as close to the fence as he can without touching it. "I love you, Jade."

"I love you. You'll always be here." I place my hand against the middle of my chest.

"It kills me that I can't kiss you goodbye." His voice breaks.

"You will, soon."

He nods. "You better get going. Your parents, Rust, and Saffron are searching for you as we speak. Don't forget to tell my Uncle Hunter that I said hello and I can't wait to meet him. I'll find you, Jade. I promise." And then he turns around, climbs into his truck, and is gone. Somehow, I manage to make it to the truck. I crawl into the passenger side and bawl like I've never cried before.

"I heard what Ty said." She motions to the open window. "I'm so sorry, Jade. Are you sure you want to come?"

"Of course. You're my sister." I reach over and grab her hand. "And Ty will join us as soon as he can."

"It's going to be okay, Jade." She hands me the manila envelope. "Can you pull out the map, please? We'll need it soon. Main, Virginia isn't that far away." She starts the engine, pulls off her ball cap and lets her hair down. As we drive along the gravel road, she yells, "We're free!" I copy her and we yell "We're free" over and over again.

After a few minutes of driving, we pull into a parking lot with a small building.

"What's this?" I ask.

"It's a gas station but there's a store that sells snacks and water. There's a restroom, too. We don't need gas but when we do, I'll be able to pump it. Bronze taught me how to do that," she says proudly. "In fact we've been to this station a few times."

I follow her inside and we use the restroom. Then we choose cheese sandwiches wrapped in plastic and bottled waters. Peaches is still wearing sunglasses but the clerk comments on how unusual my eye color is. I'm not sure what to say, so Peaches chimes in and says they're colored contacts. After she pays, we sit outside on the little picnic bench.

"Jade, our birthday is on July 7, right?"

"Right."

"And all this time I thought mine was two days after that. How messed up is that? By the way, our birthday is the combination to our father's safe."

"Easy to remember."

"Now it is." She stands to leave. "You ready to go?"

"Absolutely."

Chapter Twenty

As we walk to the truck, I notice two men standing next to a white car with the word "Police" on it. They're wearing navy blue hats and shirts with gold badges. I assume they're Outside officials.

"Good afternoon, ladies," the older man says. The younger man tips his hat and smiles.

"Hello," we say in unison.

I wait for them to make a lewd comment or harass us in some way but they don't. They simply continue their conversation.

Back in the truck, my heart beats and my mind races because they remind me of the Nirvana guards. Why didn't the guards at least check to see if we were in the tunnel? Also, we waited nearly half an hour for Ty and no officials came. That doesn't make sense. Something isn't right.

"Hey Peaches."

She's tapping her fingers on the steering wheel to the beat of "Mother Freedom" by Bread.

"Peaches," I say louder.

"Hmm?"

"Something doesn't feel right."

She adjusts her sunglasses. "What do you mean?"

"It shouldn't have been that easy to leave." I bite my lower lip.

"I know. I'm surprised my, I mean our, father helped us."

"But once Saffron realized you were missing, why didn't she order the guards to search the tunnel?"

"She probably didn't think I knew about the tunnel. And up until last night, I didn't. She was probably more concerned with the fire burning down her precious mansion." Her voice drips with disdain.

"You're probably right." I lie.

She places her hand on her stomach. "Ugh. I think the cheese sandwich made me sick. Are you feeling okay?"

"I feel fine."

"Bronze warned me about eating at gas stations." She laughs.

I glance out the window. The paved road is the only indication we're not in Nirvana because all we've passed so far are homes and trees. However, the doors aren't painted bright colors. And there are signs indicating the speed limit which we don't have in Nirvana. I pinch myself to prove I'm not dreaming. Have we really escaped the commune unharmed? Just as my muscles relax, Peaches swerves the car off the side of the road, narrowly missing a large oak tree. I'm jostled hard against the door.

"Peaches, why did you..." I say before I notice she's bent over, clutching her stomach, with her head on the steering wheel. I scoot across the seat and lay a hand on her back. "Are you okay?"

She moans. "I think my baby's coming!"

"But you aren't due for a few months!"

"I know but I'm having contractions!"

I thrust open the passenger door, leap from the truck, and jog to the driver side. Then I tenderly guide her to the passenger seat. "Is there a hospital nearby?"

"I don't know. I've never seen one around here." She groans. "But you can ask someone at one of the restaurants up ahead." Beads of sweat cling to her forehead.

I hand her a bottle of water. "Here, drink some water and then take slow breaths." I pray the truck isn't stuck and nearly cheer when it easily scales the embankment. I wait for a car to pass before easing the truck back on the road. As I drive, my eyes dart from the left hand side of the road to the right, looking for any people to ask for help. Just as I'm about to panic, a building with a giant yellow M appears. I turn left into the parking lot. "I'll be right back, okay?"

Peaches nods weakly.

I jog into the building. A girl in a blue visor and matching shirt is standing behind a counter. Her name tag says, "Amy." When I approach her, she asks, "Would you like to try our new bacon burger loaded with onion ring combo?"

I shake my head. "Can you tell me where the nearest hospital is?"

"Are you hurt? Should I call 911?" She pulls a pink plastic object from her pocket.

I don't know what 911 is but I don't think I want her to call it. "No, my sister is in labor. She's out in the truck." I point out the window.

"Oh my gosh! There's a hospital about seven miles from here. Make a right out of the parking lot, then make a left on Jefferson Avenue, then a right on Lincoln Street. The hospital is at the end of the road. By the way, your eyes are cool."

"Thanks." I hurry from the building and jump into the truck. Within seconds I'm making a right out of the lot. "I have directions. We'll be there in a few minutes." Peaches is curled up in a ball and every so often she groans. "Left on Jefferson, left on Jefferson." I mutter to myself until I spot the street sign. Lincoln Street appears a minute later. When a massive white building emerges at the end of Lincoln Street, relief washes over me like warm water spilling over a bathtub. I swing the truck into an empty spot before running into the hospital. I grab the first nurse I see. "Help, my sister's in labor!"

She pushes a wheelchair to the truck and we transfer Peaches into it. She quickly wheels my sister into the hospital. "I'll bring you paperwork to fill out. Your sister will be in room thirteen."

"Wait." I crouch down to my sister's level. "Everything is going to be okay." I brush the hair out of her eyes.

She smiles dimly. I give her a quick hug before the nurse shoos me away. After a few minutes, the nurse hands me a pen and some papers. "Fill this out to the best of your ability. You've called your parents, right?"

"Right. They're on their way." I lie.

"By the way, you girls have some unusual colored contacts. Where did you order those? My granddaughter would love a pair."

"I-I-I can't remember."

"If you do, let me know. Bring the paperwork to the front desk when you're done, dear."

I sink into an uncomfortable chair and fill out what little I can. At least I know Peaches' address and birthday but I don't know what health insurance means or if she has any medical conditions besides pregnancy. Plus, I'm distracted by the hustle and bustle of the hospital. The man in the chair next to me is grimacing in pain because his arm is clearly broken. It's hanging at an unnatural angle. Across from me, a woman is holding a child who is covered in red spots. "Don't itch, baby, don't itch," she says repeatedly. It's awful. I drop the paperwork off at the front desk and then look for a restroom. I splash cold water on my face and stare at myself in the mirror. "Everything is going to be okay," I whisper. But when I exit, I hear a voice that makes my skin crawl and my knees buckle.

"What room is my daughter in? Thirteen? Thanks so much." Saffron's voice is so sweet it could cause cavities.

I pull my baseball cap lower on my forehead. Then I bend down and pretend to tie my tennis shoes. I tilt my head to see Saffron sashay into room thirteen. Two guards follow behind her. She's no longer wearing the faux baby pillow. My heart sinks. What are we going to do now? I should have known she'd do something like this! But how did she find us? Does she know someone who works at the hospital? That must be it.

Not knowing what else to do, I find a seat with a clear view to room thirteen. I keep my eyes locked on the door until eventually Saffron leaves the room with one of the bodyguards. In the hallway, Saffron runs her fingers through the guard's blonde hair and pulls him in for a long kiss. From his profile, I can tell that his nose is large and crooked. Oh my gosh. It's Peri, the guard who harassed my mother, Slate and I a few weeks ago. I watch as they hold hands and stroll down the hallway as naturally as if they were life partners. He must be one of her minions.

The other guard slides a chair into the hall, plops down, and cracks open a soda. Clearly he's in for the long haul. If only I had sleep inducing herbs like valerian root to dump in his drink, unless he's asleep, there's no way I'm getting past him. Unless I snag one of those lab coats. That's the only thing that seems to differentiate nurses and doctors from patients. I get up and walk through the hall, away from room thirteen. I peek in each room to no avail. But in the last room on the right, I spot a lab coat hanging on the back of an office chair. I snatch the coat and quickly put it on. For good measure, I grab a stethoscope and loop it around my neck. I try to act nonchalant as I head down the hall. I even smile at a passing doctor but he frowns. Maybe he's wondering who I am. But he doesn't ask. Perhaps he's just having a rough day.

As I approach room thirteen, my hands start to shake and my mouth feels dry. I brace myself for a confrontation with the guard but he barely acknowledges me as I pass by him. I gently close the door and breath a small sign of relief.

Peaches looks pitiful lying in the hospital bed. Her eyes are red rimmed and puffy. She remains quiet as I perch on the side of her bed.

"How are you feeling?" I ask.

"Awful. Saffron must have known about our plans. She must have slipped wormwood in my breakfast tea. Why else would I go into labor so early?"

"It could have been from all of the stress," I say softly.

"I don't think so." She shakes her head vehemently. "She let us leave because she knew we'd end up here. She's pure evil. Jade, what are we going to do?"

"Well…" I glance around the room until the window catches my eye. It's large enough for us to crawl through. Plus, we're on the first floor so we wouldn't have to worry about breaking any bones. "Are you up for crawling out the window?"

She glares at me. "The doctor said within the hour my baby will be born. I'm not going anywhere." She crosses her arms. "You might as well leave without me."

I stroke her hair. "I'm not leaving without you or my niece or nephew. I'll be planted in the waiting area until you and your baby are ready."

Peaches shakes her head. "But if you stay out there, Saffron will find you."

"Then I'll wait in the truck. I promise I'm not leaving without you."

Tears stream down her cheeks. "Jade, she's going to steal my baby," she says flatly.

I blot her face with tissues. "No, she won't. We'll find a way. We've gotten this far, haven't we?" I force a smile on my face. "Where did Saffron go, by the way?"

"To get something to eat. She's bound to return soon."

"What did she say to you?"

"She acted like nothing happened. She's crazy."

"There's no doubt about that. You're nothing like her." I rest my head against her shoulder.

"I think I hear her. You better go."

"I'm not leaving without you, I promise. I'll be in the truck, brainstorming ways to get you and the baby out of here." I kiss her on the forehead before I cross the room to the window. I raise the blinds, slide the window open, and slip into the dark night. I can't help but peek through the window. It kills me to leave my sister alone in that room with Saffron milling around. Not knowing what else to do, I jog to the front of the hospital to the truck. Inside, I remove the stethoscope from my neck but I keep the lab coat on for warmth. Then I realize I'm still wearing a baseball cap. No wonder that doctor looked at me strangely. My stomach growls but there's no food in the truck. I don't want to drive somewhere because I'm afraid I'll get lost. Plus, I don't want to leave in case Peaches needs me. What exactly are we going to do? How am I going to stop two grown men and a crazy woman from stealing my sister's baby? "She'll notice this truck," I whisper. "I've got to move it." I start the truck and drive around the parking lot. Where can I hide a rusty old truck? Then I notice a small parking lot with rows of large white vehicles. I swing the truck into the lot and find a space at the end.

For the next hour, I rack my brain for other ideas but nothing materializes. All I've realized is I'm no help to anyone sitting in the truck. Cold, hungry, and frustrated, I leave the truck and head to the window outside my sister's room. At least I'll be able to see what's going on. I peer through the window to find a doctor and several nurses at the foot of Peaches' bed. Saffron stands off to the side, watching. Peaches feet are in stirrups, her skin is beat red, and her face is crumpled like a tissue. Every now and then, her mouth forms an "O." This goes on for what seems like forever but is probably only a few minutes. Finally, the doctor holds up a tiny blue-colored baby. My sister lies back against the pillows, with her arms outstretched. But instead of handing her the baby, the doctor places the baby on a table, places a mask on its face, and breathes into the baby's mouth. Then he presses several times on the baby's chest. Peaches tries to get up from the bed but the nurses restrain her. Eventually, the doctor injects the baby with a needle. Finally, he wraps the baby in a blanket and brings it to Peaches. She clings to her baby and sobs. The experience feels surreal, as if I'm watching a movie. My sister has just lost her baby and it's all Saffron's fault. I race to the hospital entrance, fling open the doors, and sprint towards my sister's room.

"Miss, miss! Can I help you?" A nurse reaches for me but I swat her arm. I rush past her and crash into Peri. He grabs me by my left arm. "Let me go!" I flip flop like a fish caught in a net trying desperately to get loose. My actions only cause the other guard to grab hold of my right arm.

"Is there a problem, miss?" A security guard employed by the hospital asks.

"Yes, they won't let me go!"

"Boys, let her go," Saffron says. After they release me, I angrily rub my arms. "Come in here, Jade." She motions for me to follow her.

"Are you okay, miss?" The security guard asks.

"Yes, I'm fine." I lie. Inside room thirteen, Peaches is cradling her dead baby and sobbing.

I clench my fists and with what little restraint I have left, hold them against my thighs. "What did you do to her?"

"Calm down. Have a seat." She points to a chair.

Reluctantly, I sit down and glare at her and the guards who stand behind her.

"I would never hurt my daughter—"

"She's not your daughter." I practically spit the words at her.

Saffron straightens her spine. "Do you have any idea how much trouble you're in, Jade?"

"Trouble? I don't think so. You do know that the commune leader is my father, right?"

Her lips quiver and her eyes bat back tears. I'd feel sorry for her if she wasn't such a wretched woman. "I won't sit here and take abuse from you." She rises from the chair and stares down at me. "You are banished from Nirvana, so don't you even think about coming back. It's time for you to leave now. Peaches is coming home with me."

"I am not going anywhere with you!" Peaches hollers.

Saffron looks shocked. "Darling, you don't mean that. Come home with me and we'll start fresh. We'll forget this nightmare ever happened." She steps toward the bed.

"Get away from me! I hate you!"

I rise from the chair and stand next to my sister's bed.

Saffron's yellow eyes look like washed up pools of sadness. She opens her mouth to speak but no words come out. Instead, she nods and spins on her heel. "Let's go." She tells the guards.

Peri wraps his arm around her. "Are you sure? I can make her come, you know." He pulls out a long needle from his pocket.

Peaches screams.

"Put that away." Saffron hisses. She grabs onto Peri's arm. "I said, let's go."

She doesn't turn back.

I turn to see my sister cradling her dead baby. "I am so sorry." Tears stream down my face.

"She's beautiful, isn't she?" Peaches caresses the baby's cheek.

"Yes, she is."

"Can you get your camera? I'd like to take Anna's picture."

***

The next few days are horrible. Peaches is discharged from the hospital the next morning and that afternoon we visit a funeral home to make arrangements. We stay in a hotel for two days until the service. At the cemetery, I watch helplessly as the tiny wooden casket is lowered into the ground. My heart breaks when Peaches tosses a bouquet of miniature white roses onto the casket. When men arrive with shovels, I place my arm around my sister's shoulders and guide her away from the grave. We find a bench beneath a weeping willow tree where my sister weeps for her lost child. I cry for Anna, Peaches, Grandmother Ruby, and for all I've left behind in Nirvana. When no tears are left, I gaze at the sun which reminds me of a lone balloon floating through a brilliant blue sky.

"I'm ready to go." Peaches says.

"Are you sure?" I ask gently.

She nods. "I'll keep memories of Anna here." She places her hand on her chest. "Along with my memories of Bronze." She pauses and stares off into the distance for a moment. "We have to make sure Saffron and Carmine don't hurt anyone else. We need to meet our grandparents and Ty's uncle. Hopefully they can help us." She rises, reaches for my hand, and then we walk out of the cemetery.

Chapter Twenty-One

When we reach the truck, Peaches insists on driving. From her solemn expression, I can tell she doesn't want to talk. Since I forgot my reading glasses, I have to squint at the map but fortunately the directions seem simple.

"It looks like the most direct route to Main is I- 77. You'll want to make the next right turn."

Peaches takes the turn faster than necessary which makes me grab the bar above my head. Ty and I call it the "oh crap" bar. Thinking about Ty causes a wave of sadness to thump against my chest. I close my eyes to stop the tears from spilling down my face. I can't focus on him right now; I have my sister and this trip to worry about. When I open my eyes, I notice Peaches is sitting straight up and gripping the steering wheel. One glance out the windshield explains her obvious discomfort. Cars and trucks are speeding and weaving in and out of *one, two, three, four, five, six, lanes of traffic*!

"Wow. I am so glad you're the one driving," I say.

She forces a smile. "How long are we on this highway?"

"Twenty-eight miles."

"Can you find a decent radio station?"

"Sure." I search through the stations and stop at "Highway to Hell" by AC/DC. "How fitting is this?"

"It's perfect."

After the song ends, she says, "Are you nervous about meeting our grandparents?"

"I was nervous but now that we're on this road, I'm terrified."

"Me, too. I'm also worried about my, I mean our dad. Saffron is bound to find out he helped us."

"Maybe she'll be so upset she'll leave Samsara, and then Rust will have some peace."

Peaches snorts. "Fat chance. If anything, she'll force him to move out. I'm so relieved she isn't my mother."

I can't say the same about Royal. Even though I've been referring to him as my "fake-father," I still love him and most likely always will. And even though my mother lied to me many times, I will always love her. I wish I could call them to let them know we're okay, but Saffron and Rust are the only ones with access to Outside phone calls.

"Peaches, if we call Rust, do you think he'll let our mother and Ty know we're okay?"

"He'd definitely do that. Maybe we can call from our grandparent's house."

"I hope they'll be glad to see us."

"How could they not be? We're super cute." A genuine grin spreads across her face; it's the first one I've seen in days.

"Speaking of cute, do you think Ty's uncle will be good looking?"

"If he looks anything like Ty, he will!" A blush immediately spreads across her face. "Okay, now I'm embarrassed. Let's change the subject, better yet let's play a game. Turn the radio up. The first person to correctly identify the most songs before we exit the highway wins."

The first song is familiar but I can't think of the title or the name of the band.

"Hotel California by The Eagles," she says with a fist pump.

After a total of seven songs, Peaches wins by correctly identifying five song titles and their respective bands.

"You're going to take the First Street Exit, which is on the right," I say. After she takes the turn, my senses are assaulted. My nose fills with the smell of hotdogs, sweat, and smoke. My ears ring with the sound of horns, people yelling, and brakes squealing. And even thought the buildings are predominantly gray, everything else is colorful: cars, people's clothes, and various signs.

"What is this?" I ask.

"I don't even know but it's chaotic, that's for sure. Make sure your door is locked. Better yet, let's roll up the windows."

"Good idea."

"What street do they live on, again?"

"Eighteenth. Keep going straight and it will eventually be on the left. Fortunately, the streets run in numerical order."

Even though it's only a few minutes away, it takes longer because the streets are so congested with cars, people, and bicycles.

"Finally, Eighteenth Street," Peaches mutters. "But where am I going to park?"

"Can you park in there?" I point to a building featuring a sign that reads: "Eighteenth Street Parking Garage. All Day Parking: $15."

"Looks like our only option." She turns left into the building. A man in a little yellow hut hands her a ticket. When he smiles, I notice his two front teeth are missing.

After several loops around the garage, Peaches finds a parking spot.

"Oh my gosh, we're really here, aren't we? Pinch me so I know I'm not dreaming," she says.

I pinch her lightly on the arm.

"Ouch."

I grab my backpack and sweatshirt, we lock the doors, and we're on our way.

"This feels so weird, doesn't it?" I ask.

"Extremely weird."

"Should we take the steps?" I point to a stairwell.

"Sure."

As soon as I open the door, we're hit with the smell of urine.

"Gross," we say and hold our noses. I'm incredibly relieved when we reach the sidewalk.

Peaches grasps my hand. "I'm scared."

"Me, too. But we've got each other, so we're going to be fine."

"Would you like to buy your girlfriend a flower? A dollar for a carnation, two dollars for a rose." An elderly man asks me. His arms are filled with wilted flowers.

"I feel sorry for him," Peaches whispers in my ear. "Should we give him money?"

"No," I whisper back. "We don't have much."

"No, thanks," I tell him.

"I want you to have them." He hands each of us a yellow carnation. "Peace be with you," he says before he haggles an elderly couple.

"Thank you," we call after him.

Peaches breaks off the stems and tucks one flower behind her ear, and the other behind mine. She reminds me of our mother, who must be worried sick about us. I feel a sharp pain in my heart. We'll call Rust soon and he'll let her know we're okay. Everything is going to be fine.

"Which apartment building do they live in? There's a bunch," I say.

"I'd say the one directly across the street."

"What makes you say that?" I glance across the street to find an older version of Ty. My heart drops in my stomach. "Oh my gosh." I watch as he opens the door and slips inside.

We cross the street, even though cars are honking and people are shouting at us. We loiter in front of an old brownstone building until Peaches asks if I'm ready. I nod.

But when she attempts to open the scuffed red door, it won't budge. "Now what?" she asks.

"I think we have to wait for someone with a key."

We wait for a few minutes until a woman with hot pink hair unlocks the door. Fortunately, we're able to slip in behind her.

"Wow, this is nice," Peaches says.

Everything is white- the couches, the walls, the front desk... it reminds me of the second floor of Samsara, where the intraocular eye procedures take place.

"Should we visit our grandparents or Ty's uncle first?" She asks. "From the apartment numbers, I assume they're both on this floor." I follow her down the hallway.

"Since we know Ty's uncle is here, let's knock on his door, first. It's right up here, apartment 99. What are we going to say?"

"First we'll say hello. Then I'm going to ask if I can use his bathroom." She knocks on the door.

Within seconds, Hunter opens the door. He looks only a few years older than we do and he's the spitting image of Ty. He's even wearing clothes similar to the ones Ty wears to work: white tee shirt, flannel shirt, jeans, and work boots. But Hunter's eyes are the color of pine trees.

"Can I help you?" He asks pleasantly.

"Hi, I'm Peaches and this is Jade. We're friends with your nephew, Ty."

The color drains from his face. "Is he okay?" He whispers.

"Yes, he's fine," Peaches says quickly. "We were wondering if we could come in."

"Of course." He opens the door wide. We step into a large living area with hardwood floors and black leather furniture.

"Please, have a seat. Would you like something to drink?" He asks.

"Iced tea if you have it, if not water is fine. Also, may I please use your restroom?" Peaches asks.

"Of course. Second door on the right." He points down the hallway.

"Iced tea for you too?"

"Yes, please." I gingerly take a seat on the couch and allow my eyes to dart across the sparely furnished room. Colorful paintings align the wall and there's an easel in the corner.

He places three iced teas on the coffee table. Then he collapses on the love seat and yawns. "You'll have to excuse me; it's been a long day."

Before I have a chance to respond, Peaches plops down next to me.

"So how do you know Ty?" He asks.

"We grew up with Ty in Nirvana," she says.

"I can tell from the color of your eyes. People always ask if I'm wearing colored contacts. So you're close friends with Ty?"

Peaches glances at me. "Actually, Jade is Ty's girlfriend."

Hunter smiles. "Oh yeah?"

I blush. "Yes."

He runs his hands through his dark hair. "I haven't seen him since he was a kid. Where is he? Didn't he want to leave with you?"

"Yes, he wanted to come. He helped us escape but in the end he decided to stay," I say.

"Why?" He asks.

I take a deep breath and slowly let it out. "His father had a heart attack."

Hunter grimaces. "Is my brother going to be okay?"

"I'm not sure. I'm really sorry."

"Thank you." His eyes drift off for a moment. He cracks his knuckles before he says, "So who are you related to?"

"This is going to sound weird, but here goes. Jade and I are fraternal twin sisters but we were raised separately. Rust is our father and Jonquil is our mother, however, I was brought up thinking Saffron was my mother and Jade thought Royal was her father. Not long ago Rust broke down and told us everything."

Hunter raises his eyebrows. "So that means Rue and Goldie are your grandparents. They live right down the hall, but you probably knew that, right?"

"We did. Do you think they'll want to meet us?' She asks.

"Rue and Goldie are two of the nicest people I know. They'll definitely want to meet you. Should I call them?"

I chew on a piece of ice and glance at Peaches before answering. "I'm nervous but yes, I'd love to meet them."

Hunter picks up a small device, punches in numbers, and then places it against his ear. "Hi, Rue, it's Hunter. I have two people I'd like to introduce you to."

Peaches squeezes my hand.

"You're in the courtyard? Excellent, we'll be right there." He slips the device into his back pocket. "You ready?"

"Yes," we reply in unison.

We follow Hunter into the hallway. "The courtyard is right through these double doors." He holds the door open and Peaches and I walk out onto the patio. They walk ahead but I hesitate.

I notice a lone weed growing between the bricks. I pick it and blow the seed head off of the mature dandelion. I close my eyes and make a wish that our grandparents and Hunter can help us reunite with our parents, Slate, and Ty. In the meantime, I pray they stay safe. I watch as the seeds travel through the sky, destination- anywhere.

###

About Kristy Feltenberger Gillespie

Kristy Feltenberger Gillespie lives in Warrenton, Virginia with her husband, two cats, and three dachshunds, and they're expecting their first child in July of 2015. Gillespie is a middle school counselor, graduate student at Longwood University, (pursuing a degree in School Library Media) blogger, short story and Young Adult novel writer. When she's not working, she's traveling or dreaming of traveling. She's been on several cross country road trips with her mom. In fact, Hawaii and Alaska are the only states she hasn't been to.

CONNECT WITH KRISTY ONLINE:

Keep Calm and Write On Blog:
http://kristyfgillespie.com

Facebook:
https://www.facebook.com/kristy.feltenbergergillespie

Twitter: @KFGillespie

CHECK OUT KRISTY'S YOUNG ADULT THRILLERS:

Hunted: http://www.amazon.com/dp/B00UPLMQUG

Blinded: Coming Soon!

CHECK OUT KRISTY'S SHORT STORY COLLECTION:

Even In Death: http://www.amazon.com/dp/B00MFV0V24